The West Indian

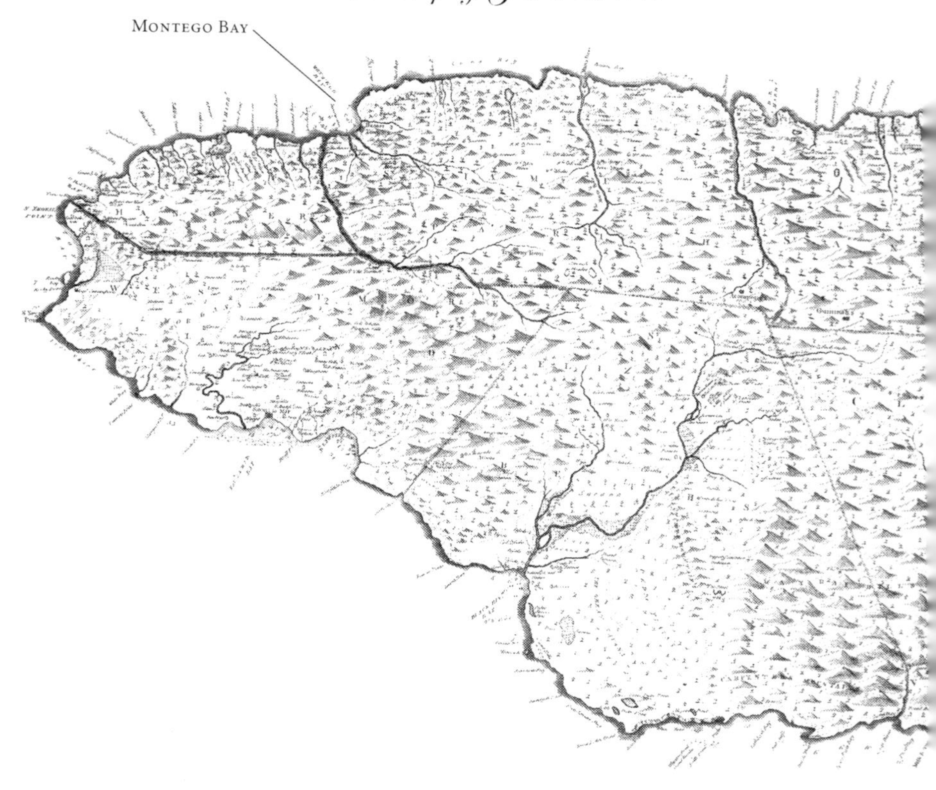

VALERIE BROWNE LESTER

The West Indian

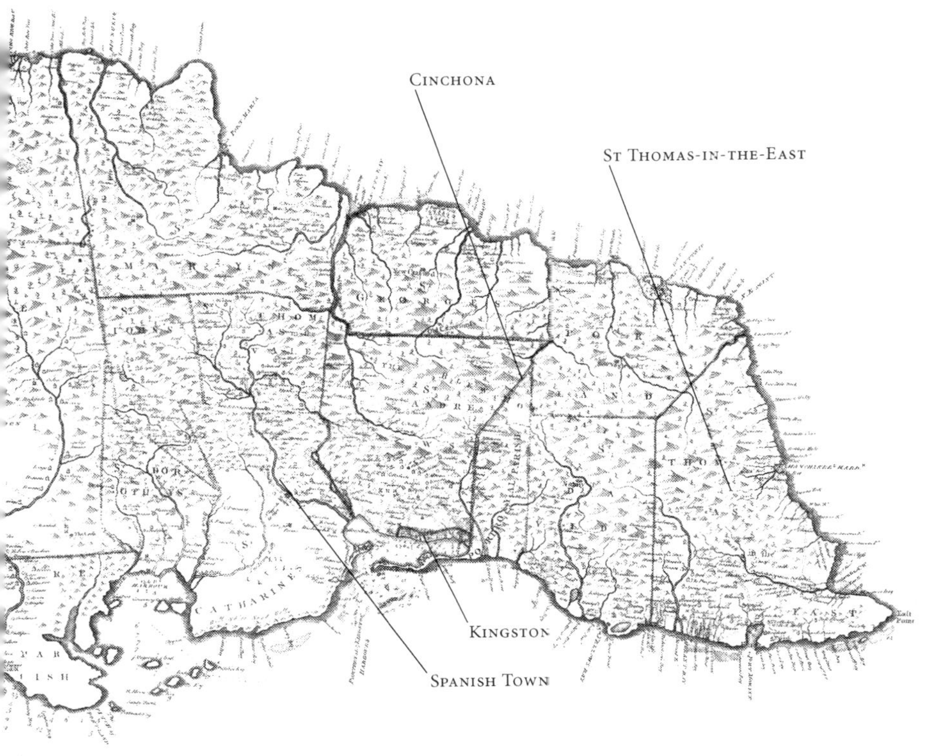

Mason & Fraser

2019

Print Edition ISBN 978-1-7335984-0-8
Electronic Edition ISBN 978-1-7335984-1-5

AUTHOR'S NOTE

I am indebted to the following for their contributions:
William Beckford, George Bridges, Charlotte Brontë, Emily
Brontë, Robert Burton, George Chapman and Musaeus, Lord
Chesterfield, William Diaper and Oppian, Charles Leslie,
Matthew ("Monk") Lewis, Edward Long, Memorials of Liverpool, Maria Nugent, Diana Phillips, Sappho, Enid Shields,
Laurence Sterne, and Theocritus with Anon.

My deepest thanks go to my critics: Diana Phillips, Sue Ramin,
Alison Jean Lester, Toby Lester, Bruce Kennett, Marcus Bicknell,
Mary Ann Frye, Gale Clifford, and Arthur McNeil.

IT IS JUNE THE THIRTIETH, 1770. All night Peter hears the screaming, and just before dawn he creeps out of bed, tiptoes down the stairs, softly crosses the dining room, and tugs open the doors to the gallery. Cool air streams in. He pads past the rocking chairs and down the steps into the garden. He picks up a stick and drags it all the way to the tamarind tree, scuffing his feet on the pathway and making a wake of dust behind him. He hauls himself onto the owest branch, and it sweeps the ground with his weight; then limb by limb, he makes for the top. The sky is grey but shifts to rose in the east, then orange, and Peter watches the colours slink around the horizon.

The screaming stops.

There is a pause, a heartbeat, and COCK-A-DOODLE-DOO pierces the vacuum of silence. Another heartbeat; a horse whinnies in the distance, and a sudden breeze rustles the leaves of the tamarind tree. Peter climbs down again. He must, he must-must-must find out about the screaming. He starts running; he runs to the back of the house, to the kitchen and finds Monimia, sitting at the scrubbed wooden table, head down on her arms, fast asleep. He stands beside her, level with her ear, breathing loudly, breathing as loudly as he can, trying to wake her without disturbing her. He inspects a fly on her arm. He peers down the shiny dark hole of her ear and blows into it. She jumps up and unleashes a torrent of curses at him. He waits until the storm has passed, tugs her hand, and asks if someone was killed during the night.

She sits down heavily again, Ooof, and pulls him onto her lap. Then he learns that entering the world can sometimes be noisier than leaving it, and now there are two where there was only one, but the new one is very little and the older one is very tired. He wants to see the new one, but Monimia cautions him not to go upstairs. She gives him an orange, and Peter goes outside, kicking a stone all the way back to the tamarind tree.

He climbs up again and, straddling a branch, sticks his thumb into the eye of the orange, then swiftly strips the rind away and lays out the sections one by one along the branch. He counts them — ten — and eats them slowly, spitting a seed with deadly accuracy at a lizard on the ground below. In his ears, Peter still feels the vibration of the screams from last night. He is determined to see the new one.

Peter drops from the tree, rolls on the ground, and wipes his hands on the grass. He skulks to the gallery and climbs the steps. His bare feet feel their way cautiously over the rough wood — he doesn't want another splinter — and a rocking chair sways as he passes. Crossing the threshold into the dining room, he moves faster as he reaches the cool mahogany sheen. When he enters the hall, his feet sink into the turkish carpet, and he follows its serpentine pattern to the foot of the staircase. He climbs each wide step, creak creak, holding on to the stair rail, and counts as he climbs — ten steps to the turning and nine more to the top. He walks the length of the upstairs hallway in the direction of the screaming room. The door is open, and for the moment all is quiet. Peter stands in the doorway. The woman is lying on her back with her long black hair spiraling across the pillows. Her face is pale, with dark rings under the eyes, but it is more peaceful than he has ever seen it. The air is still, the rising sun flares in the mirror and throws a slice of light across the bed, across the embroidered sheet, and onto a gauze-covered crib. Peter tiptoes along the length of one floorboard from the door to the crib. If he treads on a crack, he will fall into the sea and be eaten by sharks. He tries not to breathe. At last he reaches the crib. Through the mosquito net he spies a small shape, but he cannot see it clearly through the gauze. He slowly draws the netting back.

The baby stirs and purses its mouth. Its hair is like a dark brown cap. One hand escapes from its swathing, and Peter gazes raptly as the tiny white fingers stretch open. He reaches out his own brown hand to make sure the fingers are real, and, like a spring, they snap fast over his index finger. The baby opens its eyes and stares so hard at Peter that its eyes cross, and Peter laughs out loud. The woman sits bolt upright, the peaceful face contorts, the screaming starts again, the huge mouth is a cave with a giant clapper, the tranquil hair shudders, and the baby wails. The midwife comes running. Peter notices blood on her shoes as she sweeps him from the room. Monimia, bustling from the kitchen, breathless at the top of the stairs, yanks his hand and hauls him down the stairs, bump, bump, bump, drags him across the floor, swoosh, out the door, thump, and back into the kitchen, slam. She grabs him by the shoulders and shakes him. The door flies open again. Henry Mason looms huge in the entrance, his shadow stretching across the floor.

"Why did you let him go upstairs?" he shouts at Monimia.

"Me don' see him go."

"You must keep him away from her."

To Peter: "Do as you are told."

Peter knows how to soften his father's heart. He smiles; he reaches up his arms, and Henry Mason bends down, scoops him up, and ruffles his hair. Peter lets his eyelids flutter in the breeze of his father's breath. He wraps his arms around Henry's neck and brings his mouth close to Henry's ear.

"That baby," he whispers, "Is boy?"

"A girl."

"What she name?"

"Bertha."

A girl. Peter must warn her about her mother.

*   *   *

In September 1762, eight years before the screaming, a certain Martha Grant received a letter from her cousin Henry Mason in Jamaica. It contained a proposal of marriage. At the time, deeply saddened by the death of her fiancé, she was working in Yorkshire as governess to her sister's children. Isolated in the sodden countryside and longing for a change of scene, she was tempted by her cousin's offer to join him in Jamaica.

Martha weighed the pros and cons of Henry's offer and made lists. On the pro side she listed:

Adventure

Living in Jamaica, where her beloved Arthur had died

Seeing her cousin again and renewing their friendship

Escape from becoming an old maid

Sunshine

Colour

Unfamiliar natural history

For the cons she listed:

Leaving behind her father

Leaving behind her sister and her family

The balance swung sharply in favour of Henry's proposal. Martha promptly made the decision to accept, and four months later, she sailed across the Atlantic. Having arrived in Spanish Town, she wrote to her father about her journey and her first impressions of Jamaica.

Spanish Town. January the eleventh, 1763

Dearest Papa,

I hasten to assure you of my safe arrival, and I send you my tender regards. You must know that you are constantly in my thoughts and prayers, as are Lizzie and Jack and their little ones. Please read this letter to them, so that they too may experience my Atlantic crossing.

My voyage was, in the opinion of the captain, a pleasant one and free of incident. I beg to disagree. Weather conditions in December make for a fast, rough trip as far as Madeira, and for me it seemed like a world gone mad, a world turned topsy-turvy. The three weeks after we sailed from Liverpool were cold and brutish, and the Bay of Biscay is sadly misnamed; it should rather be referred to as the Jaws of Hell. Mountainous waves and foul winds. Sudden, deceptive calm by day, which stalled us. Terrific storms by night, which made me believe that a hell of fire would be preferable to that hell of intolerable noise and endless rocking. It was all sensation. I felt sick to death. My temples throbbing, my head burning, my limbs freezing, my mouth all fever, my stomach all nausea, my mind all disgust. Then the intolerable noise — the cracking of bulkheads — the sawing of ropes — the screeching of the tiller — the trampling of the sailors — the clattering of the crockery! Of all the inconveniences attached to a vessel, the incessant noise appears to me the most insupportable.

Everything above deck and below was all in motion at once. Chairs, writing desks, books, boxes, candles, flew to one end of the room; and the next moment, as if they had made a mistake, flew back again to the other with the same hurry and confusion. I leave it to you to imagine the extent to which I was subjected to sea-sickness. I am surprised I survived at all. And even when the worst was over, I might have starved to death had it not been for Lizzie's thoughtful gift of gingerbread. It was unfailingly tasty when all else, such as the stewed goose or salted cod of the ship's menu, had scant appeal.

*Alas, Papa, reading was impossible. Just a glance at
a printed page caused the words to blur, the head to spin,
and the stomach to heave. All my hopes for hours of long,
uninterrupted reading were dashed.*

*During those first three weeks of our eight-week voyage,
three weeks that were more terrifying than the worst
nightmare, it was impossible to venture into the open air
for fear of being swept overboard, and we were obliged to
remain below deck where all was stuffy and confined, and
we were overwhelmed by the stench of molasses which had
seeped into the very fibre of the ship. We shared our space
with any number of fellow creatures; the ship at the start of
the voyage resembled a cross between a floating menagerie, a
market garden, and a grocer's shop. There were on board two
Pekingese puppies, one English bulldog, several cages of doves
of different breeds, my canary until he died, and the ship's
cat, who surveyed the whole scene with a baleful eye, and
slunk around on stealthy foot, close to the ground. In addition
to the pigs and fowl destined as our shipboard fare, there
were above deck, poorly sheltered, and looking as miserable
as I felt, three elegant horses, a dozen Jersey cows, and an
enormous bull, named Hercules. One of the horses fell ill
and died, and it took eight sailors to lift it and throw it over
the ship's side to its watery grave. The other two managed
to survive the journey. It turns out that they, along with the
bull and the cows, were on their way to Henry's cattle farm,
which in this country is called simply a "pen."*

*Seven other passengers made up the ship's complement,
all, with one exception, embarking on a new life in Jamaica
for one reason or another. The one exception was a Mr John
Eyre, who disembarked at Madeira where he has recently*

started business as a wine merchant. It turns out that he is Henry's Funchal agent! Isn't life full of the most amazing coincidences? A generous man, he came back to the ship before we left Funchal, bearing with him a case of best Madeira wine as a wedding present for Henry and me.

Another passenger of whom I became particularly fond was a Mrs Jamison, who was joining her husband in Jamaica after two years of separation. She and I suffered through our mal de mer together and exchanged many pleasantries during the course of the voyage. I am saddened that she will be living at Savanna-la-Mar rather than in Spanish Town; as I look at the map of Jamaica I see that it must be a two-day ride away at least. The shape of Jamaica puts me in mind of a sea-turtle, head protruding from shell towards the west, shell rising from Montego Bay in the north, tail forming the easternmost point, and one flipper paddling to the south.

Conditions improved the farther south and west the ship sailed, and our crossing was aided by northeast trade winds and a favourable current in the range of half a knot. The auditory nightmare abated, and as soon as we fell in with the trade wind, we proceeded both rapidly and steadily. As we neared the Caribbean Sea, the weather became delightful. We ceased to pitch and roll. The sun was bright, and cool breezes sent us forward steadily. The swell of the waves was scarcely perceptible, and the ship moved along so steadily that the deck afforded almost as firm a footing as the dry land. I picked up my books again. My spirits, which had been dashed on the rocks of despair by the combination of mal de mer and mal de pays, were suddenly lifted and I felt like Belinda admiring the Thames:

Smooth flow the waves, the zephyrs gently play,
Belinda smiled, and all the world was gay.

Our ship was joined by schools of porpoises who entertained us greatly by playing alongside the ship and tumbling directly under its nose. When in their gambols they allow themselves to be seen above the surface, they are of a dirty blackish brown, and as ugly as the heart can wish; but in the waves they acquire a fine sea-green cast, and their spouting in the sunbeams is extremely ornamental. We were also visited by several man-of-war birds and a species of gull, whose nautical name is "the boatswain." It is white and is distinguished by a single very long feather in its tail. The birds followed our ship closely, ever watchful for an easy meal. And our own meals sometimes arrived out of the air, in the shape of flying fish that threw themselves recklessly onto the decks. Catching them was easy — I picked one up in my hands and enclose a drawing of it, which I made from memory after I had held it a moment. I watched its mighty struggle to survive in the foreign element, before I cast it back into its true home. Regaining the water, it seemed un-affected by its reckless adventure, and swam merrily away.

The task of eating flying fish is more difficult than catching them because they are largely made up of skin and bones; but whatever morsels one can extract taste fresh and sweet, and after several weeks at sea, anything that tastes fresh tastes appetising.

It is now three days since I set foot on land and around me all is strange and wonderful. I am writing to you by candlelight because I cannot sleep. The tropical night is full of strange, piercing noises, which could frighten me except that I chant, like Caliban:

"Be not afeard: the isle is full of noises,
Sounds and sweet airs that give delight and hurt not."
But I must admit that the drone of the mosquitoes and their
insistent stinging are intolerable. I shall endeavour to write
under the mosquito net that covers my bed, my safe haven.

Henry came on board our vessel to meet me on my
arrival in Kingston. He is tall — he towers over me
now — dark-haired and well-favoured, of a somewhat
sallow but smooth-skinned complexion. This sallowness I
have remarked on many of the English faces here. It must
come from a want of cool breezes and good English beef!
My luggage was put on a wagon drawn by eight oxen, while
Henry and I rode in a handsome phaeton — which was so
hot that I wished I had not worn my best black silk — to
Spanish Town, which was even hotter than Kingston, being
inland and not fanned by breezes from the sea. The journey
took nearly five hours and the road was very poor. I tried
not to complain of the heat, but Henry noticed my discomfort
and promised to take me up to his little house at Cinchona,
high in the Blue Mountains, for our voyage de noces. He
says that up there the weather is cool, the mountain mists are
reminiscent of England's mist, and the mosquitoes are non-
existent.

My ankles in particular are covered in mosquito bites
and the itching is intolerable. It seems that these insects lurk
in invisible hiding places during the day and venture out
at night to prey on the blood of innocent newcomers, while
the sun-tough skins and rum-infused blood of the long-term
residents act as deterrents.

Our route to Spanish Town took us through the endless
sugar plantations and little settlements of Caymanas, and

*now I have become acquainted with the sight of the crop
that delivers so much revenue to the plantation owners.
Each individual plant resembles a giant grass plant; tall and
waving when the wind blows, the canes make a sound like
the swishing of the sea.*

*When we arrived in the capital I was quite taken aback
by the noise and bustle of the place. Everywhere there are
"higglers," itinerant vendors selling their wares à haute voix,
all with individual cries, the inflections rising and falling,
and a fierce insistence on selling such things as live pigeons,
young cocoanuts, the fruit of which is like jelly, meat pasties,
hot peppers, sticks of sugar cane, and herbs and spices. Our
carriage moved with the greatest difficulty through the
town, at one point stopping so that Henry could show me
the emporium his father established for the sale of goods from
England. Henry has continued to operate it successfully in
partnership with another merchant, Thomas Fraser and, at
least nominally if not successfully, with his feckless brother,
Jonas. Hence Mason, Mason & Fraser. As we walked
around the emporium's dark and glittering interior, I uttered
appropriate noises of admiration, even as I was longing to lie
down and go to sleep.*

*We continued our journey, and it was a relief to arrive at
our destination, the house of Mr and Mrs Fraser. In aspect
they appear a very Jack Sprat and his wife, but they seem to
be the souls of kindness, and I am to stay with them until I
am married. I was immediately surrounded by the household
staff, who ogled me and giggled, before bursting into a song
of welcome and presenting me with a fan made from palm
fronds. This welcome was thoroughly amusing, and yet there
was something in it by which I could not help being sadly*

affected; I believe it was the consciousness that all these human beings were slaves.

Mrs Fraser invited Henry and me to relax with some lemonade on a shaded gallery where I tried to steady myself from the infernal phantom rocking of the ship. Henry seemed unwilling to converse with me at any length, but perhaps that was because of the intervention of Mrs Fraser's incessant chatter. I believe him to be quite shy. He sat with us for just a few moments before he had to leave again for Kingston in order to supervise the transport of Hercules the bull and his harem to his pen.

Henry lives in a great house called Beverly, some short distance from his cattle pen. He took me there yesterday and showed me around. He told me how, in a country where gentlemen's houses are generally built low, of one storey, to withstand the shock of earthquakes and the fury of hurricanes, his father decided to defy convention and built a two-storey mansion. He copied a house he admired fourteen miles away, just outside Kingston, a house called Prospect Pen that had already stood firm in the face of hurricanes and earthquakes for a hundred years. His Spanish Town replica does not have Kingston's backdrop of the Blue Mountains, but is otherwise identical, even to the avenue of yokewood trees leading to the front steps. The house itself is spacious and is topped by a little lookout. Long windows and high ceilings take best advantage of the breezes. The kitchen is in a separate building close by, joined to the house by a covered walk. Set at some distance is a string of small wattle cabins for the slaves, all situated in little gardens and bowers of sweet smelling shrubberies.

A thin, fierce housekeeper from England rules the large

staff of domestic slaves. Mrs Perkins came to Jamaica with Henry's parents and remained after Mrs Mason returned to England and Mr Mason died. Henry told me that she is competent and trustworthy, and I hope that she and I shall be able to work together to make the house more habitable. I have found very little comfortable furniture; what exists is often broken, uncomfortable, or aesthetically displeasing. The mansion is in sore need of a loving touch and a more artistic eye.

My first encounter with Mrs Perkins was hardly a resounding success. After I greeted her, she announced: "You are aware, I trust, that the running of the household is entirely my business?" To which I responded: "For that I am grateful. As a newcomer to the island, I would not know how to begin." She drew herself up to her full height — considerable — and glared over her beak at me. "Indeed," she snapped.

Everything around me is new and strange, and your absence hurts like a throbbing wound. However, I hasten to reassure you of my safe arrival and my interest and amazement at my surroundings. Although I have yet to establish a complete rapport and marriage of the minds with my husband-to-be — he reads little and his mind is, necessarily I fear, focussed on commerce — I am confident that we can be mutually supportive as we set forth on our marital journey.

Dearest Papa, this letter is far too long, and I hope I have not wearied you. My candle, by its guttering, tells me it is time to put down my pen; the first pale light of dawn is showing at the edge of the sky and Venus gleams, a beacon of promise for the new day. Soon the dawn chorus will commence, a strange group of singers whom I have yet to identify. Their song makes up for in raucousness what it lacks in harmony.

A thousand kisses shower on you, Papa. May the Creator who fashioned us both look kindly on us, keeping us together even as we find ourselves an ocean apart.

Your loving daughter, Martha

January the twentieth, 1763

Since my arrival, my hosts Mr and Mrs Fraser have taken me for several expeditions by carriage into the countryside. Jamaica appears beautiful — such hills, such mountains, such verdure; everything so bright and gay, it is delightful. Nothing, certainly, can exceed the beauty and enchanting scenery of this country. It is strange to imagine the daffodils and apple blossom of an English spring while I look on in amazement at Jamaica's natural life, which seems to have no pause in its riotous and amusing disregard of the seasons. Indeed, I have heard it said about Jamaica that "'Tis here an eternal spring, the beauties of December equal the bloom of April."

"Do not become too enamoured of the island," warned Mrs Fraser on one of our expeditions when she noticed how enchanted I was with everything I saw. "The advantages of Jamaica are balanced with some things that are disagreeable enough. The rivers contain the dreadful alligator; the fens and marshes, the guana and the galliwasp; the mountains are some of them impassable and breed numberless snakes and noxious animals."

In spite of her dire warnings, we continue to tour the nearby foothills and the fertile plains with their plantations and pens. In the distance, immense mountains rise up, some covered with the thickest woods of the most lively green; other mountains, rocky, appear quite blue. Here and there, tufts of green sprout upon their craggy and tremendous sides. When the sun first rises, all this is particularly beautiful, for the mist is cleared away gently, lifting like a large gauze curtain, until we can see the silver hills and bright green woods. The dew is heavy in the early morning, and all the animals seem to enjoy the coolness of the ground in consequence. By the middle of the day, they are panting and appear miserable with the heat, their mouths hanging open, and the poultry with their wings distended. All seek the shade.

However, we do not need to travel far to find shade and to gaze at one of the most beautiful sights I have come across yet: a giant silk-cotton tree found right here in the Frasers' garden. It has grown to a magnificent height and has magnificent proportions. Most cotton-silk trees are straight, and the most beautiful throw out no branches till they have reached a height greater than that of any ordinary tree in England. Nature, in order to sustain so large a mass, supplies it with huge spurs at the foot which act as buttresses, connecting the roots immediately with the trunk as much as twenty feet above the ground. The most striking peculiarity of these trees consists in the parasitic plants by which they are enveloped, and which hang from their branches down to the ground with tendrils of wonderful strength.

Sometimes a tree has reached its full growth before the parasites have fallen on it, and then, in place of being strangled, it is adorned. Every branch is covered with a wondrous growth — with plants of a thousand colours and a thousand sorts. Some droop with long and graceful tendrils from the boughs, and so touch the ground; while others hang in a ball of leaves and flowers, which swing for years, apparently without changing their position. I am in awe of the Frasers' wonderful specimen with its startling adornment, growing right here in their garden and offering us its cooling shade.

I am well, which is an unusual condition in this climate. Life, which each day presents a new challenge to health, seems especially precarious here. So far I have not fallen prey to the myriad ills that plague even the strongest of constitutions, although I do admit to a nasty case of prickly heat, and it is in vain that I try to avoid encounters with mosquitoes for they are legion.

I limit what I eat because it seems clear that many of the diseases here stem from a disregard for moderation of appetite. Everyone considers himself a gourmand, although I would prefer to use the word "glutton." I am stunned by the quantity of food consumed; although perhaps it is profusion rather than consumption which counts in the hosts' anxiety of making welcome and of crowding their tables. But on second thoughts, I must declare I have never seen such abandoned eating and drinking. I don't wonder at the fever the people suffer from here. They eat such loads of all sorts of high, rich and seasoned things, and drink really gallons of wine and mixed liquors! I observed some people eat of late breakfasts as if they had never eaten before — a dish of coffee, a bumper of claret, another large one of hock-negus; then Madeira, sangaree, hot and cold meat, stews and fries, hot and cold fish pickled and plain, peppers, ginger sweetmeats, acid fruit, sweet jellies.

Last night I encountered such a mountain of rich food at a party given in my honor that I could not begin to do it justice, and I fear I may have offended my hosts because of my timid efforts. The first course was entirely of fish, excepting for the cook's *pièce de résistance* in the centre: jerked hog, complete with ears and tail. There was also a black crab pepper-pot, for which I have kept the receipt. It is as follows:

> *a capon stewed down*
> *a large piece of beef and another of ham, also stewed to*
> > *a jelly*
> *six dozen of land crab, picked fine, with their eggs and fat*
> *onions, peppers, ochra, sweet herbs, and other vegetables*
> > *of the country, cut small*
> *Stew all ingredients well*

The second course was of turtle, mutton, beef, turkey, goose, ducks, chickens, capons, ham, tongue crab patties &c. &c. &c. The third course was composed of sweets and fruits of all kinds.

In short, the eye is astonished even as the stomach is overwhelmed.

I see little of my husband-to-be because of the demands of his business; not only does he supervise his pen, with assistance from an overseer, and run his emporium in Spanish Town, he also owns a warehouse and counting house in Kingston and a sugar plantation in St Thomas-in-the-East. When I do see him, he is tired, and his mind is distracted. He looks at me and straightway looks away. He sighs. There is nothing left of my dear, talkative childhood companion. I fear that I have failed to satisfy his hopes for an attractive wife, being so small and plain. In turn, I am dismayed by his size. He is well over six feet tall and, although handsome enough, is showing signs of corpulence. The contrast is striking between him and my dear lost darling, my gallant Captain Clarke, so lithe and so neat in his appearance. Oh, Arthur!

The wishful thought that Henry and I would be perfect companions because of my stimulating conversation remains merely wishful. We have no time to practise the art of conversation in his scheme of things. Pools of silence spread in place of dialogue. If I play my clavichord, he leaves the room.

We have yet to set a wedding date, although Henry grits his teeth and intimates that we shall be married soon. In the meantime, the ladies of Spanish Town come to call on me and to inspect my English clothes.

"Show us everything!" they cry.

"Let us see every item in your wardrobe!"

"We are starved for the latest fashions!"

I notice that their usual morning habit is a loose nightgown, carelessly wrapped around them; but before dinner they dispense with their dishabille and show themselves in all the advantage of a becoming rich neat dress, but none of them wears corsets. The latest designs from England are eagerly awaited, even though the winter fashions inevitably arrive in time for the hot season in Jamaica. There is an element of ostentation amongst the women, and undeterred by this timing and in the grip of their desire to be observed wearing the very latest fashions, the ladies stuff themselves into the most unsuitably warm garments and, perspiring profusely, parade up and down the square in Spanish Town.

"Do you not have something more elegant, more colourful, more in the new style?" they moan, wistfully rubbing fabric between their fingers, examining seams and trimmings, and making sure that buttons and buttonholes are compatible

"Is this all you have?"

I am a sore disappointment to the ladies of our fair city, caring as I do more for neatness of attire than for flamboyance, and they are unable to hide their disappointment at the paucity and plainness of my clothes. Even my attempt at finery for the ball at Government House last week disappointed them. They put their hands in front of their mouths and I could almost hear them whispering behind my back:

Isn't she small? Isn't she plain?
Isn't she bookish? At least, she's not vain.
Did you see what she wore to Government House,
To the ball held last week? She looked like a mouse.
So dull and so small, unspeakably plain,
But kind, so they say, and at least she's not vain.

In turn, these women are a disappointment to me. I had hoped to educate myself about the island by questioning them about its geography and natural history, but on these topics they are mute. It seems that they cannot forget the charms of the English robin nor the white cliffs of Dover. Their eyes are closed to the world they live in. Such nostalgia is dangerous and enervating, and I try to fight it in myself. I have to forcibly suppress my rage at their idleness, their apathy, and their hyperbolical and most asinine stupidity!

The heat makes heavy clothes intolerable for the men, and therefore they generally wear only thread stockings, linen knee breeches, a waistcoat, and a handkerchief tied around their heads with a hat above. Wigs are never used except on Sundays and in court time, and then the gentlemen appear very gay in silk coats and waistcoats trimmed with silver.

The servants wear a coarse frock, which buttons at the neck

and hands, long trousers of the same, a speckled shirt, and no stockings. The servant maids have generally a linen or striped holland gown and plain headcloths. The servant men who attend gentlemen, are dressed in their master's livery, which gives utmost pain to the uneasy slave.

I sometimes wonder, when all seems to contrive against me, when I face the prospect of a loveless marriage half a world away from home, why I do not run away and board the first ship back to England. Strange to say, I am not homesick. I certainly do not miss the drip and drizzle of England. My dear Arthur often wrote to me about the wonders of Jamaica; everything I look at, I see through his eyes and am joyful to observe what he has seen before me. More than that, I am invigorated to shoulder his cause. Influenced by his Quaker uncle, Arthur became an ardent abolitionist before he died and now, seeing what I see each day, I can comprehend why. It became his mission to improve the lot of slaves in Jamaica, and he wanted me to work at his side after we were married. It is up to me to fulfill his dream. How can I best accomplish this? I must observe, assess, and act.

I rejoice in the way each day bursts open with sunshine. I feel my soul expanding, exulting, with the strangest sense of freedom, of triumph. An invisible bond has burst, and I struggle out into unexpected liberty. Now I remember that the real world is wide, and that a varied field of hopes and fears, of sensations and excitements, await those who have courage to go forth into its expanse, to seek real knowledge of life amidst its perils. I have fallen in love with Jamaica, and this love for the island is what Henry and I truly have in common. May it serve us well.

February the first, 1763

In the mornings, I leave the Frasers' house to spend time at Beverly, readying it for my married life with Henry. I have a formidable task ahead of me.

"Tut tut," snaps Mrs Perkins, spindle-thin and iron-grey, whenever I make a suggestion for change. Jealous of the fact that someone other than she will be mistress, and in spite of my efforts at friendship, she has retreated into an icy silence from which the only sound that emanates is the occasional sniff of disapproval from her long, narrow nose. But I am determined that we shall be allies and not antagonists; I will not allow her to distance herself from me. It is only a matter of time before I will prevail.

She breaks her silence to bark orders at the servants.

"Do as I tell you! Don't drop that! How can you be so stupid?"

I deplore the manner with which she treats the domestic slaves, referring them to the bookkeeper's whip for the merest infractions of her iron rule. They tremble at the sight of her and are much inclined to drop things in her presence purely out of fear, thus perpetuating her anger and their inability to control the natural gravitational inclination of crocks and pitchers, cups and saucers.

It is extraordinary to witness the immediate effect that the climate and habit of living in this country have upon the minds and manners of Europeans, particularly of the lower orders, who consider the negroes as creatures formed merely to administer to their ease, and to be subject to their caprice; and I have found much difficulty to persuade that great person and superior being, my white domestic, that the blacks are human beings, and have souls.

My constant companion is Pearl, Henry's fifteen-year-old "outside sister" who, sorely in need of company, follows me around the house any time she can escape Mrs Perkins's iron grip. Henry's father Silas Mason engendered several children of colour, but this one was his favourite. She has lived within the house since her birth — making her his inside outside child! Her beauty is dramatic, and she is at the very peak of desirability. Her eyes are dark and light at the same time; her shiny black hair bounces under a saucy bandana; her form and features are statue-like; her complexion has no yellow in it — it is more of an ash-dove colour than anything else; her teeth are admirable both for colour and shape; and her face is broad enough to give it all possible softness and grandness of contour. She usually wears a mixed dress of brown, white and yellow, which harmonises excellently with her complexion; and she often throws one of her beautiful arms, glittering with bangles, across her brow in a most dramatic manner. Pearl is ripe for admiration.

Her official title is assistant housekeeper, but her workload is light. As Henry's half-sister, she is not expected to work in the same manner as the other domestics. She sings and dances as she works and is the sole individual who can charm a smile out of the dread Mrs Perkins. Mrs P. has taught her, quite well I must admit, to read and write and to do her sums. While Pearl has had limited material to enjoy until now, she is obviously a competent and enthusiastic reader. She borrows my books and we have already had several conversations about their subject matter.

"Come along now, Pearl," Mrs Perkins calls, interrupting our discourse.

"Wait a moment," cries Pearl.

"Come along at once!"

"Let me finish . . ." begs Pearl.

"At once, I said. And that is that."

Pearl looks at me despairingly.

Whenever I desire Pearl's company, Mrs P. insists that the girl has work to do. But there are moments when I am firm, which is hard in the face of that disapproving sniff, and insist on Pearl's help in sewing such things as curtains and linens. Her work is neat and imaginative; when I draw roses for her to embroider, she changes them into the native flowers of Jamaica. While we sew, she talks in a voice that is saturated with the singsong accent of the island but is more distinct to my ear than the voices of others born here. This must be because of the influences of Henry and Mrs Perkins. When she concentrates, her English is perfect. Any excitement causes her to relapse into the vernacular.

"One time, my father took me in a boat, and we capsize and nearly drown! 'Help, help,' I cry, and he catch me up and save me, quick, quick, from the teeth of one big barracuda," she says, kicking off her shoes and launching into another tale of adventure. Pearl's stories are filled with drama and mimicry, and if I did not know otherwise, I would believe that she had been influenced by frequent visits to the theatre. She dramatises everything she recounts or reads to me, setting the scene and changing her voice for every speaker.

When I ask her about her ancestry, Pearl is at first reluctant to speak, but as our friendship grows she shares more and more of her confidences.

"My father Mr Silas Mason tol' me that the father of my mother come from Scotland. And my grandmother was a fierce Coromantee, from the Gold Coast of Africa. That is where I catch me temper!" says Pearl, laughing.

"My mother, I never saw," she continues, "but my father him say she very beautiful and still loves me very much, although I cannot see her."

Henry and Pearl are clearly much attached to each other. Their eyes light up when they see each other, and Pearl loves to throw her arms around him when he comes home at the end of the day. Then she sits on his lap like a large, purring kitten, while he strokes her hair. Poor child, she has no equals and no associates in this household because of her age, her colour, and her position. She is as eager for my company as I am for hers for we are both fish out of water. It is through her that I learn about the island, and it is through me that she learns about the wide world beyond Spanish Town.

February the seventh, 1763

Even though educating slaves is a revolutionary idea here, I have decided to start a small school for the offspring of household slaves in Spanish Town and, in that way, I shall begin to fulfill my dear Arthur's desires. I shall employ Pearl as my assistant because of her competence with reading and writing and her aptness with arithmetic. It is ridiculous to confine her to the making of puddings and embroidering of bags. She needs exercise for her mental faculties.

While there is already a school for the poor children of Spanish Town, it seems that only poor whites or poor slightly coloureds may attend. I can see no reason why the blacks, who are also children of God, should be deprived of his greatest gift: the ability to read. I cannot bear to describe the condition of slaves in this country, the hardships of their lives. I believe sincerely that a country is rotten at the center if its subjects are oppressed.

The ladies of Spanish Town insist that educating slaves will have the effect of inciting rebellion, and they try to discourage me by regaling me with stories of dreadful uprisings, which loom huge and terrifying to a newcomer because of their immediacy. Fear is catching, and, to my shame, I find myself susceptible. I do not respect my fear and I work hard to overcome it.

The favourite story with which the ladies like to terrify me is that of Tacky's rebellion, and they delight in invoking his ghost. Their eyes widen and their voices tremble as they intone the tale of Tacky, a Coromantee slave, who had been a chief in his own land.

"Tacky believed he could catch bullets in his mouth and throw them back at the soldiers who fired them. Imagine that!" they cry.

"Tacky made his plans like a general," they concede, "and chose Easter for a surprise attack." Their voices sink dramatically.

"Before daybreak, he and his followers crept down to Port Maria on the north shore of the island and murdered the fort's sleeping storekeeper!" Horror and more horror.

"They then supplied themselves with arms and ammunition from the arsenal, and hundreds . . . "

"No, thousands, my dear . . .

" . . . of discontented slaves heard the news and joined Tacky."

Now, this is the favourite part with which the ladies love to regale me. Their eyes widen further and their voices lower ominously as they intone the litany of horrors perpetrated by Tacky and his followers.

"They overran the estates," they say, their eyes fairly gleaming.

"They slit the throats of the sleeping owners," they insist, punctiliously pronouncing each letter of the word 's-l-i-t,' lingering especially over the 't'.

And then their voices lift again as they describe how the gallant white troops came to the rescue and overpowered most of the slaves, but their voices sink again as they tell how Tacky, accompanied by a fiercely loyal few, continued the struggle.

"Many months passed before the revolt was completely subdued, and when it was all over, sixty good white people and about three hundred and fifty wicked black slaves were dead, including Tacky." They breathe a sigh of relief.

In Jamaica, they have the severest ways of punishing. People here say that no country excels it in the barbarous treatment of slaves or in the cruel methods in which they are put to death. A rebellious negro, or he that twice strikes a white man, is condemned to the flames; he is carried to the place of execution, and chained flat on his belly, his arms and legs extended, then fire is set to his feet, and so he burns gradually up. Others they starve to death, with a loaf hanging before their mouths; I have heard tell that these unfortunate wretches will sometimes gnaw the flesh off their own shoulders. Where does it come from, this instinct to torture and maim?

"Henry, Henry," I cried later that day, "how can you justify the employment of such bands of unfortunate slaves and then treat them with less respect and kindness than barnyard dogs?"

Henry reacted with irritation.

"How often do I have to explain to you that the production of sugar requires a vast amount of human labour?" he asked.

"You have explained it often enough for me to comprehend, but what I cannot understand is your lack of comprehension of what is patently evident to my newcomer's eye. Namely that the smooth running of the estates would be enhanced and the threat of rebellion diminished if planters paid attention to the conditions of those upon whose sweat they depend for their profit."

"Leniency inevitably leads to rebellion."

"I understand with all my heart the slaves' urge to revolt."

"This urge must be suppressed."

"Shortly before I left England, I read Dr Samuel Johnson's speeches against slavery. He is not of your opinion."

"Let Johnson come to Jamaica and run a sugar plantation then!" Henry's temper rose, and he slammed out of the room. His words enrage me and further inflame my own opinions, opinions that are considered completely inappropriate in the society in which I must move. Such confrontation is valueless; I might as well ask the Thames to reverse its course. I need to calm down.

There is a large tamarind tree at some distance and to the east of the house. Its branches spread far and wide, with some limbs even sweeping the ground, hiding from view a person standing below; they form an enclosure that resembles a giant arboreal circus tent. Having been put in mind of a circus tent, I asked Cuthbert, the butler, to arrange to hang a swing from one of the great branches, and this morning he and several other fellows carried out my request. In the afternoon, following a short postprandial nap, I crossed the garden where the sun continued to beat relentlessly down. Having thrust my way through the spreading branches, I found myself in another realm — a realm of green shade and dappled, feathery light, where the air was cool. The slightest breeze set up a susurration among the leaves. I sat upon my swing, its ropes and the tree's branches creaking slightly with my weight, and pushed myself off. What pleasure! What a lifting of spirits! I must have passed a full hour there, swaying back and forth, cool and calm under the spreading branches. I need never feel alone in the company of this dear tree.

February the eleventh, 1763

I still suffer from sleeplessness. The tropical night is much too entertaining for sleep, being far more alive than the torpid day. My candle draws around it a host of flying creatures, mostly moths of various sizes and designs. There is also a large, earthbound cockroach to entertain me, one that Pearl informs me is known as the "drummer." This fellow acquires his name by drumming on the woodwork of the house. If he is the kettle drum of the interior nocturnal orchestra, the huge string section is made up of whining mosquitoes.

When I step outside into the garden in search of a breath of wind, I am awestruck by the glory of the universe. It seems that I am closer to the stars here in the tropics than I ever was in England. I feel that with the smallest of effort I could pluck one of these glittering baubles and hold it in my hand. But closer by and easier to reach are crickets and tree toads, chirping and squawking. In the midst of their cacophony, suddenly the song of the Jamaican nightingale bursts forth. Such a declaration of passion! Such ardent courtship! Surely this cannot be the same fellow as the timid, reclusive English nightingale, whose little song is oft repeated? This bold singer has an endless repertoire.

The Spanish Town ladies condemn my nightly excursions as dangerous and foolhardy because of the "Noxious Dew." Their voices go round and round in my head. I can hear them chanting, admonishing me thus:

Beware, my dear, of the Noxious Dew.
If you step outside, it will fall on you.
If you step outside to admire the view,
to look at the stars, to gaze at the moon,
the noxious dew will take its cue,
and drizzle down on poor little you.

I refuse to pay attention to their nonsense.

February the fourteenth, 1763

Henry is no ardent nightingale, I fear, and I have yet to hear his courtship song. Some days ago, we sat down together in the dining room, for all the world like two business partners, to negotiate a date for our wedding; we did finally succeed in naming a day. This date, however, has now been cancelled because of the unexpected early docking and forthcoming departure of the *Leviathan*, a ship filled with merchandise for Mason, Mason & Fraser, merchandise for which Henry alone, he insists, can supervise the unloading and distribution since his brother Jonas is nowhere to be found. And then Henry must organize the cargo for the ship's return trip to England.

Nothing, not even a wedding, can stand in the way of the business of Mason, Mason & Fraser, and all of Henry's promises to take me here and there on the island have come to naught in the face of the pressure of commerce. I decided to send a note to him at his warehouse in Kingston.

Dear Henry,

May I suggest that I accompany you to your plantation in St Thomas-in-the-East next time you travel there, a place I would be most interested to see? Perhaps I could be of assistance to you, and I would certainly enjoy the change of scene.

His response:

Dear Martha,

If you came with me to St Thomas, Mrs Fraser would have to accompany you as a chaperone, and I would be concerned that the rigours of the journey might have an adverse effect on her health. I would have no time at all to spend with you, and your presence would act as a hindrance to the speed with which I could transact my affairs.

You have our wedding trip to Cinchona in the cool Blue Mountains to look forward to.

Henry was clearly trying to mollify me with this promise of Cinchona.

His absence has left me with time on my hands. I have now finished sewing my trousseau, and for one who finds sewing to be the least rewarding of female accomplishments, this is a considerable triumph. Pearl has embroidered a border of Jamaican birds and flowers all around the hem of my wedding dress and has signed her name to her work in neatly executed chain stitch. The colours she has chosen for the birds and flowers — magenta, orange, purple, pink — add a garish, tropical touch to an otherwise simple, traditional gown.

I have also had time to consider the question of a school for the children of household slaves in Spanish Town, and I am planning my course of action, even though it will be against Henry's will. The curate at the church of St Iago, Mr Kenet, is of like mind on the subject. He is a most tender-hearted man, a bachelor, two or three years older than myself, tall and thin, with bright blue eyes, and receding sandy-coloured hair. His hands are long and bear a thin coat of reddish hairs; his neatly-trimmed nails are immaculately clean. I find him most agreeable. He suggested that I might be able to use the church hall for two hours each morning. He offered to approach the rector for me, and did so, but the said gentleman turned down his request. Learning this, I decided to try my own powers of persuasion, and last week had the most appalling encounter with the Reverend Mr Rutter, he of the nasal bleat and whining argument. I should not have been surprised to find him adamantly opposed to the idea of educating the negro slaves. Like many churchmen on this island, his Christian charity extends only to those with white faces. He quickly turned the conversation from the education of slaves to his personal hobby horse.

"Who was it that discovered the New World?" he bleated at me, lowering his brows, and pinning me with a fixed stare.

"I have been told that Christopher Columbus was the first European to set foot on the islands of the West Indies," I responded cautiously, knowing that the trap was sprung.

I had walked straight into it, of course, and he launched immediately into a diatribe, swelling up with his theory, and whining thus:

"But it cannot be supposed that the children of Noah should be excluded from one entire quarter of the globe when they found themselves obliged to separate, in order to fulfil the designs of their Creator. Nor is it impossible that Noah himself, who lived three hundred and fifty years after the Deluge, should have undertaken the re-establishment of America. It is not probable that he would remain so many subsequent years without performing great exploits and undertaking noble enterprises. He, the inspired and experienced navigator, could he not build another ship, his own remaining fast on the mountains of Ararat, to repair the desolation of the earth? He who possessed a knowledge of a thousand things we are yet unacquainted with, by the tradition of sciences with which our first father is inspired, and whose children he had conversed with, could he be ignorant of these western lands, in which it is even possible that he himself might have been born? It cannot be imagined that the artisan of the largest ship the world ever saw, a ship destined to float upon a boundless ocean, agitated by an overwhelming and miraculous tempest, would have been unable to communicate to his children the art of navigation upon a sea reduced within its natural limits, comparatively tranquil, safe, and narrow. We must rather believe that he possessed means of fulfilling the decrees of Him who had especially elected him for the purpose of regenerating the race of man. Yes, yes. What, what? Speak up."

I allowed that, in the hands of our Creator, anything was possible.

"And," he continued, drawing a deep breath and surging forth again, "Procopius, during the reign of Justinian, mentions in *Vandalica* I.2. that there were in his time, standing in Africa Tingitana, two columns, erected by the Canaanites who had fled from Joshua, the son of Nun, and Eusebius says that the Canaanites, who were expelled by the Israelites, conducted colonies to Tripoli in Africa, and navigated the western ocean. Now, do you still believe that Columbus was first, eh? What?"

And here he clamped his jaw shut and thrust out his chin.

I allowed, once more, that in the hands of our Creator, anything was possible, but I tumbled into Rutter's trap once again by admitting that I personally might desire to have some proof of Noah's voyage to Jamaica and evidence of Canaanite settlements in the West Indies.

"Proof!" he puffed, and a fleck of spittle flew from the "f" of proof onto my dress. "Would you dare to ask God for proof of his ability?"

I agreed that it would be presumptuous to ask God for proof and bid Mr Rutter good day. As I drew my handkerchief from my reticule and wiped the spittle from my dress, I acknowledged to myself that I would never be able to change his mind about his decision on the church hall. This has not altered my determination to educate the children of slaves; it has instead strengthened my resolve. I will establish my school on the west gallery at Beverly.

Thus far I have but one desk, my own that I brought from England, with which to furnish the room. I need small desks for my pupils, slates, and a blackboard. I have asked the coffin-maker to fashion the desks. The slates and blackboard will be harder to come by.

I have already gathered four children of slaves who live at Beverly, and they are eager to commence. Mr Kenet promises me more, and Pearl, of course, will be my able assistant. This plan of action does not sit well with Mrs P.

Because Henry is away so often, I have not had the opportunity to discuss my plans for the school with him, but when I talk about them to the ladies of Spanish Town, they remain horrified.

"Knowledge will give these children a will to revolt!"

"Subjugation is the only fit way to treat the slave population!"

"Only by harsh punishment and the strictest discipline can the slaves be prevented from rising and killing off their masters, whom they outnumber so greatly!"

These women are clearly influenced by their husbands, whose eyes are so fixed on profit that they are unwilling to give even the smallest children the time for education. Such hardheartedness towards children is unusual in women. These children are barely walking before they are made to totter off to weed the gardens and feed the animals, closely watched by one of the old estate women, who rules them with a switch in the manner of those who rule her. I spit on the attitudes of the Spanish Town ladies. I will not listen. I will not be cajoled into thinking that these littlest of God's creatures can foment rebellion just because they can write their names. Should I be afraid of them? I should not, but still those women's voices ring in my head, condemning my every move:

Did you hear that she wants to set up a school?
A school for the slaves! Why that poor little fool!
It's doomed from the start. It will never succeed.
How can she teach savages? They simply can't read.
Arithmetic, too, is beyond their ken.
Have you heard them count? They never reach ten.
It will never succeed. It's doomed from the start.
She'd better forget it. Please pass the jam tart.

February the nineteenth, 1763

I have spent time at Beverly every day this week, making improvements to the furnishings and escaping the company of the Spanish Town matrons. I am gradually breaking down the wall of ice between Mrs Perkins and myself by acknowledging her greater knowledge and experience at Beverly and expressing my deep gratitude for every jot of help she occasionally extends. She is indeed thawing a little.

Because Henry is away at present at Reward, his plantation in St Thomas-in-the-East, she and I have found ourselves alone in each other's company more often than usual. One afternoon when I was reading on the gallery, she approached me, bearing a message from Henry. I thanked her for it and begged her to sit down and take a glass of lemonade with me. At this request, she found herself completely flummoxed. Was this gesture on my part acceptable?

"Sit, please, dear Mrs Perkins," I insisted. "Excuse me while I call for some lemonade." I left the gallery quickly, pre-empting her next move.

When I returned, she was sitting awkwardly on the front edge of a chair.

"You have worked so hard, today," I said, "Today and every day. You deserve a moment of rest and conversation." At this she slowly slid herself back in the chair, leaned into the cushion at her back, crossed her feet at the ankles, and let out a small, audible sigh.

"I have so many questions. You are the only one who can recount the full history of Beverly and its owners for me; Henry avows that he never has enough time to do so. But first, please tell me how you came to Jamaica."

At this moment, Celia, who will be my principal maidservant when I move from the Frasers' house to Beverly, arrived bearing a large jug of lemonade and two glasses. I poured one for Mrs Perkins and one for myself, and after she had drained half her glass, she looked down at her hands as though trying to make a hard decision. Finally, she looked up, and her eyes bored straight into mine. She paused.

"Please, Mrs Perkins, I so desire to learn about the path that brought you to Jamaica, and what kind of place you found it to be on your arrival."

Her inner struggle was almost palpable. I could see her wondering whether telling me her history would be caving in to the enemy, but then I saw a wave of satisfaction cross her face as she acknowledged to herself that she held all the cards in this particular game. She was taller, older, wiser — in her opinion — more in control of Pearl, and clearly far more valued by Henry than I. Revealing her history and that of Beverly would only place me more firmly in her debt.

She drank off the rest of her lemonade, settled herself down into the chair like a scrawny hen on its nest, cleared her throat, and began. Her voice changed. In place of her usual sharp, snappish whip of words, came a deeper and slower cadence and her voice rose and fell almost melodiously. She had fallen under the spell of that special demon, her own narrative, recalling incidents and conversations as though they had occurred yesterday.

"I had known the Grant family for many years. Silas Mason married my particular friend Eliza Grant, your aunt, and when he decided travel to Jamaica in search of wealth and sunshine, Eliza pleaded with me to accompany them. In fact, she completely refused to travel to Jamaica unless I came along."

I caught sight of a little smirk of self-satisfaction on Mrs Perkins's face.

"Indeed, I witnessed one of her tantrums to this effect. 'I have heard descriptions of Jamaica that stand my hair on end,' she shouted at Silas, with tears pouring down her face, 'tales of rebellion and mysterious sicknesses, of ghouls, of teeming mosquitoes and rat-sized insects whose stings can kill a man, of house-flattening hurricanos, and winds that drive a person mad.'"

"'We believe what we want to, my sweet,' replied Silas. 'As for me, I look forward to adventure, sunshine, and the promise of unimaginable riches. The tales of Jamaica I have heard include those of fortunes doubled, tripled, quadrupled, of fields of sugar cane waving in the gentle trade winds, of the richness of molasses, and the pure gold of rum. The rest is fickle rumour and speculation. Do not be afraid, my dear Eliza. My friend, Partridge, who has invited me to Spanish Town to become his partner, promises we will be comfortable and well-situated. Accompany me to Jamaica and see for yourself; then decide how you like the island, my angel.'

"'How can I survive in Jamaica without the company and encouragement of my dear Priscilla? I refuse to go without Priscilla.' At this, Eliza stamped her foot.

"'Very well. Priscilla shall accompany us,' he conceded. 'That is, if she is willing.'

"And here Eliza pressed her advantage. 'And Fanny must come too.'

"'Of course,' replied Silas, and groaned. Fanny was Eliza's coddled King Charles spaniel.

"Was I willing to join them? Indeed I was. I was no longer tied to England. Both my parents were dead, I had no brothers and sisters, and my husband, that foul-mouthed drunkard, had succeeded in killing himself five years previously by falling over a cliff at Filey and breaking his neck. I admit that I liked the idea of a bit of sunshine."

Here Mrs Perkins paused for breath, and I offered her more lemonade. She shook her head. She had warmed to her tale and did not wish to be interrupted. She was a surprisingly eloquent narrator, even going so far as to imitate the voices and physical mannerisms of Eliza and Silas. On she surged.

"On April the 12th, 1739, we set sail for Jamaica aboard the *Good Fortune*. Eliza spent the first two weeks of the voyage in her cabin, ill, tearful, and convinced the ship was about to sink.

Fanny trembled and whined at her feet. I strode around the deck, in the firm belief that exercise and fresh air were the best cures for seasickness. I was right. Finally, when the weather improved and the seas calmed, Eliza appeared on deck, only to complain about the glare and the stench of molasses.

"Silas told her that she'd better get used to the stench because it was the smell of lucre. He explored the *Good Fortune* from stem to stern, pronounced her trim, and told the captain that if he weren't about to make his fortune in Jamaica, he would sign up as first mate. Then he invited the captain to play a game of cards. By the end of the voyage, he had played cards with every member of the crew, and thereby enriched his inheritance."

"What was Silas like?" I asked.

"He had a mind turned to commerce and gain, and a body with a wide girth, meaty hands, a red face, and a bald head. His laugh was raucous, and he ate far too much."

"Do continue."

"For our accommodation in Jamaica, Mr Partridge made available to us a large house on the east side of Spanish Town. Eliza immediately retired to her room, with Fanny panting at her feet. The heat prostrated them both. Not me, though. She remained there, emerging only at meal times, for weeks on end. Her prostration meant the administration of the household and its servants fell directly into my hands. When Silas realised how great a task it was, he gave me the title of housekeeper, and began paying me for my work. Quite right too."

"He must have been delighted by your efficiency," I remarked. Again came that little smirk of self-satisfaction.

"At first, I was daunted by the size of the task, although I never let him know this. Frankly, I was surprised by how many slaves were required to run a household, slaves that I would have to manage. Sometimes I felt it would be simpler to do everything myself. I was even more surprised by the various domestic animals that considered the interior of the house their territory; chickens roosted on the gallery, horses peered through the doors, pigeons flew in and out the windows, and pigs rooted for crumbs in the dining room. Disgusting! It seemed that it was my job to shoo all these creatures away.

"I admit that I was not a little angered when my friend Eliza began to treat me like a serving woman and Silas treated me like a slave. Apparently in gaining the title of housekeeper, I lost the position of cherished friend. One evening Silas shouted at me, 'Don't just stand there looking disapproving — get that hog out of here!' pointing to a large animal that had just trotted into the dining room.

"I countered, 'I take leave to remind you, Silas Mason, that you have no right to shout at me. Even though I am now officially your housekeeper, I am not your slave. The animal you wish removed is none of my business. I shall summon your manservant to take care of the matter.' I swept out of the room. Subsequently, Silas treated me with more respect. He knew he could not afford to lose me."

"Bravo, Mrs Perkins!" I said, clapping my hands with approval.

At this point, she took a deep breath, folded her hands, and let out a sigh of satisfaction. Night was falling and the mosquitoes were beginning to feast on our ankles.

"Shall we go inside and continue?" I asked, even though I knew it was time for me to return to the Frasers' house for the night.

"That's enough for now." Mrs Perkins's eyes, which had become almost dreamy as she recounted her past, suddenly switched back to the present reality. "I must lock up the stores," she said, and with that she stood up briskly, smoothed down the creases in her skirt, jangled the keys that hung from her waist, turned on her heel, and left the gallery.

I wanted more. I wanted to learn about Silas Mason's rise to prosperity, about the birth and childhood of my husband-to-be, about Henry's brother Jonas, and about all the circumstances surrounding my arranged marriage.

February the twenty-first, 1763

Yesterday, I lay in wait for Mrs Perkins all day, hoping she would return to the gallery so that I could encourage her to tell me more, but when I finally cornered her, she said she was far too busy. This afternoon, however, she did reappear. After settling down with a glass of lemonade, she began again and had soon warmed to her subject. Once more, I was surprised and delighted by her quick memory and her fluency. It was as though she gained actual flesh by living in the past, and the past filled out those dry bones of hers, allowed her blood to flow more freely, and loosened her tongue.

"Unlike Eliza, Silas was roused by the climate and the change of scene. He rolled up his sleeves, squared his Yorkshire jaw, and set to work to make his fortune. He examined the premises of Partridge & Partridge (which as you know is now a major import-export business that ships sugar, rum, coffee, allspice, and mahogany to its correspondents for sale in England. They in turn send out all the supplies needed for the plantation here in Jamaica). He was appalled by the dust and disorder of the premises, but before he set to work to improve matters, he insisted that Partridge change the name of the establishment from Partridge & Partridge to Partridge & Mason, since the younger Partridge had returned to England some years previously. He had the new sign painted in black and gold and hung it where it could be seen by all who made their way along Monk Street.

"Silas then balanced the books, took inventory, stirred up the workers to clean and paint, and entered into a battle with rats, ants, and cockroaches in the storerooms. Having set all to rights, he suggested to Partridge that they open a retail shop in the front part of the building. Partridge protested that his business was wholesale not retail, but Silas insisted the time was ripe for retail since so many people continued to move to Spanish Town from England, and these people needed somewhere to spend their money. Silas won his point, and soon enough Partridge & Mason opened their doors to those who could pay for luxury items from overseas. With the shelves in the new retail shop loaded with merchandise from England — all sorts of fabrics and fancy goods and condiments — all Spanish Town came to buy. The business flourished from the start."

Suddenly I had a vision of those eager, greedy Spanish Town matrons fingering the goods, and in my head I heard their gloating voices:

> *What delicious delights are now to be found*
> *at Partridge & Mason! Such treasures abound!*
> *I bought some preserves. I bought some lace.*
> *I bought a bracelet. I bought a case*
> *of madeira and a very large tin*
> *of sultanas. It's such a sin-*
> *ful paradise, a garden of Eden.*
> *A trip to the store is a trip to heaven!*

Just at this moment, Pearl wandered onto the gallery.

"Why you talking so much?" she asked.

"Mrs Perkins is telling me about her early days in Jamaica."

"I want she should tell me too."

"Pearl! You know better than to speak like that! Kindly rephrase your remark." Mrs Perkins had swiftly reverted to her usual snappish self.

"Please, please, may I listen too, Auntie darlin'?" asked Pearl, kissing the widow's unyielding cheek and stroking her clenched fist, uncurling the fingers one by one.

I saw no reason why Pearl, too, should not hear the tale, and so I spoke up for her. Once again, I perceived Mrs Perkins's quandary; but who does not appreciate an attentive audience? Who, when she has been starved for attention for years, does not relish a moment in the light?

She stood up, stretched, and sat back down again. Pearl curled herself up like a cat at her feet and started to inspect Mrs Perkins's shoes with an inquisitive finger.

"Business prospered beyond Silas's expectations, and Partridge & Mason soon acquired a warehouse in the port of Kingston for the storage of merchandise coming to and leaving Jamaica. Leave my feet alone, Pearl, or leave the room.

"Soon after our arrival, Fanny came on heat, and crowds of howling, mangy dogs assembled outside Eliza's bedroom window. 'Get away from here, you vile creatures!' Eliza screamed. She screamed at Silas to make the dogs go away, screamed at me to make the dogs go away, screamed at the slaves to make the dogs go away. Silas appointed a dog chaser, armed with a large broom, to shoo the animals away, but still they came, those scavengers from the streets and alleys of Spanish Town. One big, ugly dog managed to streak past Eliza just as she opened the door to her bedroom. He leapt past her to the windowsill from where Fanny was watching her circling admirers. In a flash, he covered the little bitch while Eliza screamed and flapped her arms. Too late."

Mrs Perkins's eyes glinted with excitement, and colour flooded her usually pale face. I had never seen her this animated.

"Oh, no," cried Pearl. "What happened?"

"Fanny died giving birth to one enormous living black puppy and two smaller ones, stillborn. Eliza, prostrated with grief, would have nothing to do with the lone survivor, who was tall and short-haired like his father, except for the long, feathery ears and tail of his mother. Silas, believing that Eliza would learn to love the dog, optimistically named him Beau, and left him in my care. I had absolutely no intention of being the animal's caretaker, so I handed him over to Cuthbert, the butler. Beau soon learned to stay well away from Eliza, who always shrieked 'Keep away from me, murderer!' each time he came in view.

"In 1740, Partridge's wife died and he returned to England, having first sold his interest in the business to Silas. Three days later, on May the ninth, Eliza gave birth to Henry. The birth was surprisingly easy for someone who always considered her health precarious — Henry was born a mere four hours after she felt her first pangs — but she found the experience brutal in the extreme. I was tending to Eliza when Silas first saw Henry. He was overjoyed.

"'Never again,' Eliza moaned.

"'You will soon change your mind, my darling!'

"'Never again.'

"'Come, come, my dear. Think only of the product and not of its delivery. Look at this wonderful child and see how peacefully he sleeps. We shall have lots of these little fellows.'

"'Never again,' moaned Eliza. But, even so, she smiled at the sleeping baby in her arms.

"The next morning Silas took down the sign at his store, telling the clerk, 'Paint it in blue and gold, and let it read "Mason & Son" in large letters.'

"From the moment of his birth, Henry was well-behaved, and his parents adored him."

"Sweet baby Henry," murmured Pearl.

"Silas called for him each evening on returning from work. He would bounce the child on his knee and tell him stories about the life of a merchant. Thus Henry's first words had much to do with commerce, and his favourite bedtime tales were those of buying and selling, of ships and cargoes and pirates, of bidding at auction, of sugar crops, and of the amassing of fortunes. He became familiar at an early age with a world where anything could be bought or sold.

"Two years after Henry's birth, Eliza struggled to deliver another boy, and nearly died in the process. When the midwife summoned Silas to come and inspect his new son, Eliza wailed, 'Never, never again,' and turned away from the angry, howling baby."

"Naughty Jonas from the day he born," muttered Pearl.

"'A second son. Hooray! Hoorah! I say, well done, Eliza!' crowed Silas, snatching the baby from the midwife and joggling him roughly up and down. The baby howled, and Beau barked outside the window.

"'Kill the dog,' ordered Eliza."

Pearl leapt to her feet. "Kill Beau? Oh, no!"

"Don't be silly, Pearl," said Mrs Perkins. "You know perfectly well your grandfather never had the heart to kill Beau. Sit down and let me continue." She wrested Pearl back to the floor and proceeded.

"'Look at the size of the child's nose,' groaned Eliza, 'Where did that come from?'

"'Why, it resembles the elegant proboscis of my uncle, Jonas Mason, the erstwhile mayor of Scarborough! If he turns out to be anything like his illustrious relative, he has a fine future in store. We shall call him Jonas after my uncle.'"

I was again surprised by Mrs Perkins's ability to imitate Silas. She dropped her voice, swelled her narrow chest, waggled her eyebrows, and to the degree she was able, boomed like a very Cicero. Then her voice screeched as she assumed the role of Eliza.

"'Your side of the family. I knew it. Oh, what frightful screaming. Why will the child not be quiet? My head is splitting.'

"'My own empire,' cried Silas.

"The next day, Silas asked his clerk to change the sign once more, this time adding an 's' so that it read 'Mason & Sons.'

"When Jonas was old enough for conversation, Silas offered him the same stories about commerce he had offered Henry. Jonas showed no interest. He was wild where Henry was mild. He climbed on chairs and tables, and leapt to the floor, while Henry sat still and did as he was told. He played in the dirt and no matter how often his nursemaid changed his clothes, he was always filthy. He persisted in stealing Henry's toys, and bit his brother when Henry tried to reclaim them. He far preferred the company of his young nursemaid to that of his mother or father. She threw him high in the air when his parents were not looking; she taught him songs from Africa, songs of which his mother and I did not approve; she gave him sugar cane to chew on instead of the rusks I recommended. Later, when I started to teach him his ABCs, he spat at me when I insisted that he sit still. He was always a very wicked little boy."

Pearl leapt up, and shouted, "I hate Jonas. One time when I was lickle . . . "

"Little," snapped Mrs Perkins.

"One time when I was lit-tle, Jonas he grab me pigtail an' stuff red ants down me back." Pearl began to sob at the painful memory.

"My pigtail. My back," interrupted Mrs Perkins again. I wished to heavens she would leave the girl to proceed with her story.

"'Cry baby, cry baby,' Jonas say and pull my plait again and t'row me down on the floor. He mash me down with he foot . . . "

"His foot. Come along, Pearl. You can speak better than this."

"Go on, Pearl," I said encouragingly.

"Then Jonas said 'Baby, baby on de floor. Cry again, I pull some more.' And I said, 'I go tell Aunt Priss.' And Jonas said, 'Tittle tattle, butter for fat, if you kill my dog, I kill your cat.' And I yelled for you, Auntie, and you come running, but when you reach, Jonas him gone." Pearl's eyes were dancing as she took the stage. I found her story-telling delightful and was in no way disconcerted by her grammatical errors, which seemed to increase the more excited she became.

"One night I wake up and see a duppy standing in me doorway. White, white. I was so frightened. It raised its arms and moved toward me, waggling its fingers. I scream an' scream, 'Aunt Priss, Aunt Priss,' but when it hear your footsteps it flit away."

Here Mrs Perkins intercepted the tale.

"I made straight for Jonas's room, and found him on his bed, rolled up in a sheet. 'Leave the child in peace,' I said. 'You can't fool me, young man. I know precisely what you are up to.' And that insolent boy shouted back at me, 'What you talkin' about, ole woman? Priss, Priss, Prisssss.' In truth, I had begun to fear Jonas myself. He had raised his arm to strike me more than once."

The widow shuddered, and I was afraid she might leave off her narrative, so I swiftly spoke, "Dear Mrs Perkins, pray let us leave Jonas and return to Henry."

"Is there time? Is that not enough for today?"

"There is plenty of time. You must take all the time you need."

"Very well. When Henry was eight years old, Silas took the decision to send him to boarding school in England. He made the announcement to Eliza and me early one morning, first clearing his throat and thrusting out his stomach before launching into his argument." Here Mrs Perkins stood up and raised her right arm, pointing her index finger in the air.

"'Gentlemen of fortune, like myself, hem hem, send their sons to Great Britain to have the advantage of a polite, generous education, since learning in Jamaica is at a low ebb these days. Boys who do not have this advantage become spoiled and lethargic. Now that Henry is eight, he must go to England. As for Jonas, he's not worth the brass. If he learns anything at all, he'll learn it from me, right here, under my eye.'

"Eliza seized the moment, announcing excitedly that she would accompany Henry to England, and then she asked me to come immediately and help with her packing.

"'Not so quick, Eliza,' said Silas, holding up his hand. 'How will I live without my poppet, my sweet poppet?' I wished he would not use that silly lovey-dovey language in front of me. 'Perhaps Priscilla should accompany Henry to England instead of you? What do you say, Priscilla?' he asked.

"I had no time to respond before Eliza shrieked, 'Oh no, dear husband. I could never, never remain in Spanish Town without Priscilla's dear company. And you could never manage without her running your household. She must stay here to take care of you. I am the useless one. I should be the one to go. I promise I will come back as soon as Henry is settled. I shall be here again before you've even noticed I have gone. Now, come at once, Priscilla, and help me pack.'

"'Just a moment, my sweet. Let Priscilla speak. Now, what say you, Priscilla, my dear? Will you accompany Henry to England or will you remain here?'

"'Priscilla likes it here. She told me so,' whined Eliza.

"I took a long time before responding. They both held their breath. And then I spoke.

"'As I am a childless widow, with no pressing need to return to England, it would be better by far for all concerned if I remain here to run the household.'

"Eliza clapped her hands with joy, and so the matter was settled. But poor little Henry was unhappy about the decision. He could not understand why he was being banished. He asked me how his father, whom he loved so much, could bear to part with him. He believed Silas must hate him to do such a terrible thing. I tried to comfort him, but he was inconsolable. I heard him several times say to Silas, 'Papa, Papa, I do not want to go to England. Why must I leave you?'

"Silas repeated again and again that Henry must go to England to become an educated gentleman, and that he must be a brave boy. He insisted that when Henry returned they would work together, side by side, always with the interests of Mason & Sons at heart. Henry pleaded that he was ready for work even now and that, thanks to me, he could add and subtract, so he would be an excellent bookkeeper."

At this, Mrs Perkins gave another of her little smirks of self-satisfaction.

"For the first time in his life, that mild little boy lost his temper and shouted at his father that he refused to go to England, that he wanted to stay in Jamaica for ever and ever, that he was a good boy and should not be punished, and that Jonas should be the one to be banished. But Silas was not a person who changed his mind when he had made a decision. He patted Henry on the head and assured him he was receiving a privilege rather than a punishment, and that he would write to him every week. He advised Henry to make a plan to work hard, look forward, and always keep the best interests of Mason & Sons at heart.

"And that was that. Eliza and Henry sailed for England six weeks later." Here Mrs Perkins drank some lemonade and uncrossed and re-crossed her ankles before she continued. Pearl stretched out flat on the floor, lying there, arms outstretched like a gorgeous starfish, but Mrs Perkins seemed not to notice.

"Eliza wrote to me about their voyage on the *Betsy*. Strangely enough she suffered not at all from the seasickness she endured on the journey out, and by the time the ship arrived at Liverpool, she had completely recovered her health and good spirits. She was revived. She wrote to me that she had managed to banish Jonas almost completely from her thoughts, even going so far as to blot out the sight of him as he stuck his tongue out at her at the moment of farewell. She felt well rid of him, and only had the slightest twinge of guilt when someone asked her, 'Didn't I understand that you had two sons?'"

With this, Mrs Perkins snapped back to the present, and that was that for the day. Our eloquent rhapsode had suddenly returned to her snappish self, and the flesh seemed to recede from her bones. She stood up and instructed Pearl to do the same. Together they marched from the gallery into the dining room. Pearl looked back at me over her shoulder and gave me a wink.

I remember Henry so well when he first arrived in Yorkshire off the *Betsy*. It was 1748 and he was thirteen years old at the time. He was a sallow, sad-looking lad, who preferred me above all his cousins, undoubtedly because I alone expressed an interest not just in him but in the island from which he had just arrived. My questions about Jamaica seemed to ease his homesickness. We enjoyed each other's company.

Aunt Eliza invited her friends to bring their children to meet him, and along came those mothers with their primped and polished darlings who bowed on cue, spoke when they were spoken to, and who could parrot Latin precociously while basking in adult adulation. Henry, in contrast, refused to talk in company, cringed when he was spoken to, and clung to his mother's side looking miserable and dull.

"Oh, isn't he charming!" the friends cooed falsely. "So quiet and so shy." And then stretching hard for one more adjective that could possibly please Eliza,

"So . . . tall."

I witnessed Aunt Eliza drilling Henry in the art of conversation, stressing to him that "manners maketh man." She strove to drive away any vestige of a Jamaican accent, which I felt was a pity because I loved that singsong speech. She then hired an elderly tutor, much vaunted for his immense knowledge of Latin and Greek, to educate Henry up to the same level as English boys. Henry hated the beaky, dusty scholar on sight and told me so.

Even though I was five years older than he, I spent a great deal of time with him in the months before he departed for boarding school. I was his only true friend, and he would converse happily with me about Jamaica. It was as though talking about the island loosened his tongue, and this was good for me because I wanted to learn everything I could about the exotic island from which he came, the island where my beloved Arthur had spent his final days.

"What is a galliwasp, Henry?"

"How high is Blue Mountain Peak?"

"What is the colour of orange blossom?"

"Is it true that there are alligators in Jamaica?"

Then he would talk incessantly about his island, and sometimes his eyes would fill with tears. Poor fellow.

Soon enough the day came for him to leave for school. He made me promise to write to him, which I did, and in return I received letters in which he tried to be brave although it was clear he hated the place. He was always cold, always hungry, always disgusted by the monotonously grey diet of stale bread, grey bacon, and watery cabbage. He was forced to labour at studies that he scorned, his natural intelligence revolting against the relentless regime of Latin and Greek. Only in the subjects that might prepare him for the life of a Jamaican merchant did he excel: arithmetic, reading, and writing.

Henry was reunited with us during his longed-for exeats and holidays, joyous times that were inevitably spoiled for him by his mother's unwillingness to talk of their return to Jamaica.

It was as clear as crystal that Aunt Eliza had absolutely no intention whatsoever of returning to Jamaica, and I believe she harboured the illusion that Henry would refuse to return to Jamaica when the time came. What a vain hope.

He matured early, growing whiskers and towering over other boys his age when he was only fourteen. He hated sports, cold water, and the itch of woolen clothes; he was the victim of persistent colds and of chilblains on fingers and feet. He remained an outsider at school, was bullied by the older boys and referred to as "The Idiot" or "The Creature." What little remained of his gentle singsong speech was cruelly mimicked by his schoolfellows.

February the twenty-fifth, 1763

Three days still remain before Henry's return from Reward. I have refused all invitations from the Spanish Town matrons so that Mrs Perkins can continue her tale, in the morning, in the afternoon, in the evening, whenever she is available. This morning, at last, she revealed some of the secrets that had still mystified me. We met again on the gallery; again Pearl drifted in and arranged herself decorously, this time on the swing seat, idly moving it back and forth with one bare big toe. Mrs Perkins was eager to continue her tale; she had been captivated by her own narrative powers and her willing audience.

"Mason & Sons prospered so much," she began, "that Silas needed a way to spend his profits. Because he had no one else to talk to about this, and because he knew I was completely trustworthy, he described to me what he had in mind." Here again came that little sniff of self-approval. "First he needed a house in Kingston, where he could spend the night when ships arrived with cargo from overseas. 'Kingston is a fine town these days,' he said, justifying his action, 'well situated at the base of the Blue Mountains — bustling, spacious, a place of vast trade, with never less than two or three hundred vessels in the bay before it. Yes, yes, I need a house from whose windows I can watch the vessels as they come and go in Kingston harbour, a house with comfortable accommodation where I can entertain ships' captains and visiting merchants.'

"He soon found a house on Harbour Street which fitted his needs. Next, with his import-export business continuously thriving, he was ready for another challenge. He determined to try his hand at farming, and if that were successful, he would purchase a sugar plantation. 'That's when the money will really start rolling in,' he said, rubbing his hands together before devouring a large meal of suckling pig and fried plantains. I watched him unbuckle his belt. He remarked that his clothes were uncommonly tight. I refrained from remarking that he was uncommonly fat.

"He purchased 137 acres of farmland on the banks of the Rio Cobre, just outside Spanish Town. He acquired oxen, donkeys, horses, cows, and mules. He operated his pen in cunning fashion, raising working animals, which he sold to plantations where they were used for transportation and to power the sugar mills. In turn, he purchased worn-out working cattle from the same plantations and fattened them up for the local meat market.

"Having bought the land and the animals, he decided it was time to build his residence, a house that would express his character. Generous and stable is how he put it."

I interrupted Mrs Perkins here because Henry had already told me about the building of Beverly — a safe topic of conversation between us. I have yet to live in the house, but I can already tell it is truly admirable, although the furnishings still leave much to be desired. It is a large establishment, and to think that I am to be its mistress fills me with a mixture of happy anticipation and a fear that I may not be up to the task.

"Now, Mrs Perkins, tell me about when you moved in to Beverly," I said, and she picked up the tale again.

"Silas was delighted that I was so efficient and trustworthy and that his household ran so smoothly under my management. But I was not delighted by his behaviour. What would Eliza, his wife in England, think of the fact that he continually brought Chloe, the mulatto laundress, into the house?"

"Chloe!" cried Pearl. "She my mother." Here she jumped up and performed a regal little dance, lifting her head high, holding out her skirt, and pointing her toes. "Martha, did you know that my grandmother was a Cormantee princess? A real princess!"

"And your grandfather was slave trader," said Mrs Perkins.

"I don't want to know about him. Tell me more about my mother, Aunt Priss."

"Your mother was tall and good-looking, and she was soon visibly with child."

"Me!" said Pearl, distending her stomach and waggling her hips.

"Indeed. But I could never bring myself to speak to her, and this made Silas angry. He constantly justified his immoral behaviour, blaming it on Eliza's absence from Jamaica. 'What's a man to do?' he asked. What indeed? A promise before God between man and wife must not be broken. Look at me; I stayed faithful to that drunken lout because of my promise to him. It should have been far easier for Silas to remain faithful to dear Eliza, even though she had not yet returned to Jamaica, than for me to remain loyal to Ernest Perkins."

The widow's voice rose in this paean to her own self-righteousness, and then she stood up suddenly and launched into a diatribe, stamping her foot and shaking her fist, once again a very Cicero.

"It is my strong belief that it would be far better if in Jamaica the white men would abate of their infatuated attachments to black women, and, instead of being graced with yellow offspring not their own, perform the duty incumbent on every good citizen, by raising in honourable wedlock a race of unadulterated beings."

Good heavens!

"I'm not yellow!" shouted Pearl, pinching her cheeks to make them turn pink. I hastily intervened.

"Tell us about the birth of Pearl, dear Mrs Perkins. She must have been a beautiful baby." At this, Pearl brightened up, but the widow pursed her narrow lips and shook her head.

"The birth was difficult. The mother died, but Monimia saved the baby."

"Monimia, the cook?"

"Yes, Monimia. She fancies herself a midwife."

"I killed my mother!" shrieked Pearl, bursting into tears.

"You most certainly did not kill your mother, you silly girl," I said, reaching over to the swing seat and stroking her hair. "Your mother's body failed her, and this was not your fault. Go on, Mrs Perkins."

"Silas was undone," she said with a slight sneer that seemed to say that Chloe's death served him right. "And the same day he insisted that I was to be in charge of the child and it should be raised in the house. First a dog, and then a child. I ask you. I choked at the notion. But when Silas put baby Pearl into my arms and I saw how beautiful she was, something strange came over me." Mrs Perkins shook her head from side to side as if trying to understand how this could be.

Pearl looked at me and smirked.

"I was so beautiful that Aunt Priss she love me straight away!"

Mrs Perkins ignored her.

"I told Silas that Eliza would never forgive me if she found out I was caring for his bastard, and he responded that she need never know because he believed she would never return to Jamaica.

"'Take her, love her, teach her,' he begged. And I looked down into that little sleeping face, and there and then, on the spot, I promised to do all those things."

"And you did, Aunt Priss, and look how lovely I am now!" said Pearl, striking a pose.

"And conceited, too," snapped Mrs Perkins, and then changed tack.

"Silas decided to release Henry from boarding school when he was sixteen and sent him to a merchant's counting house in Bristol to learn business. Here at last Henry came to grips with matters that he considered important, matters such as trade, accounts, and bills of lading. He succeeded beyond everyone's expectations. The Bristol merchant was delighted with his new recruit, and when, after a year, Silas insisted that Henry return to Jamaica to put truth into the sign 'Mason & Sons,' the merchant was unwilling to part with him. But there was nothing he could do; Henry was like a racehorse at the starting gate. He packed his bags at once and travelled to Yorkshire to bid farewell to his mother and her relatives before leaving for Jamaica."

"I remember when he came back," I interrupted. "After

his year of working with the merchant, Henry was a changed person. He was no longer a lanky, fearful lad; he had become a confident young man. Aunt Eliza was clearly proud of the transformation but desolated that he was returning to Jamaica. She had been convinced that after several years in England, he would never leave. I must admit that I, too, shed a few tears to see my dear cousin depart for such a distant country. I made him promise he would write me letters full of descriptions of Jamaica and its natural wonders. I promised him that I would sooner or later visit him there. And then I overheard the farewell instructions his mother gave him as he was setting off. She clung to his arm as he prepared to leave, her voice rising in her desperate need to control his actions.

"'Do not sit outside at night in the noxious dew; do not ford rivers in flood; do not climb mountains during or just after it rains for fear of landslides; do not cross bridges unless you first ascertain that their supports are firm; always sleep under a mosquito net; never smoke in bed; avoid rum.'

"And then, unable to contain herself, she ran after him and grabbed him by the arm as he mounted the first step into the coach. She uttered her parting words vehemently, her voice rising to a crescendo: 'Do not be tempted by the charms of slave women. Marry soon and marry an Englishwoman. Promise me, Henry.'"

What could Henry do in the face of such an onslaught? He simply nodded his head and waved goodbye.

And then Mrs Perkins commented, "Henry shook off England like a dog shakes off water."

Pearl sat up suddenly. "I remember when Henry first arrive. So tall, taller than my father, and so well-dress. I run to him and t'row my arms around him."

"Throw," said Mrs Perkins involuntarily and then continued. "Silas revealed to Henry that Pearl was his half-sister, and that he should accept her and love her. Henry extracted himself from her embrace and held her at arm's length. He was naturally astonished to have suddenly acquired a nine-year-old sister of mixed blood. He had no idea how to address the creature who had thrown herself at him so precipitously.

"'My two favourites, together at last!' crowed Silas, advancing on them and binding them together in a tight embrace. 'You have only to regard Pearl to love her, Henry. Take a good look, son.' And Henry stepped back and gazed at Pearl for a long time. Then he opened his arms and embraced her."

"And him twirl me roun' and roun'."

"For heaven's sake, child. And he twirled me."

"What were you wearing, Pearl?" I interjected.

"I was wearing me best white muslin dress with scarlet ribbons t'readed — th-readed — t'rough — th-rough the sleeves and the neck. And I had a big hibiscus flower in me hair. Henry say I was beautiful, and he kiss me."

"Silas was so happy." Mrs Perkins resumed. "He then took Henry on a tour of the pen even before he would let him sit down and have a meal. Pearl dragged me by the hand and insisted that we follow them. As we trailed behind, I listened to Silas boasting about his possessions. I remember almost exactly what he said: 'Over there I have 100 acres in Guinea grass, up there I have 150 acres in Scots grass and rushes, and down by the Rio Cobre I have 125 acres in common pasture. In that direction you see five acres of slaves' housing and gardens, and seven acres for the horses. The seven remaining acres are old river courses and wasteland. I keep a Scottish overseer, 40 slaves and a domestic staff of eleven, consisting of my butler, Cuthbert;

the cook, Monimia; a footman; a coachman; an assistant cook; a waiting maid, Celia; two house-cleaners; two washerwomen; and a seamstress. What d'ye think of that, Son? Not too bad for a lad from Yorkshire!'"

"What a memory you have, Mrs Perkins!"

She shrugged and admitted that the possessions were all still in Beverly's inventory. Then she continued, "As we returned to the house, Henry asked Silas where his brother was, and Silas replied that he never knew where Jonas was from one moment to the next. Finally, he allowed Henry to retire to his room, where the servants had prepared a bath for him. I caught Pearl peeping through the keyhole as he bathed, and I had to drag her away."

I stifled a giggle.

"Henry was singing," said Pearl, as though that were the perfect excuse for spying on her brother. Quickly changing the subject, she asked, "Do you remember, Aunt Priss, what happened that night when we was eating?"

"Were. I'd rather forget it."

"Martha, I will tell you," said Pearl. "Jonas let an alligator loose in the dining room. It go snap-snap with its jaws, and waddle straight towards Henry. Henry jump up on him chair and spill pumpkin soup all over the table. 'JONAS!' yell me father, but Jonas disappear. The servants come running, and they chase the alligator all roun' the dining room. Monimia she come with a sack and a stick, and she make the alligator walk into the sack."

"It sounds as though Jonas was still behaving like a little boy, playing practical jokes," I said. Then I turned to Mrs Perkins and asked her to tell me how Jonas had spent his time while Henry was in England.

"Jonas's schooling was patched together in Jamaica: various tutors, all of whom left in a hurry, followed by some schooling in a religious establishment. When he was fifteen, he was expelled for drinking and whoring. Now he is supposed to be working for Henry, stocking the shelves at Mason & Sons. In truth he spends most of his time playing cards and gambling. On the rare occasions he stocks shelves, he also stocks his pockets." Here Mrs Perkins gave a sniff of disapproval.

I had wanted to give Jonas a fair chance and not decide what his character was until I knew him better. But I must admit that my first impressions of him were most unpleasant. He seemed the direct opposite of Henry. Where Henry is tall, handsome, and reserved, Jonas is short, wiry, and gleams with wickedness. Where Henry's eyes are dark and still, Jonas's flash with light and mischief. Where Henry appears prudent, quiet, and circumspect, Jonas is profligate, violent, and mercurial. It is hard to imagine two brothers less alike. My initial encounter with Jonas shocked me. It occurred on my first visit to the Spanish Town emporium with Henry. I was examining the goods for sale, when Jonas suddenly leapt up from behind a counter like a Jack-in-the-box springing from nowhere. I gasped in surprise, and he laughed a hollow, rum-soaked, mocking laugh right in my face. I had to step backwards to avoid the stench of rum. Henry reprimanded him, and he laughed again before skipping nonchalantly out into the street, whistling.

"That is my brother," said Henry. "Now you know."

Mrs Perkins continued her narrative. "Henry began working with his father immediately, making constant use of his facility with arithmetic. He soon grasped that in the world of the merchant, he must expect the unexpected and count on nothing. He learned that ships regularly sank, crops regularly perished, cattle sickened and died as often as they reproduced, and slaves could most fearsomely revolt. But he perceived that, in spite of all these setbacks and, in some cases, because of them, people needed the provisions that only the merchants provided. He ignored Jonas, whose rare appearances at the shop he discouraged.

"Silas stepped aside once Henry had proved himself competent. He had other fish to fry 'It is time for my sugar estate,' he announced one day. 'I believe that St Thomas-in-the-East is the place to investigate.' Soon enough he had found a perfect site, and set about the business of establishing a plantation, building the works and a residence, and buying more and more slaves. Like everything else he touched, it began turning a profit within a couple of years. As you know, he called his plantation Reward, and reward him it did.

"And he believed in rewarding himself by reaching for the rum bottle. He reached for the rum bottle again and again. Ugh! And his capacity for food knew no bounds. Monimia, who had been warming his bed ever since the laundress died and had borne him two sons . . . "

"Freddie and Augustus," interrupted Pearl.

" . . . was up to the culinary challenge. As you have already noticed, she is a good cook." This was said somewhat grudgingly. "With her own large appetite, she was only too willing to abet Silas in his quest for the most extravagant table in Jamaica. Henry confessed to me he was dismayed to witness his father becoming fatter and fatter, and sinking into drunken stupours. He suspected that he was taking risks with the profits from Mason & Sons and speculating with slave ships.

"And now I come to the terrible part of this tale." Mrs Perkins sat bolt upright and grasped the arms of her chair, her knuckles white, her eyes staring into the long, dangerous territory of this particular recollection.

"I had always insisted on a family meal late each afternoon, a meal where we practiced good manners and engaged in polite conversation, something I deemed important for Pearl if she were to make a fine marriage with an Englishman."

I found this remark interesting. It seems that for her Pearl is an exception to the rule that Englishmen should marry only pure-blooded Englishwomen. Pearl, under her expert tutelage, had miraculously become completely white!

"However," she continued, "Silas's manners had become abhorrent. Dear Eliza would have been horrified to see him apply himself to a plate of food with the enthusiasm of a hog at a trough, all the while throwing bones to his hound, that ancient, ugly Beau. And Jonas invariably appeared late at the dinner table and often drunk, while Henry regarded the scene in silence and with disdain. Only Pearl and I made any attempt at social intercourse."

Pearl preened.

"On the evening I bring to your attention, Silas was particularly gluttonous. Monimia had served his favourite meal of roast chicken, plantain, and rice and peas. I could not believe my eyes as he put an entire chicken breast into his mouth at one time."

Then Pearl sprang to her feet and took over, gesticulating wildly. "He choke on the wishbone! Him face turn red, den purple. My father fall down on the floor. Aunt Priss stan' up and scream. Henry just stare. Jonas jump up, trip over Beau, and fall flat. Only I, Pearl, only I do something! I stick me hand down me father t'roat but I cyan't reach the bone."

Mrs Perkins resumed, "Throat. Soon the whole household

was surging around Silas, who battled for breath on the floor. That fool Monimia flung her heavy self on top of him, shrieking and covering his face with kisses.

"'Out of the way, all of you,' I commanded, elbowing my way through the crowd and kicking Beau, who was trying to lick his master's hand. But still the crowd pushed in and the air was full of the wailing of the servants. Beau let out a dreadful howl and all of a sudden, silence fell."

Pearl, wide-eyed, took over again. "Then Monimia screamed 'AIEE! I hear Master spirit leave him body. I hear him rise up. Look, look, Master him fly t'rough de window.' And she jump up and push t'rough the crowd, and lean out the window, and shout, 'I see him. Look, look. I see him spirit go. Look up in de sky. AIEE! My master gone.' She fall down on the groun', and slap the floor with she hands."

Mrs Perkins jumped in, "Ignoring her prone figure, even trampling on her, the slaves ran to the window for a glimpse of the departing soul. I never heard such rubbish. Who can see a soul? Then I had to kick that stupid dog away again in order to cover Silas with the table cloth."

"What a terrible story!" I said.

"My poor old Papa, my dear Papa," sobbed Pearl. I moved over to the swing seat and hugged her to me.

Mrs Perkins continued: "Jonas left, and spent the night in a rum house. Henry quit the dining room and went to his father's desk. He sat there all night with his head in his hands. I gave instructions to the servants to clear the dining table and to lay Silas upon it. Monimia washed him with more loud tears than water and dressed him for the last time. When all was finished, old Beau curled himself up at the foot of the table, and promptly died. When I told Henry about this, he decreed that

Beau should be placed in the coffin with his master. I responded that it would be a tight fit, but he insisted, and so the carpenter sawed and hammered all night to produce a coffin large enough for those two big creatures."

"What did I do?" asked Pearl. "I don't remember."

"Celia put you to bed and sang you to sleep. The following day, as soon as the funeral was over — immediate burial is a necessity here before the corpse turns black and stinks — Henry locked himself in his father's room. For the next three days he refused to unlock his door and turned away all offers of nourishment. We could do nothing for him."

"But then I cure him! I make him eat!" said Pearl. "I save an orange from my supper, and I put it in my pocket, and in the middle of the night I climb out my bedroom window onto the roof of the gallery. I walk all along one side of the house, turn a corner, and climb in Henry's window. Henry wake up when the floor creak. I lift the mosquito net and sit down cross-legged at the foot of the bed. Then I peel the orange so the skin come off in one twirl. I separate the pieces and hold one out to Henry.

"'Eat,' I say."

"'Feed me,' he say."

"I crawl over him and place the piece between his lips. He bite it and he chew, and then he eat another piece, then another and another. And then I wrap my arms around my brother and rock him back and forth and comfort him. When I get tired, I push him back on the pillow, and stroke his forehead. Then I lift up the mosquito net and I gone. Like duppy."

"Yes, that was when Henry started eating again," said Mrs Perkins.

"Well done, Pearl!" I said.

"Tomorrow I shall tell you about the reading of the will.

I have a copy of it. Goodnight to you both," said Mrs Perkins, pulling herself back to the present, becoming thinner and paler, and then disappearing.

Pearl and I swung gently on the swing seat for a while without talking. She was content in the knowledge that I admired her tale more than the grammar of its telling. Then I took my leave and returned to the Frasers' house for the night.

February the twenty-seventh, 1763

There remained just one day before Henry's return from Reward. We three assembled on the gallery early in the morning in the hope that an early start would give Mrs Perkins enough time to finish her tale. Pearl arrived bearing a bowl of genips, a fruit that resembles grapes but has a hard skin and a single large, white seed; the sounds of her popping their skins with her teeth to get at the cool, orange-coloured, jelly-like flesh and then spitting the large stones from the gallery into the garden accompanied Mrs Perkins's story. Fortunately, the widow seemed unaware of these sounds once she had immersed herself in the narrative.

"Silas's estate lawyer arrived to read the will. The poor old man had to shout it through the door because Henry still refused to leave his room. When he had finished reading, he gave me a copy of it, thus demonstrating once again my trustworthiness. I have the copy here," she said, producing it from a deep pocket in her skirt. "Henry, the firstborn, the apple of his father's eye, inherited Beverly and its contents, the cattle pen and its animals, the business in Spanish Town, the warehouses in Kingston, the plantation at Reward, the domestic staff, and all the slaves. At that time the domestic staff consisted of . . . " And here Mrs Perkins broke off and consulted the paper.

"A negro man named Cuthbert

"A ditto named Paul

"An elderly ditto named Hannibal

"A negro woman named Monimia

"A ditto named Quasheba

"A young ditto named Clare

"A ditto ditto named Jenny

"A ditto ditto named Hannah

"A negro girl named Celia

"A mulatto girl named Pearl left free by testator's will

"A mulatto boy named Augustus, Monimia's son, left free
    by testator's will

"A ditto ditto named Freddie, Monimia's son, left free
    by testator's will

"Henry was required by the terms of the will to make certain that his mother in England wanted for nothing in the way of financial support. The other inheritors were Jonas, Pearl, and me. Jonas received a sum of money and the house in Kingston. When Pearl reached the age of eighteen, she was to receive a generous allowance and two slaves. On me, Silas settled a sum of money. Next came the inventory of the contents of the house."

Mrs Perkins dropped the will onto her lap, and I thought she was going to stop there. I quickly asked her to read the inventory aloud, thinking that it would be of interest to see how much of what Eliza brought to Jamaica remained.

"Not all the items came from England, of course. The mahogany furniture was made here. But this is the whole list: 45 silver spoons, a knife case with 24 knives and forks; 8 silver salvers; 4 pairs of silver candlesticks; 3 silver ewers; a mahogany book case filled with 56 books; an old portmanteau;

a chest containing numerous pieces of Irish linen, mosquito net lawn, baize, and blanketing; 3 chamber chairs and pots; 5 tables and washstands; a large mahogany dining table and 12 mahogany chairs; 6 side tables; an old writing desk; 2 sofas; 6 old chairs; a cedar chest; 3 bedsteads with mattresses, mosquito nets, bolsters, and pillows; 3 looking glasses; 4 old chests of drawers; a bunker for liquors, containing 27 bottles of Madeira wine; a card table; plates, cups, saucers, glasses; 6 sugar bowls; decanters; a water jar and frame; a japanned coffee pot, tea pot, and milk pot; an eight-day clock; a map of the world; a spyglass; a large Bible; a small prayer book."

"Thank you. That was indeed interesting." My impression was that almost everything had remained in place at Beverly, all the items of value having been locked up safely by Mrs Perkins. I doubt, however, that any Madeira remained. Jonas would have taken care of that.

"Henry pulled himself together eventually and returned to work. It did him good. He restored and enlarged the premises of Mason & Sons and took on the merchant Thomas Fraser as a partner. Even though Jonas was nominally a partner, Henry banned him from work at Mason, Mason & Fraser in Spanish Town, and insisted that he work in the warehouse in Kingston and live the house he had inherited there. Henry could not bear the disorder that Jonas caused, and as head of the family, he finally felt he could wield power over his brother. I overheard him instruct Jonas to put away childish things now that he had attained his majority. It was time to measure up, to put his shoulder to the wheel, to be cooperative, to learn the language of commerce, and to stay away from rum and whores. Jonas wriggled and sulked and slammed out of the room.

"Henry had few friends and deeply missed his father. He was lonely, and he was forced to spend more and more time with Pearl and me when he was not working. He sorely needed distraction from the world of commerce and cows. But most of all, he needed a wife. The ladies of Spanish Town appreciated this all too well and set about match-making."

Again I heard those voices, those conniving voices in my head:

> *Henry is lonely. Henry is sad.*
> *Oh, it's too bad. Henry is sad.*
> *Would he like Julia? Would he like Maud?*
> *She came in to thousands, so I've been told.*
> *Frances is lovely — if a tiny bit fat.*
> *How about Jenny? Consumptive? No? Mad!*
> *Perhaps Antoinetta from out in the east?*
> *But her manners are dreadful;*
> *she behaves like a beast.*
> *We'll soon think of someone; we'll dangle our wares*
> *At Henry, dear Henry, to banish his cares.*

"I wanted he should marry me. I love Henry!" cried Pearl.

"Silly girl," snapped Mrs Perkins. "Back in England, Eliza was well aware of Henry's predicament. She wrote to him repeatedly about her concern for his welfare and his need for an English wife. She insisted that he would never find happiness with a local woman. When Henry reported in his letters to her that there was no young Englishwoman suitable for him to marry in all of Spanish Town and Kingston — in fact, in all of Jamaica — his mother decided to arrange a marriage. She wrote to him accordingly. Soon after her letter arrived, I found it on Henry's desk, and I felt duty bound to read it."

"Aunt Priss, you naughty!" said Pearl.

"I most certainly am not. It was my right to know what was going on."

"What did it say, Mrs Perkins?" I asked. The widow pulled a document from her other deep pocket, and began to read. She had certainly come well prepared.

"My dear Son,

If I could, I would have you be, what I know nobody is — perfect. As that is impossible, I would have you as near perfection as possible. I know nobody in a fairer way toward it than yourself, should you so please. Never were so many pains taken for anybody's education as for yours; and never has anybody had those opportunities for know- ledge and improvement which you have had. Yet you are incomplete without a wife. Should you marry soon and well, my constant anxiety will be put to rest — anxiety that you may fall in with the prevailing custom in Jamaica, become infatuated with one of the black women of the island, pro- duce yellow children, sink into indolence, and lose interest in the business of Mason & Sons.

Do you remember your second cousin Martha? Do you remember how kind she was, how she was your favourite companion, and how you and she used to play cards together for hours on end? Do you remember how sweetly she played the clavichord when we visited her family at the vicarage each Christmas? Two years ago she agreed to wed Captain Arthur Clarke of the Royal Navy, and plans were well under way for their marriage when he was suddenly called upon to sail to the West Indies. His bravery and success in the expeditionary force at the siege of Havana became legendary.

But, alas, although Captain Clarke's life was spared in the battle, he subsequently succumbed to dysentery.

Since the death of her betrothed, Martha has been grieving. She lives with Lizzie, her married sister — you remember Lizzie — whose husband is a gentleman farmer. There she acts as governess for their children. While she enjoys her task and is, in fact, a skilled teacher, she remains restless and broken-hearted. Through his adventures, Captain Clarke had brought the world outside England to her door and she had looked forward to her future with gladness and curiosity. On the occasions when I visit the family, Martha is always at pains to persuade me to describe my life in Jamaica, the flora and fauna of the island, and my voyage to and fro. She pesters me for information about flowers and butterflies; she hangs on my every word. I describe as much as I can remember, simulating enthusiasm for her benefit.

Martha's present situation is far from an ideal one in which to encounter any kind of adventure which might offer the opportunity for travel or the chance to meet the right partner. The only buildings she sees are farm houses, the only men for miles around are farm labourers. Left to her own devices, she has ventured farther and farther into the world of books. I have never known such an omnivorous reader; her knowledge, already considerable under the influence of her learned father, is now encyclopedic and her conversation is sprinkled with references to what she reads. She is never without an apt quotation or an idea that has been born out of something she has read. This makes her a most delightful companion."

"This is true, Martha," interrupted Pearl. "I find you are a most delightful companion."

"Thank you, Pearl."

Mrs Perkins continued reading the letter.

"Her mother and I have agreed that you and Martha make an ideal match, and her father has already raised the possibility of such a match to her. You would offer her the chance to leave the path labelled 'Old Maid.' If you were to marry her, she would become mistress of her own house in a part of the world that she desires to see. In turn, she would make you a trustworthy partner, a suitable mother for your children, and a companion of the most mentally invigorating sort. Although she will undoubtedly be sorry to leave her little pupils here, she seems more than willing to entertain the idea. As she said: 'I have always longed for the opportunity to travel and am eager to broaden my horizons.'

"Now, Henry, although I know that she might not be your first choice in terms of physical attributes, and although she is a little older than you are, I also know that you are not the kind of person who thinks merely of surface beauty. Martha's beauty flows from inside, and you know how much her inquiring mind and lively conversation captivated you in the past."

"Martha, how can she say this?" said Pearl, stroking my hair. "You beautiful all over, not just inside."

"It is your duty to your late father to marry so that his business may be handed down, in all its prosperity, to another generation of Englishmen. It will prosper if you marry to the purpose; do it thoroughly, not superficially.

Please send me your response on the next packet. Do not delay. Letters take long enough to cross the ocean without your dawdling for weeks over your reply. This only I am sure of, that you will prove either the greatest pain or the greatest pleasure of, Yours."

So this is how Eliza challenged Henry to marry me! I had always wondered how she persuaded him. To think that I was so easily manipulated.

Mrs Perkins folded up the letter, put it back in her pocket and said, "This put Henry in a quandary, but as he always had, he bowed once again to Eliza's strong will."

"And that is when he wrote to me?" I enquired.

"Yes, indeed."

"I still have that letter, and I brought it with me today. I thought you might like to hear what he said. It is a beautiful, persuasive letter, and I could not refuse his offer."

"Read it to us!" said Pearl, and Mrs Perkins's eyes glinted with curiosity.

"Dear Martha,

You have, no doubt, been approached by my mother concerning the question of marriage — our marriage. To her approach, I lend my own voice. Martha, will you marry me?

Will you venture across the Atlantic Ocean to an island that has too many beauties not to engage your attention? Jamaica produces a thousand surprizing curiosities. Kind Nature in return for sultry sun has blessed it with varieties of trees and flowers, birds and butterflies that few countries can boast of.

Spanish Town itself is situated in a pleasant valley on

the banks of the Rio Cobre and has all the advantages you could wish for in a small city. You would not be deprived of entertainment. Merchants here live after a very gay manner; they have frequent balls, and have lately got a playhouse, where they retain a set of extraordinary good actors.

An orange tree, laden with fruit, grows against the window at which I am writing. I look out over groves of citrus, plantains, cocoanuts, and pepper trees. A large spreading tamarind tree is the centerpiece of the more formal gardens. From my vantage point, I can also see the stables, which are attractively formed of open wickerwork.

Because you and I hail from the same family, we have much common ground. We will understand each other and will work together towards a common good.

I remember you with fondness and admiration. Say yes, and you will delight your loving cousin, Henry

Postscript: I remember well the raspberry jam you made one summer. Please bring some with you if you decide in my favour."

I folded the letter up and looked across at Mrs Perkins. She nodded her head and began to rise from her chair. She seemed deflated, a much smaller, paler person than the one who had recounted the narrative. I thanked her profusely for her time and generosity in telling the tale. I almost wished to throw my arms around her in gratitude, and indeed started forward as if I might do so, but she sidestepped, and grabbed Pearl by the hand.

"Come along now," she snapped. Together they left the gallery, with Pearl dragging her feet and glancing back at me.

April the twenty-third, 1763

The banns have been announced in the church of St Iago for the past three Sundays, and I am to be married there this Thursday. I know the church well now, having attended Sunday services there ever since my arrival and having studied it closely during the Reverend Rutter's appalling sermons, trying to shut out the sound of his voice.

I believe my father would find St Iago a fitting church for his daughter's marriage. An elegant structure of brick, in form of a cross, it consists of four aisles, of which the main aisle measures one hundred and twenty-nine feet in length, and twenty-nine in breadth. As it is without a tower, the congregation is summoned by a small bell hung in a wooden frame in the churchyard; the pulpit, pews, and wainscoting are of cedar and mahogany; and the aisles for the most part paved with marble. The altar-piece is handsome and adorned with carved work. The ceiling is neatly coved and graced with two magnificent chandeliers of gilt brass; the walls are hung with several monuments of marble, plain, but well executed.

I recently learned that the building was erected in two years, at the parochial expense, on the foundation of the former one, which was irreparably damaged by the hurricane of August 1712. And in 1762, just last year, it received a thorough repair and at present yields to none in the island for a becoming neatness. It is indeed a delightful building, and I wish my father could be the one to perform the ceremony. How I shall miss the attendance of my family and friends, supporting me throughout the day. Even Mrs Jamison, my shipboard friend, is unable to be by my side because she is grieving over the recent loss of her husband and planning to return to England.

I have little of the eager, blushing bride about me. I fear I have failed to gain the confidence of my husband-to-be, and what hopes I had for a marriage of true love springing out of this marriage of convenience and familial fondness are now slim at best. I am not proud of this litany of complaint. I know I should be filled with joy at the idea of my impending marriage and the joining of two souls in a common life, but I fear that these two souls will have to leap across a chasm of estrangement. We are no longer the loving companions we were in England. Henry has withdrawn his affection from me, and if I did not know better —there is no one else here on whom his affection might turn, as far as I can see — I might suspect him to be in love with somebody else.

I have no feelings of reluctance about living in Jamaica because I continue to be daily charmed by its beauty and its natural history. To be sure, I have travelled little as yet because of the pressures of Henry's business, but in the last two weeks Mrs Fraser has again taken me for rides in her carriage to points of interest within easy reach of Spanish Town. Just yesterday, we took the road alongside the Rio Cobre and followed the rushing torrent up through its narrow valley. Trees hung over the road and the river, making the valley cool and vibrantly green. Colourful birds flashed overhead, gleaming vermillion, yellow, blue. The doctor bird is the dashing favourite of Jamaica, a hummingbird in formal attire, with two extremely long black tail feathers, which whir mysteriously as he flies.

Mrs Fraser is a whirlwind of activity as she supervises the preparations for the wedding breakfast. She has planned an elaborate menu to which I fear I shall be able to do scant justice because any kind of nervousness never fails to steal away my appetite. Henry, however, will be certain to make up for my failure.

Mr and Mrs Fraser are unfailingly kind. Mr Fraser is a quiet, thoughtful man, quick to console and slow to condemn. Although also quick to console, Mrs Fraser is quite his opposite in other ways, and I must admit I am wearying of her unending torrent of words. Every time I settle down on her gallery with a book, she flies at me, showering me with conversational gifts, gifts that — to my mind — are mere soufflés: snippets of gossip, receipts, comments on the weather, advice about clothing. If I look on the bright side of my married state when I leave Frasers' care, I can appreciate that life with Henry will afford plenty of silence and plenty of time for reading.

Pearl will be my bridal attendant, and the glory of my attendant should do much to distract the attention of the onlookers from the apprehensive bride. Working together at Beverly, she and I are making a gown of yellow silk for her, which, on her insistence, we are adorning with gold sequins. She had been greatly struck by the effect of sequins when she saw a band of roving actors, gleaming in satin and sequins, proclaiming their forthcoming event in Spanish Town. She was not only attracted by their sequins; she was seduced by their recommendations. She listened carefully, memorized their announcements, and made her case to Henry when he found us together, working on her dress.

"Henry, Henry, take me to see the play!" Pearl begged.

"What play is that?" Henry asked.

"'The Fair Penitent', an excellent, excellent play by Nicholas Rowe, to be performed by a talented cast of players who have come to Spanish Town all the way from England. Please, please,

Henry!" Pearl jumped up and down with impatience, and then wrapped her arms around him.

"What do you think, Martha?" he asked, looking at me over her shoulder. "Is this suitable fare for a young lady?"

"It is a tragedy," I responded carefully, not wanting to say anything that might jeopardise this opportunity for Pearl.

"I love tragedy!" cried Pearl. "It is so much more interestin' than comedy!"

"Well, well! Martha, shall we attend a performance of 'The Fair Penitent' since Pearl recommends it so highly?" asked Henry.

"But what about me?" shrieked Pearl, hitting him on the chest.

Henry laughed and grabbed her by the wrists. "You, too, of course, you silly goose."

Three nights before Henry and I were married, we went, all three, to see the play. It turned out that the "The Fair Penitent" herself was suitably fair but unsuitably penitent, to my mind, but Pearl was enthralled.

"I intend to become an actress," she announced to me the following day.

"This would be a most inappropriate path for one as young and tender as you," I responded, discouragingly.

"I am older every day, and I am NOT tender," Pearl countered. "I can memorise parts with ease. Listen. Listen."

And here Pearl ran to the staircase, climbed a few stairs, and draped herself over the banister.

> *O Romeo, Romeo! wherefore art thou Romeo?*
> *Deny thy father and refuse thy name;*
> *Or, if thou wilt not, be but sworn my love,*
> *And I'll no longer be a Capulet.*

I was amazed; I had lent her my copy of "Romeo and Juliet" just a few days previously. I decided to test her further and made a cruel jump to the end of the play, lowering my voice in an approximation of Friar Laurence.

Come, go, good Juliet; I dare no longer stay.

Pearl paused for the briefest moment before she spoke:

Go, get thee hence, for I will not away.
What's here? a cup, closed in my true love's hand.

She wrapped her hands around an imaginary goblet and sniffed it.

Poison, I see, hath been his timeless end.

She paused, at a loss for a moment, and then she grasped the air.

O happy dagger!
This is thy sheath; there rust, and let me die.

With this she pretended to stab herself, fell on the stairs, and rolled down, thumpety-thump, until she arrived on the dining room floor, crumpled and apparently insensate.

"That was, indeed, a tragic piece of acting!" I cried enthusiastically.

Pearl stirred, rose to her feet, and curtseyed to her audience of one. Unless I am mistaken, she had tried to memorise the entire play.

The yellow silk dress is her first such gown and she is fascinated by how elegant she suddenly appears. As she glances at herself in the mirror, she flirts with her reflection, lowering her eyelids, pursing her mouth, and smiling broadly at her beauty. She is right to smile at the radiant heroine of her own particular drama.

Of all my wedding presents, I treasure most the silver brush and comb and hand mirror from my sister, Lizzie. This little mirror is my reassurance. So often in this strange land, among people whose ambitions or lack thereof are foreign to mine, I lose sight of myself. I cease to remember Martha Grant and what she cared about. But when I go to my dressing table and pick up my mirror and see my plain, familiar face staring back, I recall myself and all that I believe in.

My plans for the little school are stalled until the wedding is past, but I am eager to start work, and will waste no time in doing so as soon as we return from our wedding trip. I have much to learn from the lore of children on this island, with its mixture of tales from Africa and England and the memory of its indigenous Arawak past. What a jumble of language and ideas!

"Come, Martha, come and taste," Mrs Fraser calls, inviting me to taste the batter for the wedding cake.

The next time I write on these pages, Martha Grant will be Martha Mason. I pray that I may prove myself a proper wife for Henry, and that he will turn his face towards me and appreciate the loyal and loving partner that I intend to be.

Santiago de la Vega Gazette

MAY 18, 1763
MARRIAGES

Early on Thursday morning, in the parish church of St Iago de la Vega, Henry Mason, Esq., of this island, elder son of the late Silas Mason, Esq. and Mrs Eliza Mason of England, to Miss Martha Grant, of Yorkshire, England, elder daughter of the Reverend Percival Grant, a lady in every respect qualified to render the married state compleatly happy.

May the twenty-first, 1763

"In every respect qualified to render the married state compleatly happy"? Me? With Arthur, perhaps, but with Henry I fear "compleat happiness" will be elusive.

Words cannot describe how much I missed my dear papa and sister on my wedding day, and yet I was not totally miserable. I observed so much that was amusing and extraordinary and was obliged to suspend my knowledge of English weddings and to enter into the spirit of a strangely different kind of adventure.

The night before the wedding, I could not sleep. I tossed and turned. I chased mosquitoes. I brushed my hair. I went onto the upstairs gallery and examined the stars, happy in the knowledge that those to the northeast were the same stars that look down on Papa and Lizzie. By candlelight, I embroidered a four-leaf clover among the tropical flowers that Pearl had sewn on my wedding dress.

Finally, I returned to my bed and fell into a fitful sleep. It was still dark when I awoke to hear Phyllis, the Fraser's domestic into whose care I had been delivered, calling at my door.

"Mistress Mart'a! Dolly Bride! Wake up. Is now your wedding day," and in she came jiggling and giggling to my room bearing hot water, fresh towels and a lantern. She lifted up the mosquito net and pulled me to my feet, again calling me "Dolly Bride" because, compared to her, I am as small as a toy. Soon Mrs Fraser joined us, squawking and fluttering around me as I dressed, turning a simple task into an elaborate ritual. She clucked as she buttoned me into my white, high-necked, long-sleeved wedding dress, and tied its apron around the front. Then with a mighty crowing she placed my mob cap on my head, admiring its height and the manner in which it was caught around the head by a frill.

While I was being attended to at the Frasers' house, Cuthbert was assisting his master at Beverly. Henry had visited the tailor in Spanish Town, who with a mighty effort had created an outfit such as a European gentleman might sport on his wedding day. Consequently, Henry suffered, sweating, throughout the whole event in a medium length dark blue woolen jacket trimmed with brass buttons, light blue knee britches, and a white striped dimity lapelled waistcoat. He wore his wig tied back in a black silk bag.

Thus polished and dressed, we set off from our separate residences in the soft light of early morning to meet each other at the parish church of St Iago de la Vega. When arriving at the church, I was delighted to learn that the Reverend Rutter was suffering from a bilious attack and unable to perform the service, and that Mr Kenet was replacing him.

The words of the marriage ceremony differed in no way from the one to which I was accustomed. Everything else, however, was astonishing in its variety. Henry and I were married at 7.30 in the morning in order to benefit from the relative coolness of the air. The newly refurbished church was a bower of riotous colour, most of the flowers being of red or purple hues, to which the brilliant yellow satin of my bridal attendant's attire added its golden glow. All the many doors were wide open to catch the breeze, but the breeze was not the only thing the open doors invited to enter. A crowd of curious onlookers formed at the back of the church, and a scrawny cat strolled in and settled down to scratch itself in the middle of the aisle just as I was walking down on Mr Fraser's arm. Then came the sound of horse's hooves, and "Whoa! Whoa!" as Henry's brother Jonas arrived from Kingston, hitched his horse to the wooden bell frame, came flying up the steps, tripped and fell, cursing, into a pew.

I trembled my way to the altar, clinging to Mr Fraser's arm. Once delivered there, I was greeted by Mr Kenet who stepped forward and took my hands in his, holding them firmly until I stopped shaking before he began the wedding service. In the absence of my dear father, there was no one I would rather marry me than Mr Kenet.

As Henry and I recited our vows, the morning sentinel marched proudly in front of the altar and crowed loudly. Throughout the entire ceremony bats, whose efforts to sleep had been rudely disturbed, squeaked shrilly. Finally, as we left the church, four mangy dogs on the steps entered into a vociferous altercation over what looked like the jawbone of an ass. Henry kicked them out of the way and I cried at him to desist.

My new husband and I rode with Pearl in a carriage back to the Frasers' house, cheered along the way by higglers and followed by a crowd of whooping children and barking dogs. The Frasers' entire staff was out to greet us on our return, shouting and laughing, dressed in their best, the women wearing their brightest kerchiefs. They gathered around us singing and dancing in a circle. What a contrast this outpouring of high-spirited congratulations was compared to the tepid festivities I have witnessed at many an English wedding!

Having accepted interminable good wishes from the crowd, we went inside to a cool room. Here was Mrs Fraser's *pièce de résistance*. Everything gleamed: the silver, the crystal, the gilt-framed portraits, the mahogany. Shafts of bright sunlight sliced through the shutters only to be softened by filmy curtains. The sideboard groaned with the weight of the wedding breakfast; the groom and guests gave it their full attention, but the bride was only able to peck at her plate and take little sips from her goblet. After we had dined, we all left the house, goblets in hand, and strolled on the lawn among the flowering shrubs and beneath the shade of the spreading branches of the Frasers' great silk-cotton tree.

Mr Fraser then proposed a toast to Henry and me and our future happiness, to which Henry responded with a few short platitudes. The guests cheered and clapped, and the Spanish Town matrons gathered around me to admire my dress, the only item of my wardrobe that they have pronounced fit.

Next, a breathless messenger arrived with news that a fire had broken out in the warehouse in Kingston, and that the partners, Mason, Mason, and Fraser, must come immediately. Without a word, Henry snatched the goblet from his brother's hand, and cast it to the ground. Jonas staggered and tried vainly to execute an elaborate bow while Henry dragged him away, followed by Mr Fraser. Pearl ran after them, screaming, in a fruitless attempt to persuade them to stay.

Having my wedding breakfast interrupted by a fire struck me as more deliverance than disaster. Of course, I was concerned that lives might be endangered and the partners would suffer a loss, but for my part, I had gained a sudden reprieve from society and a chance to return to my reading. A collective tut-tutting emanated from the ladies of Spanish Town, who were socially flummoxed. Should they leave or should they stay? Eventually, taking the partners' departure as a cue for their own, they gathered up their parasols and reticules, and prepared to leave. As they bade me farewell, their expressions of congratulation turned to ones of sympathy for the poor bride over the sudden departure of her groom. Frankly, I was in no need of their sympathy; what I needed was peace and quiet.

As soon as all the guests had left, I changed from my wedding gown into a day dress and packed my portmanteau. Thomas

Fraser called for a carriage, summoned me and his wife, and then we three set off for Beverly, my new home.

"Let me help you unpack," cried Mrs Fraser when we arrived, fluttering around me again like a hen with a chick.

"No, no, my dear Jessica," I insisted, "you have already outperformed yourself at the wedding and in all your months of hospitality. It is now up to me to establish myself in these new surroundings. You cannot do it for me. Farewell, farewell, and a thousand thanks to you both."

"Farewell, dear Martha. You shall be much in our thoughts," responded Jessica, wiping a tear from her eye, and giving me an anxious glance. Mr Fraser pressed my hand encouragingly. I restrained my own tears, embraced the dear couple warmly, waved them farewell, and turned from their arms straight into the path of the ever-vigilant Mrs Perkins.

"Where is Pearl?" I asked her. I had seen her leave the wedding with Mrs Perkins, shortly after Henry's departure.

"She is in her room, attending to her studies, and must not be disturbed," she insisted, and then turned to order two slaves to carry my portmanteau up the stairs. She preceded me to the large, airy bedroom I would share with Henry. Having directed the placement of the portmanteau, she shooed the slaves away.

"I trust that you will find everything to your satisfaction, Mrs Mason," she said, daring me to find fault. Gone was the storyteller; the housekeeper had returned in full force now she had a new mistress with whom to contend.

"Entirely, Mrs Perkins. Thank you."

Without another word, she left the room, shutting the door firmly behind her. I flung myself face down on the bed, and gave my tears free rein, muffling my sobs with a pillow. I wept and wept. What had I done by marrying Henry? How could I endure the consummation of a loveless marriage? Who could console me now?

Through my sobs, I heard a sudden fluttering of wings. I raised my head and saw that a pigeon — I believe it was the Jamaican ring-tailed pigeon — had flown into the room through the open doors of the upstairs gallery. She landed on the dressing table, settled, squatted, and laid an egg, appearing just as surprised by the event as I was. I could not help but laugh out loud, and on hearing the sound, she glanced at me with a stern pink eye, and quickly flew away.

Ah, kind Nature! When we believe that all is lost, you send your message of Life.

THE WEDDING NIGHT

Having overseen the containment of the fire, which was merely smouldering by the time he arrived in Kingston, Henry returns to Beverly, and is to be found drinking rum as he sits smoking on the gallery. He is thinking, on some level, "Tobacco, divine, rare, super-excellent tobacco, which goes far beyond all their panaceas, potable gold, and philosophers' stones; a sovereign remedy to all diseases!"

Martha is reading in the bedroom she is to share with Henry.

Mrs Perkins is in her bedroom, in her nightgown, working on the day's accounts.

Pearl has tiptoed down from her bedroom. Still wearing her yellow dress, she is in the dining room, dancing and singing to herself, golden in the candelight, two Pearls, the real one captivated by the one reflected in the gilt-edged mirror.

Henry can see Pearl from the gallery.

Cuthbert is the last of the servants to leave the house and return to his quarters.

"Goodnight, Master," says Cuthbert, grinning. "I hope you have a good, good night."

Mrs Perkins closes her accounts book, blows out her lamp, lies down on her bed, and folds her hands over her narrow chest. She falls quickly into the sound sleep of the self-righteous.

Martha pours water from the large, blue-flowered pitcher into the hand basin. She disrobes and washes herself, and then pulls on her nightdress. She unpins her hair and brushes it while she looks at her tired, anxious face in the hand mirror. She lifts the mosquito net and climbs into the big bed that once belonged to Silas Mason. The mattress is lumpy, but the linen is smooth and comfortable, and the pillowcases are embroidered with flowers. Martha is overcome with weariness. To her surprise she finds that she is still clutching the ornamental bodkin she had removed from her mob cap. She slips it under her pillow. She slaps at her arm in an attempt to kill the lone mosquito that always seems to find its way inside the net. She is too weary to sleep. She selects a volume from her bedside table, spreads her hair out on her pillow to cool the back of her neck, but cannot concentrate to read.

In the dining room, Pearl lifts the hem of her dress and watches her feet as she dances.

Mrs Perkins snores.

Henry rouses himself from his chair.

Martha closes her book.

Pearl curtsies to herself in the mirror, lowering her eyelids.

Henry crosses the gallery and enters the dining room.

Mrs Perkins twitches.

Martha grinds her teeth.

"Go to bed, Pearl," says Henry.

"I am not tired," answers Pearl, from deep in her yellow silk curtsey, gazing up at him.

Strips of moonlight slash through the shutters of Mrs Perkins's room.

Henry turns away from Pearl and moves to the staircase. He grasps the handrail and climbs the creaking steps.

A dog howls.

Henry flings open the bedroom door. Martha gasps, draws her knees to her chest, and clutches her arms around her legs. She makes herself as small and safe as she can. Henry looms in the doorway. Martha shuts her eyes. He walks across the room, raises the mosquito net, and opens his mouth to speak to her. She turns away from him. He tries to pry the fingers of one hand free. She flinches. He lowers the net and goes to his dressing room and disrobes. She exhales. He pulls on his nightshirt. She notices a blur of insect and a streak of blood on her arm. He returns to the bedroom and crosses the floor. She stretches out, stiff as a board, toes pointed, neck rigid, jaws clamped. He raises the mosquito net again and clambers onto the bed.

The mattress sags under his weight as Henry Mason crawls over Martha's unyielding body and hovers over her on all fours. He lowers himself on top of her and squashes the breath from her lungs. She is suffocating, she is dead, except for one hand that remains alive and agile. It slips under her pillow. It grasps the bodkin, surfaces, flies up, flies down, striking Henry on the flank. He roars into the pillow, he rolls, he falls from the bed, pulling the mosquito net down from its frame. He breaks away from it as he stumbles to his feet and runs to his dressing room. Martha lies ramrod still, scarcely breathing, and then she stirs, struggling to free herself from the netting. Shakily, she stands on the bed, inside the net, in an attempt to hang the fabric back on its frame, but trembles so vigourously that she loses her balance and falls back down, still enmeshed.

Uneasy clouds cross the face of the moon. The night thickens and darkens. Henry's muffled roar has disturbed Mrs Perkins and she stirs but then dozes back to sleep and dreams of Tacky roaring for revenge.

From the top of the stairs, Henry looks down on Pearl, his delight, spinning around and around, her skirt flaring. As if in a trance, he descends the stairs, drawn into the vortex of her dance. She holds out her arms and they swirl around together.

Spinning, giddy, she kisses him; he misses a beat and swoons, swoons from having wanted her so long, knowing as he falls that it would be bad but heaven to die like this. Her arms sling round him as he swoons, or he might crack his head on the floor, and she holds on to him, and sinks down with him, dizzily, scratching him on her sequins, nesting him in her yellow silk, nesting right there on the glossy floorboards.

When he comes back, through the stinging stars, and gasps, and breathes her breath breathing his, and sees her eyes' concern, and feels her fingers fluttering around his face, he wills himself another spell, wanting this loving to last forever, and rolls, with Pearl, over and over, and under the dining room table.

The wind picks up. A shutter bangs against a wall. Mrs Perkins starts awake and tries to shake off her nightmare. A flash of lightning illuminates the reassuring familiarity of her room. No sign of Tacky there. The shutter bangs again downstairs. The smell of advancing rain creeps across the pasture, creeps into her room, sharp and sweet. The shutter bangs once more.

"I must shut that shutter," she grumbles to herself as she climbs out of bed and lights her oil lantern.

"Shut that shutter," she mutters again, dazed with sleep, as she crosses her room and opens the door.

"Emily, you must shut that shutter," she mutters through a yawn, as she crosses the landing.

"You must shut it. No one else will," she grumbles as she starts down the mahogany staircase to the ground floor.

She enters the dining room, leaving it immediately for the gallery where she finds the flapping offender. Lightning flashes as she fastens the latch. Thunder jounces and rolls, and the clouds unleash rain directly overhead in drum rolls on the roof. Sheets of rain fall in solid curtains from the gallery roof, making the house safe from all intruders.

Mrs Perkins, satisfied with a job well done, turns back into the house. From the threshold, she looks across the dining room, and the light from her lantern picks up a glint of yellow silk spewing from below the table. She bends forward as she circles the table, her lantern illuminating every detail of what she sees. Her mouth gapes open in a speechless cry. She breathes in and tries to scream but the howl sticks in her throat. She turns her back on the devil's work, and flees up the stairs, trips at the top, and drops the lantern. Plunged into utter darkness, she feels her way along the landing, enters her room, and slams the door behind her.

The rain beats down. The air inside the house is close and fetid, but the air outside is suddenly cool.

June the second, 1763

Henry did not return to our nuptial bed. He slept from that night forward on a truckle bed in his dressing room. In the days that followed the wedding, we circled around each other like two wary cats, speaking little, addressing each other formally, never looking the other in the eye, neither of us willing to examine our circumstances too closely. We had satisfied Henry's mother and were married under the law, and that, for the time being, was that. The consummation of our marriage would have to wait.

Having been consoled by the pigeon on my wedding day, I now derive even more consolation from another source. I have just received Parts V and VI of *Tristram Shandy* from my sister, who admits to having had the utmost difficulty in obtaining copies, so enthusiastic has the public's response been to these latest volumes. I try to read slowly, savouring every morsel, and limiting the amount I consume each day. Why am I so taken with Sterne? He is bawdy — he is scattered — he rolls around in the filthy matter of life. He hurls venom — he retracts — he inserts his knowledge of trivia in the most unseemly places — one cannot read him with a straight face — one must twist and turn and most of all understand that life is to be laughed at and that every word that is written is heaped, in Sterne's case, with innuendo and connotation. I can only conclude that it is his boisterous energy sailing right off the pages that catches me up in its wake.

Until Tristram's arrival, I had been forced to re-read the books I brought with me, and while they are all good company — especially Mr Crusoe, whose hardships on his island make my life here appear the height of luxury — I was ripe for something fresh.

My sister informs me that Samuel Richardson has called *Joseph Andrews* "a lewd and ungenerous engrafture" of *Pamela*. I do not agree with this opinion. To be sure, there is no question that Fielding disliked the priggishness of *Pamela* but parody was his intent, and parody is not "engrafture." It may lean at first on its object, but soon enough it takes on its own life. This is true of all writing, is it not? And particularly true of Mr Sterne. Each new book must necessarily lean on what comes before. This does not make it lewd and ungenerous. Authors have always plundered and parodied the works of Homer, and Homer remains unscathed. Shakespeare himself shamelessly plundered Plutarch and Plautus for his own miraculous invention, but we still read Plutarch and Plautus for their own sakes, and they remain unscathed.

I have recently begun plundering Mr Fraser's library. His leaning is toward history and I have come away with a seven-volume history of Europe, a five-volume history of France, Bundy's *Roman History,* a three-volume biography of Charles XII of Sweden, Puffendorf's *Introduction to History,* and, *mirabile dictu,* the histories of Herodotus, in Greek. I have set about making my own translation of his introduction and this will make my father most entirely happy. One of Papa's main concerns upon my departure was that I should continue to exercise my facility for translation, and that I should not lose all the knowledge of the Greek he had so painstakingly taught me. His fondest dream had been to raise a son well-versed in the classics, but Mama's untimely death cut short that dream. However, I think he is proud of the fact that he has two daughters who know some Greek and Latin. Mr Kenet, the curate at St Iago, has agreed to scrutinise anything I translate. In turn, I have offered to do the same for him. I find translation a good excuse to spend time in his agreeable company, but we must be careful not to become a source of malicious gossip by spending too much time together.

The above display of available reading material reminds me why I fell so ravenously upon *Tristram Shandy* — Vol. V is the wittiest yet, to my mind — and why I feel a great need to discuss what I read, but conversation about books is rare in Spanish Town. And I find it poignant and exasperating that I should be reading so much about Europe when my interest, one might say my passion, is so aroused by my surroundings. So far the only book I have been able to pry from Mr Fraser about the island on which we live is *The Laws of Jamaica,* but he promises me he will soon obtain a copy of Sir Hans Sloane's great illustrated work on the natural history of Jamaica. This will unravel many of the mysteries of the island.

Beverly still needs much attention. Much of the furniture remains broken or worn and is retained because it belonged to Mr Silas. Having spent so many weeks among the white paint and cheerful accessories of the Frasers' house, I feel ill at ease among these dingy relics. But in time, I will make a difference.

While Henry is away in St Thomas-in-the-East again, I am taking the opportunity to move forward with my plans for a school for the children of slaves. He was called upon to make an emergency trip because his overseer at Reward had finally died of bilious remittent fever, and he needed to find a replacement. This unexpected emergency meant we were unable to take our planned wedding trip to the Blue Mountains. I had so looked forward to exchanging the heat and mosquitoes of Spanish Town for the cool and misty climate of Cinchona. However, I had not looked forward to spending so much time alone with Henry, although I doubted that he would ever venture into our marriage bed again. Strangely enough, since our marriage, Henry appears happier and our conversations have been cordial. We are civil to each other; we run Beverly in a cooperative manner. Without the weight of the marital obligation, something of our old childhood friendship has returned.

June the twentieth, 1763

On one subject, I have made no progress. I have tried to talk to Henry about my idea for a school several times, but each time he has been distracted by his own work and has given me no straight answer. He has not actually voiced an objection, so today I went ahead and met with my first pupils, now seven in number: three little girls and four little boys, one of whom is a half-wit. I still have no desks for them, but they sit happily on the floor of the gallery. Their names are Rose, Susan, Psyche, Cupid — Cupid and Psyche are brother and sister! — Augustus and Freddie, Silas's sons by Monimia, and Henderson, the half-wit. They call me "Miss Tress" and delight in singing songs for me, about me.

My little school, the source of much caustic comment among the Spanish Town ladies, is, however, my source of constant delight. Mr Kenet has miraculously — the good Lord must have intervened — produced some slates and my seven students have now mastered the capitals A and B. We sing counting songs loudly and vigorously, and the whole classroom jumps to its feet and dances, starting slowly and solemnly with "One, two, t'ree," but rising to a rousing and swirling crescendo on "Ten." Seven, with its two syllables, is by far the favourite number. My pupils recognize that as soon as they are all assembled, they themselves make seven, and seven works magic, in that it encourages perfect attendance.

Having favourites in a classroom is something I abhor, but I must admit that my heart has been stolen by none other than the half-wit, Henderson. If he makes a mistake, and he often does, he laughs at himself and he makes me laugh too, so that I am ever ready to help him. His laughter is a tonic and gives health to my spirits.

July the third, 1763

Henry is again at Reward on urgent business. Pearl is unwell, and there is talk that she may soon leave for Henry's little house at Cinchona, where the freshness of the mountain air should improve her health and brighten her spirits. I am at a loss about the cause of her malaise. There are many tropical diseases that strike suddenly, and often fatally, and I live in constant fear of her succumbing. Her illness means that she has been unable to help me with my classes; she spends most of her time in her room, eating little and sleeping much. I miss her company and her assistance, but I have been encouraging her to read when she has the strength, and she is making her way through *Pamela*.

Mrs Perkins, too is unwell. She has been suffering from a heavy cold and waves of rage ever since the wedding. She sneezes and snorts, and there is a perpetual drip at the end of her nose.

"Dear Mrs Perkins . . . " I started the other morning, only to be greeted with an impatient toss of her head.

"Dear Mrs Perkins, take these," I implored, holding out a gift of four lace handkerchiefs. "Look, I have embroidered them with your initials."

She paused, caught on the horns of a dilemma. Would good manners triumph over disgust?

Her face twitched, her mouth turned down — and then slowly up again in the rictus of a smile.

"How kind," she snapped, taking the handkerchiefs and burying them deep in her pockets. I have yet to see her use them.

The rapprochement I felt as she recounted the history of Beverly has evaporated, and she is once again the tart-tongued widow she always was. All week she has been going about her work with her jaw clamped, slamming and crashing her way angrily through the house, which reverberates with her rage. I have begged her to explain the matter, but she snorts and turns on her heel. What has happened to cause such rage? Is this my fault? Have I stepped so far out of line that she is speechless with anger?

The very sight of her, the embodiment of fury itself, turns my stomach. But even without her help, I have been continuing to work on improvements to the house, and Beverly is taking on a new mien. I have obtained some bolts of chintz by seizing them before they made their first appearance on the shelves at Mason, Mason & Fraser — this is one of the advantages of being a merchant's wife. These colourful fabrics do much to brighten the rooms. I have also found an excellent woodworker in Spanish Town who is restoring Silas's broken furniture, piece by piece. It is now possible to sit down on a chair without living in fear of its imminent collapse.

July the eleventh, 1763

On Henry's return from St Thomas-in-the-East, Mrs Perkins became even more angry and refused to remain in the same room with him. I could be mistaken, but I believe I even saw her turn and spit in his direction when she believed she was out of sight. At once I realized that Henry was the spark and true fuel for the pyre of her rage. But why?

"What have you done to cause her to be so angry?" I enquired of him.

"I have no way of knowing," responded Henry.

"Matters cannot continue this way. You must speak to her."

"I have tried."

"What are you going to do?"

"Either she goes or we go," replied Henry, with a rare attempt at humour, "for we cannot all remain under the same roof."

He made his decision; Mrs Perkins must leave.

"What a draconian measure, Henry! How will we manage without her? What will your mother think?"

"This is no longer my mother's business."

Good heavens! Henry was growing up at last.

"How can you possibly remove her?" I asked.

"I shall find a way."

He was lucky. The position of assistant housekeeper soon became available at the King's House, the home of the governor and his wife. Henry immediately recommended Mrs Perkins for it, and his recommendation was heeded. A week later, on a Sunday, Mrs Perkins packed her bags and with never a backward glance at Beverly and never a kind word to Pearl, whom she had for so long jealously guarded, set off in the kittereen for her new employment; her departure resembled nothing more than a fierce, black cloud receding in swirls of dust.

We learned that on arrival at King's House, she immediately regained her voice and once more demonstrated her competence for organization. And thus Henry's poison became the governor's meat.

Strange as it is to say, I admit to a slight regret at her leaving. Will the household ever run as smoothly again?

"Is right I should be housekeeper," said Monimia when I asked her to replace Mrs Perkins in that role. "I was Mr Silas's love, and him my dear dead husban'." She insisted, however, that she would continue to cook as well as to housekeep.

As her assistant, I have promoted Celia, who is the butler Cuthbert's woman. I hesitate to use the word "wife," although she would use it; few slaves sanctify their relationships with matrimony. I had noticed her easy ability, but most of all I was delighted by her good humor and her conversational ability. She loves to relate a story. Words burst forth into tales that blossom with description and dialogue. I could listen to her for hours on end. She has three children by Cuthbert, a two-year- old, a one-year-old, and a baby of three months, whom she often wears on her back as she works.

I have so far no reason to regret my choice of housekeepers in Monimia and Celia. There is an air of harmony as we work together making this house more comfortable and attractive, and this harmony compares favourably with Mrs Perkins's icy, albeit competent, discord.

July the thirtieth, 1763

I tried to discover the matter with Pearl. I acted as her nurse, I concocted delicacies to stimulate her appetite, but she, who had shared her life and her every dream with me, became remote, impatient, and constantly tearful. No longer did she desire me to read plays aloud with her, no longer did she design fabulous costumes for herself as Cleopatra, as the Duchess of Malfi, as Millamant.

"Let me brush your hair and fix it in the latest fashion," I suggested one day, in an effort to soothe away her troubles. She was lying on her bed, with one arm covering her eyes. She lowered the arm, and I caught a tiny glint of interest sparking her eyes. Building on the moment, I held out the brush and mirror that Lizzie had given me as a wedding present.

"Come; get up now and sit on this stool," I encouraged, pulling her to her feet, and placing the mirror in her hand. "Do not look in the mirror until I have finished."

As I brushed her hair and piled it up on top of her head in what I asserted was the very latest fashion — ah me, what do I know about the latest fashion? — I began to make up a story for her.

"There was once a Mistress Pearl Mason, a famous actress and darling of society, who travelled from country to country conquering all in her path with no other weapon than charm."

For the first time since her withdrawal she started to smile.

"Martha, what do you think? You think I can become like her? You think I would make a Fair Penitent?" she asked, pursing her lips and widening her eyes.

"Yes, indeed," I replied, "you are already a magnificent actress."

At this, she burst into uncontrollable tears. Spasms of sobs racked her body. She threw herself on the floor and kicked her feet. She tore her hair, an action I thought had disappeared with the ancient Greeks.

I must admit I was appalled by the intensity of this display and greatly feared that she would do mortal harm to herself in her, what I then imagined to be, diseased condition. In an effort to control her hysterics, I slapped her face. She choked from the shock. I dragged her to a sitting position and pounded on her back. She gasped and flung her arms around me, and out jerked her story in fits and starts, gulps and sobs.

"Me yellow dress, oh, oh, me y-y-yellow dress," Pearl stuttered and then stopped.

"Your yellow dress?"

"Yes, on your weddin' night, I-I-I went down-downstairs in me yellow dress," she sobbed.

"Yes . . . "

"I was dancin' by meself in the dining room, spinnin' roun' and roun', watchin' me skirt twirl, lookin' in the mirror, and all of a sudden I see Henry, and Henry him, and Henry . . . " And here Pearl stopped again and covered her face with her hands as the sobs renewed. My heart started thumping wildly as a suspicion darted suddenly into my head. No, it could not be. It could not.

She removed her hands and looked me straight in the eye.

"Martha, you are my one good friend, but I cannot find words to tell you the truth."

"You must, my dear. I am your one good friend."

Pearl gasped for breath.

"I feel dizzy from the dancin', I swirl, Henry him catch me in his arms, and we fall down and . . . dr-dr-drown in love," she sobbed.

Like a bolt of lightning came the sudden realisation that the "disease" from which Pearl was suffering was no disease at all. It was pregnancy. How could I have been so blind as not to realise this before? This was the reason for Mrs Perkins's fury. She must have witnessed something.

A rage, an unadulterated, boiling, maniacal rage swept through my being. Rage at Henry and rage at myself. If only I had not refused Henry, if only I had not made Pearl such a beautiful dress, if only. But incest. Incest! How dare the man! Had he no sense, no propriety, no understanding of the ramifications of incest? I had once heard a scandalous saying which proposed that incest was the sincerest form of avarice, because it kept lust wrapped close in the bosom of the family. Hah! Yes, indeed; in someone as avaricious as Henry, this was certainly the case. But how dare he violate his own sister? How dare he, how dare he, how dare he?

Rage drove me from the room; rage raced me down the stairs; rage ran me to the stables.

"Saddle up a horse," I shouted to the groom.

I mounted, gathered up the reins, and gave her a sharp smack. I bent forwards and clung to her mane, and we travelled that mile into Spanish Town as if driven by the wind.

Breathless, I tied the horse's reins to the railing in front of the store. I tried to regain my senses, tried to impose an icy calm on my demeanour, tried to smooth down my clothes. When I felt sufficiently composed and no longer gasped for breath, I walked through the store, and made my way to Henry's office in the back. I flung open the door. He was seated at his desk but sprang to his feet when he saw me standing in the doorway.

I lost the ability to speak, but not my will. Stepping up to his desk, I snatched up his silver letter-opener, raised my arm, and lunged forwards. He saw the blade and swerved so that the dagger aimed at his heart missed its target but found a home in his arm. Blood streamed from the great wound I made as I slashed downwards.

"Martha! What in Heaven's name . . . ?"

My voice returned. "How dare you? How dare you violate that precious girl? Do you not know the meaning of incest and the havoc it causes? You are a worm, a snake, you are all that is evil!"

Henry looked at me in astonishment and then at the river of blood gushing from his arm, went as pale as a ghost, and fell to the floor in a faint. I turned on my heel and left him there. Let him stew in his own juice.

There was more to come. When I returned to Beverly, I retired to my room and washed myself, feeling not unlike Lady Macbeth as I scrubbed my hands. Soon there was a tap on my door. It was Pearl. I let her in, and she sat down on my bed.

"I have something else to tell you," she said. This time I could not have guessed in a thousand years what she was about to say.

"When I know that I am with child, I tell Henry. He look as though I had hit him with my fist, den he laugh and take me in his arms and twirl me. I feel to t'row up."

"'A baby!' he cried. 'Our baby!' and that big man did a likkle dance for joy. I ask him where we goin' to keep it, and he wait a moment, and then say, 'I will inform my mother that Martha is with child!'"

"What!! Me?" I exploded.

Henry planned it all out. Pearl explained that he intended to send her away to the health-giving air of the Blue Mountains, where there were no neighbors to gossip, for the duration of the pregnancy. Monimia would accompany her to Cinchona and act as midwife when the time came. It seems that I am to suffer a difficult pregnancy and will be confined to my room as soon as my condition begins to show. Can this be true? Have I no say in this matter? For all his gentlemanly airs, his trustworthiness in business, my cousin has now become an evil, conniving man. How can I live the lies he proposes? Must I agree to participate in his wicked plot? What am I to do?

That evening he had the audacity to call me to his room, the room across the upstairs hall to which he retired on our wedding night and where he continues to sleep. He insisted that I dress the wound I had inflicted on his upper arm. My gorge rose at the notion, and I thought first of refusing, but then I realised it offered me the perfect opportunity to remonstrate with him about his plan for "our" child and to enquire why he imagined that I would be willing to participate.

I entered the room and found him sitting on his bed, with a bowl of hot water and a pitcher on a stand beside him.

"You must clean the wound you inflicted," he ordered. "I do not trust anyone else to clean it. Then we will dress it with a salve that Monimia calls 'Heal Up.' I have seen her use it on Freddie and Augustus with good results; you may apply it once the wound is clean."

"You trust me to touch you even though I inflicted such a wound? Might I not try to strike your other arm?"

"I see no weapon." He unwrapped the bandage that covered the wound and revealed sixteen stitches sewn haphazardly over the gash with black thread, the work of the Spanish Town surgeon. I flinched at the sight but felt proud of the damage I had done.

"You have marked me forever, cousin Martha."

"I wish I had done more than merely mark you," I muttered between clenched teeth.

I stood there looking at the wound, looking with disgust at my cousin who had promised me so much, this evil man grown out of the young boy I had loved, the man whom I had chosen to marry. If I cleaned his wound, I would actually have to touch him, to risk his bleeding on me. I felt nauseated.

I turned my back on him and breathed deeply. Then, wanting

to confront him, I gathered my resolve, and with a clean cloth forced myself to bathe the wound.

"I understand you have a plan for me. Why do you believe I will comply?" I asked.

"You cannot refuse."

"I can most certainly refuse."

"You cannot and you will not."

"Pray tell me why I will not when I believe otherwise."

"You love Jamaica. You want to stay. You love Pearl, and she will bear you a child of your own blood and mine." And then Henry pointed his finger at me. "Yes, you and I will have a family, the family that you seem so intent on denying me."

I was rendered speechless with rage. Oh, the utter gall of the man to justify his incestuous act by placing the blame on me. Obliviously, I resumed my ministrations. I changed the water in the bowl and rinsed the wound, making sure that I hurt him as I did so. With a rough towel, I brusquely dabbed it dry. I brought Monimia's salve to my nose and inhaled its sharp, clean smell. I applied some to the cut, and then, as clumsily as I could, I wrapped a fresh bandage over it, all the while remaining silent. Glaring.

"Think hard about this, Martha."

I had a sudden flash of inspiration. Henry desperately wanted my acquiescence; he was in the position of petitioner and had inadvertently offered me a perfect bargaining chip. I would comply with his plan for my "pregnancy" if he made no objection to my running a school for the slaves. I made the proposal as though it were a business deal.

"Take it or leave it," I said.

Henry took it.

I left his room and went to my room. Of course, I was unable to sleep. Deep anger still roiled around in my belly even as my intellect was, I dare to admit, intrigued by Henry's proposition. I went out onto the upstairs gallery and sat in a rocking chair, and gazed at the stars for a long, long time.

The next morning, Pearl tapped on my door. She came in and climbed under the mosquito net and lay down beside me. She stroked my hair and tickled my face.

"Why you so sad, Martha?"

"I don't know what to think."

"Be happy. You and I are going to have a baby. Yes? Yes? I insist." And here Pearl stood up on the bed and towered over me. She was such a tall girl. Such a gleaming girl, so full of passion. She then spoke deliberately and without the trace of an accent: "We will have our baby together. I will make you very, very happy with this child. It will be the best gift in the world."

Yes.

August the seventh, 1763

The word is out. I am officially with child, and I can already
hear those annoying whispers in my head:

> *Have you heard Martha's in the family way?*
> *Well, just fancy that! Hoorah! and Hooray!*
> *But I hear she's not well. She's dreadfully sick.*
> *I've a pill that can quell her sickness as quick*
> *as a flash. Let's knock on her door.*
> *She won't mind, I'm sure.*
> *You dare not? I will.*
> *I'll give her that pill.*
> *What? No one allowed to enter the house!*
> *Something fishy's afoot. What? Just use your nous.*

August the eleventh, 1763

Pearl has left with Monimia for the Blue Mountains. Henry tells me he has already received word that the cool air is having a salutary effect and that she has recovered her appetite and is slowly gaining strength. Back here at Beverly, in the absence of Monimia and Pearl, Celia is managing well and proving to be entirely competent and full of her own occasionally surprising and not always appropriate initiative.

I sent a package of books along with Pearl and have encouraged her to spend time each day reading so that her mind will remain nimble while she is away. She reads perceptively and I am always delighted by her fresh views on the books I know so well. I write daily letters to her that go once a week on a mule up to Cinchona, and yesterday I received my first reply.

Dear Martha, Thank you for your letter and the books.
I shall read them all. Please to write to me again. Your
loving friend, Pearl

This brief note brought me much joy; it is the first ocular evidence I have received to prove that Pearl is gaining strength. I sorely miss her company for I am often alone these days. Henry's visits to the counting house in Kingston and to Reward keep him away from Beverly for long stretches at a time. However, I do not often seek out Henry's company because my feelings of disgust at his violation of Pearl still rankle, a violation that Pearl does not seem to regret in the least. When Henry and I inevitably find ourselves seated at the same table, it is because Pearl has seemed in no way distressed by her lot that I am able to respond to a few of his conversational gambits. In his own way, he is trying hard to please me. I hold the cards.

He has recently removed his brother Jonas from Kingston to Reward as a replacement for the overseer who died recently. As a result, Henry will make fewer visits to St Thomas-in-the-East and I will see more of him. He hopes this change will have two beneficial effects: that a member of the family will be in charge of the estate, and that the move will keep Jonas out of the rum shops and whorehouses of Kingston. In my opinion, Henry is deluded. Jonas has demonstrated time and again that being a partner in Mason, Mason & Fraser means little to him as he pursues a life of increasing debauchery.

Even when he is here in Spanish Town, Henry must spend many hours at his business or supervising the estate and visiting the animals at his pen. He has never been at home during the hours of my classes and has never conversed with me about my school. While he is at work in Kingston or Spanish Town, the pen is completely in the hands of his overseer, a cruel and incompetent drunkard who Celia told me is ever ready with his whip to lash the slaves into submission. I have begged Henry to replace him, but he will not. Apparently, ridding Beverly of Mrs Perkins is as far as he is willing to go. I have pleaded that, at least, there should be no more whipping and no vile language used in the chastisement of the slaves at Beverly.

For a few days, my pleas seemed to take effect. However, one afternoon when Henry was in Kingston and I was taking a stroll in the pasture, I crested a rise and came upon a scene such as I hope I may never witness again. The overseer, McTavish — for that is the devil's name — and the rum bottle had obviously had a lengthy engagement; the whip was out again in spite of Henry's recent injunction, and I witnessed the savage flogging of a slave.

"Halt!" I cried, running towards him. "Stop that at once!"

The brute swung around to face me, his eyes yellow, his breath reeking of rum.

"Och! Is that a wee fly buzzin' at me?" he mocked, raising his arm as if to strike me dead.

Suddenly he was interrupted by Cuthbert who, on hearing my cries, came running and leaped to my defence, hurling himself between me and the tyrant. Roundly cursing the pair of us, McTavish knocked Cuthbert to the ground, spat at him, then kicked the slave he had been whipping, turned on his heel and stumbled drunkenly away. Fortunately, Cuthbert was uninjured, and he and I lifted up the injured slave and brought him to the well beside the kitchen. I rinsed his whip-sliced flesh and Celia produced from Monimia's store of potions an unguent that she swore would heal the wounds.

While I deplore this incident, I trust that, when I describe it to Henry, it will have the salutary effect of ridding the pen of the evil, vicious McTavish.

September the fifteenth, 1763

When I was four months "with child," at a point when I would begin to show if I were actually pregnant, Henry decided it was not fitting for me to continue teaching. All my pleas, all my arguments, fell on deaf ears, and I was confined to the upstairs of the house.

How I miss my pupils! When I told Henderson that I would have to take a break of some months, he burst into floods of tears, and cried out plaintively:

"Miss Tress, don' leave we. Don' leave we, Miss Tress."

He flung his little arms around me, and all the others followed in a mournful wail, crying:

"Don' leave we, Miss Tress."

I am saddened and angered at being forced to absent myself, just as we had begun to make such good progress. Dear Mr Kenet has stepped into the breach and has promised to teach a few classes in my absence, but the poor man has little time at his disposal after he has ministered to the sick and buried the dead. We have not even had a moment in which to look at each other's translations from the Greek, although he tells me that he has been working on some lyric poetry, while I am still struggling with Book I of Herodotus's *Histories*.

I am, in effect, a prisoner in my own house. Celia, who waits on me, is my sole confidante. Henry has agreed that it would be impossible to conceal the secret from her as she is my lifeline. It has been extraordinarily difficult to keep Mrs Fraser and her cohorts at bay, but they are now informed that my health is so precarious that any excitement could precipitate a miscarriage. Barred from entry to the house, they content themselves with sending confectionery and notes that are filled with the latest in Spanish Town gossip. I feel the hot breath of their curiosity warming my neck.

I stay upstairs almost all day. I insisted that my clavichord be brought to my room, and with much heaving and pushing, Cuthbert and his helpers transported it safely upwards. With plenty of time on my hands, I am coming to terms with Messrs Domenico and Alessandro Scarlatti. I have also become the nonpareil of reading in this country. Mr Fraser now gathers books from his friends to lend to me and has recently sent along the complete works of Bacon, whose *Advancement of Learning* has done much to advance my own learning. With the advent of Bacon, I am reading in Latin again and, with the practice it gives me, I can now read Latin almost as fast as I read English.

No longer must I spend half my time in the dictionary. How delighted I am that Papa had the determination to teach his daughters Latin and Greek when most men consider these languages to be the territory of boys alone. As for me, I know no purer intellectual pleasure than that afforded by the effort of translation.

Feeling cruelly "cabined, cribbed, confined, bound in/To saucy doubts and fears," I accosted Henry on his way to bed three nights ago.

"I am going mad," I announced.

"Mad? You? Never!" was his swift, dismissive response.

"I shall go mad, I swear, if I cannot step outside," I insisted, grasping him by the wrists and leering wildly up into his face, crossing my eyes, and sticking out my tongue. "I must be allowed to walk in the garden."

"Never! What if someone should see you?"

"What if someone should see me?" I shrieked. "I shall wear a cushion of ever-increasing size under my dress. I shall devise a harness to hold it in place. I shall be the very picture of the perfect pregnant lady. I shall stroll only in the cool of dawn and in the early evening. Please, please, Henry. Grant me this one favour lest I go completely mad," and here I rolled my eyes and bared my teeth in a fearful grimace.

Henry could not help but laugh. I watched him as he struggled with my request. On the one hand, he could not bear to think that his plan might go awry; on the other hand, he clearly had some sympathy for my predicament. He began to weaken. I took advantage of the moment.

"Think of the health of our baby. A happy mother brings forth a healthy baby."

"But . . . " he started, and then he stopped as I waggled my finger at him.

In the end, Henry capitulated.

"You may walk in the garden at daybreak and dusk, but Celia must always accompany you. You should lean on her arm. If someone approaches you, feign discomfort, and have Celia return you to the house immediately. Never, never talk to anyone."

I promised faithfully to adhere to his rules. Now I walk in the garden twice a day, and the walks remind me that there is a thriving world outside the covers of books; they provide an opportunity to swing beneath the great tamarind tree and to continue studying the natural history of Jamaica at first hand. I have recently made the acquaintance of the sensitive plant whose skill is to fold up its leaves the moment they are touched. While I am charmed by its behaviour, I have learned that it is a plague in the pastures of Jamaica. It spreads fast, and because it has prickles, it wounds the mouths of cattle who munch it.

November the second, 1763

Henry has twice visited Pearl and Monimia at Cinchona and promises me that they are happy and active, much occupied by making a garden. Monimia has planted vegetables and herbs, while Pearl has planted flowers. Henry always returns with a letter for me from Pearl. The one I received today reads:

Dear Martha,

How are you? I am very big and the baby runs around inside. I wish you could visit me so that we could continue reading the works of William Shake Spear together. I am trying to teach Monimia and Cato, our caretaker, to read so that they can play parts with me the way you used to, but they are not good pupils. Monimia does not try to learn. She says she must cook and she does not need any shaking spear to help her cook. Cato tries a little harder; he has even learned to fashion his name but he changes the order of the letters so that his signature is "Coat."

In order to pass the time and to prepare myself to be an accomplished actress, I have started to learn the parts of all the beautiful young women in Shakespeare. In addition to Juliet, I have now committed Rosalind and Beatrice to memory. Write to me again soon. Yr. big friend, Pearl.

Celia sings me songs of her own invention, songs of lament and songs of joy, and she whispers about obeah, a ritualistic religion that came from Africa and involves many secret spells. When I offer to teach her to read, she laughs and asks me why she should bother, being so old.

"How old are you?" I ask.

"Fifty-t'ree," she responds.

"Fifty-three! No, no, Celia, you cannot possibly be that old!"

"Eh, eh. I wrong, Mistress. I twelve years old."

The ages of her children deny both estimates. I would guess that she is about twenty. Age and the passage of time have no meaning for her.

"You know Anancy, Mistress?" she asks, changing the conversation. "You know Crooky, him wife, and Tacooma, him son?" And then she regales me with tales of the magic spider. Being little and weak, Anancy must live by his wits; he is cunning and greedy, he is often the cause of the inexplicable — for instance, Celia tells me it is he who is responsible for why wasps sting. She always begins her tales: "One time . . ." and ends "Jack Manory, me story done." This combining of Africa's Anancy and England's Jack Manory reminds me of what a living, growing creature idiom is, every day feeding on new matter and thriving in the mouths of immigrants and in the rhymes of children.

I trust that my sister will continue to send me word of the latest publications in England. Very little that is up-to-date comes my way and I sink further and further into the words of the past. I have started reading the *Aeneid* again and I voyage with pious Aeneas towards his homeland. I read aloud to my only companion. Celia is patient and indulgent.

"And how is Mr Virgil today?" she greets me each morning.

After we converse a little about Aeneas, we move on to her preferred topic: the behavior of the immortals. While she is fascinated by Neptune's ability to ride the waves in his chariot and Venus's skill at appearing and disappearing, her supreme favourite is Juno.

"I would like to be dis Juno, an' married to the bukra god. She make big trick on him!"

She has no patience whatsoever with Dido.

In turn, I inquire after the health of the good god, Naskew, who lives in the clouds of Africa and who, in his kindness, teaches men to hunt and women to till the ground so that they may prosper.

"Him fit," she responds, but then her mood darkens as she moves from Naskew to Timnew, the evil god. It is he, she moans, who shakes the earth and brews storms, and she trembles at the very thought of earthquakes and hurricanes. This earthshaker, Timnew, sounds to me like none other than Neptune himself when he is angered.

Why do I stay in this prison? Why do I not burst my chains asunder? The truth is that I would rather be here in Jamaica, waiting for Pearl to deliver what will be my child, listening to Celia's tales of Africa, than return to England. My life in England, with Arthur lost forever, was without hope. Here I have hope at the end of my gestation. A child, a school, and an isle full of miracles.

December the twenty-first, 1763

The slaves have started celebrating the feast of Christmas. I ascend the steps to the lookout tower at the top of the house and gaze down on scenes of reckless gaiety. All work has ceased in Spanish Town, in Henry's pen, and in the surrounding pens and plantations. The days and nights are filled with the sound of drums, of singing and dancing. Every so often a solo voice will rise above the others, the chorus will respond, and the dancing will continue. All the slaves are decked out in their finest creations; there is no limit to their imagination. It is as though a floodgate has been opened, releasing a torrent of colour, of legend, and deep dark drums. The tallest men are grotesquely dressed to resemble some kind of fierce animal.

The leading masquerader, John Canoe, carrying a wooden sword in his hand, is followed by a heaving crowd of drunken women, who refresh him frequently with what I am told is aniseed-water, but is more likely rum. He dances at every door, bellowing out "John Canoe, John Canoe." I have been unable as yet to discover who this John Canoe is.

Henry is compelled to stay at home for these few days because all work on the island has ceased and because it might appear improper to be away from his legal and pregnant wife at Christmas tide. He is sullen and uneasy, resenting the hiatus and the fact that he must, by tradition at the New Year, hand out money, clothes, and provisions to his staff.

"Henry my dear, try to remember that slaves who are well-fed and well-clothed are far more likely to perform well," I say, honey-tongued, in an effort to encourage generosity. But Henry's addiction is to the making of money, which does not easily convert to the spending of it on his slaves. He is, however, profligate when it comes to his own person. He likes costly dress and equipage and lavish entertainment — and racehorses — when it suits his purpose.

During the course of my "pregnancy," on the few occasions when he has slept at home, Henry has taken his meals downstairs and has rarely paid a visit to my quarters. However, since obtaining any kind of service from the servants has been well-nigh impossible these past few days — even Celia is so drawn to the dance that majestic Juno no longer has a hold over her imagination — Henry has been forced to bring me my tray himself, for I would otherwise starve, and he has begun to take his meals upstairs with me. For the first time since I arrived, I am making the acquaintance of my husband. Let me describe him as I now see him.

He is a representative of that race of native white men, or Creoles — this is what they call persons of European descent who are born in the West Indies — who are in general tall but who tend to be corpulent. Their cheeks are often remarkably high-boned, and the sockets of their eyes deeper than is commonly observed among the natives of England; the common saying here is that by this conformation, they are guarded from those ill effects which an almost continual strong glare of sunshine might otherwise produce. Because of the brightness of the light, their sight is keen and penetrating; which renders them excellent marksmen. Henry's eyes are of a deep hazel colour; his mouth can look generous but is usually pursed. His hair is plentiful, dark brown, and wavy. If you were to stand back and look at him from a distance, you would take him for a fine-looking man. His features are regular, his face is a sallow, smooth-skinned oval; his nose is aquiline. On closer examination, however, I believe that you would detect something in his face that displeases. You would see a ruthlessness in those hazel eyes, a contempt in that pursed mouth.

Mrs Fraser has often commented that the effect of the climate is not only remarkable in the structure of the eyes of the Creole whites, but likewise in the extraordinary freedom and suppleness of their joints, which enables them to move with ease, and gives them a surprising agility as well as gracefulness in dancing. I have also noted that they have some tincture of vanity, and occasionally of haughtiness, and are much too addicted to expensive living, costly entertainments, dress and equipage, cards, billiards, backgammon, chess, horse racing, hog hunting, shooting, fishing! Unlike Henry, whose avarice drives him to excessive endeavour, most of them are possessed with a degree of supineness and indolence in their affairs, which renders them bad economists, and too frequently hurts their fortune and family.

I encourage Henry to converse with me by questioning him about his business, and on this topic he becomes animated, for commerce is a fierce goad to him. He plays at trade the way that others play backgammon, save that his gaming board is the wide Atlantic. But if I try to move the conversation from commerce into the realm of literature and the imagination, he fidgets and moves away, wringing his long hands in a gesture of impatience and despair. He wears a signet ring on the little finger of his left hand and the seal is that of a griffon rampant.

And now that Henry is forced to spend time with me, I am working on a portrait of him as we sit together in the afternoon. Seeing us like this, you might be led to believe that we are the epitome of married happiness. In some obscure sense we are, for we have found a *modus vivendi*, which is centered around the birth of our child. We await this arrival with the same anticipation that we would if this were a regular birth. It is quite extraordinary how we are able to talk with ease about the baby's future, the baby's education, the baby's name.

Henry insists that we should call it Peter if it is a boy, in spite of my suggestion of Trismegistus in honour of my dear Tristram Shandy. He has no way of comprehending my humorous allusion.

"Trismegistram?" he queried. "You have it wrong. There is no such name. There is a name Tristram. I was at school with a boy called Tristram, a bully and a liar. It's not a name I care for. We shall call the boy Peter." So Peter Mason it is; such a rocky name for a baby. Just in case it is a girl — as far as Henry is concerned this is impossible — I have suggested Catherine, and he has not objected.

My story until I came to Jamaica was trivial and predictable. I knew how each day would start and how it would finish. I had used up such life as I had in England. I desired liberty; for liberty I gasped. Even imprisoned in the confines of this room, I feel as though I am at liberty. Millions are condemned to a stiller doom than mine. Here nothing is still. Each day, I find new attractions to amaze me: a moth whose size and fur belie its ability to fly; the blossoms on the trees; the vases of flowers that Celia brings me; the doctor bird probing a red flower with his long, needle-like beak; the sudden squawk as a kling-kling lands on my windowsill. Now that I have consulted Sir Hans Sloane's natural history, I know that the kling-kling bird is the Greater Antillean Grackle. He is black, irridescent with violet, and has a fierce yellow eye and a raucous voice. He is inquisitive, gregarious, and a veritable Autolycus.

Cinchona, December the 28th, 1763

Dear Martha,

I walk like a duck and am shaped like an alligator pear, but I believe I am Miranda and that I will live in a brave new world as a fearless actress after I have the baby. Monimia says the child will come soon even though I still have two months to wait. Why is this?

I have read all the books you sent me and have just finished with Mr Crusoe. What a damn fool man. Do you think his island is like Jamaica? Do you think we have cannibals here?

I like the portrait you sent me of yourself. Did you use your mirror to draw this?

I wish to read some new plays. Please to send more books, and don't forget yr. friend.

Beverly, January 2nd, 1764

Dear Pearl,

Why do you think Robinson Crusoe is a fool? Is he not clever to fashion such a complete life for himself? Is he not like you and me, confined to a small place with few resources? Is he not an inspiration to you as you await your delivery? Remember that he says: "It was in vain to sit still and wish for what was not to be had, and this extremity rouzed my application." Does he not rouze your application?

I am enclosing a copy of "The Fair Penitent," that Lizzie was able to attain in England. I hope you will enjoy reading it as much as you enjoyed seeing it played. It certainly contains some very fine poetry. I am also sending you my copy of the sonnets of Wm. Shakespeare, with certain numbers marked for you. I would like you to learn number 143 by heart so that you can recite it for me next time we see each other.

Henry has finally decided on a course of action for the birth of the baby, a plan which brings me great joy. He has decided that my state of health has become perilous, and that the suffocating closeness of the air of Spanish Town and my long confinement in my room have given rise to a dementia of such proportions that the only possible hope for a cure is a retreat to the cool and quiet of the Blue Mountains. People in Spanish Town will mutter and cluck about the hazards to my health of such a journey but may agree that, if madness is the alternative, it is a reasonable course of action.

And thus, there, together, you and I will travail to bring forth a child, with Monimia's help. Henry has reassured me that she is a most competent midwife, having practised her skill for many years at the pen. Celia will accompany me and will act as wet-nurse for the baby. Together we four women will accomplish what no man can!

I will leave here in a few days' time, and in the meantime I am in a flurry, packing books and finishing the sewing of tiny garments. My heart rejoices at the thought of seeing you, my dear Pearl, so soon. Your loving Martha

January the eleventh, 1764

I had begun to believe that the only Jamaica I would ever see was the capital and its immediate environs, and I thought my days would always be spent in efforts to find shade and cool rooms. I was wrong.

There is another Jamaica, an island of soft mists, of verdant hillsides, of mountain splendour, but so well concealed is Cinchona that I fear I may never be able to pinpoint it on a map. Our band, consisting of Henry and me in a carriage, and Cuthbert, Celia — with her littlest offspring strapped to her back — in a wagon, accompanied by our luggage and provisions, plus six clucking chickens and three quacking ducks, set off before daybreak for Kingston. Upon reaching Liguanea four hours later, we made a stop at Prospect Pen for breakfast. This is the house that Silas Mason so admired that he made Beverly into an exact copy of it. After being welcomed by the widow Mitchell, I was whisked away to an upstairs room, a room whose proportions so resembled my own that I felt completely at home. There I consumed ass's milk, with which all pregnant women are plied in this country, and rested, moaning dementedly, clutching my large cushion, while Henry discussed some business matters with Mrs Mitchell.

From Prospect Pen, we turned north and made our way along the Hope Road and gradually began our ascent towards Papine in the foothills of the Blue Mountains. At Papine we acquired a lovely nanny goat, a fine giver of milk. From Papine onwards, the road became increasingly steep and narrow, and we stopped at the next village we came to for the night. I was immediately surrounded by the black ladies of the village who wanted to stroke me and to pat my stomach. Henry spoke sharply to them and they retreated a little, but they never took their eyes off me while I was out of doors. The next morning, we exchanged our carriages for mules and a litter, and the ladies watched with particular attention as I climbed into the litter, heaving my large pillow into it with great difficulty. I became convinced that they could see through my deception, straight to my barren state, but Henry told me that I was being foolish, and that I looked most believably with child.

We followed a trail ever upwards, and as we rode, the face of the landscape continually changed. Cool streams trickled, and waterfalls splashed like silver ribbons down the mountainside, colourful birds flashed in and out of the trees. I even saw a flock of parrots, and all the foliage was verdant and sweet-smelling. Clouds descended onto our path and continued to descend until we found ourselves suddenly riding above them, in the sunshine, looking down on billows of white.

At last, after several hours, we reached our destination, a small, framed house set in a clearing, surrounded by pimento and cinchona trees. The Spanish brought cinchona to Jamaica from Peru, and its bark is referred to as "Peruvian bark" and is efficacious in the treatment of intermittent fevers. As we approached the house, we discerned two figures tending the garden: Monimia and Pearl, a Pearl who was the very embodiment of the phrase "great with child." She screamed with delight when she saw our party and began running towards us as fast as her burden would allow. It was a fearsome sight! I thought she would precipitate delivery right there and then, first by running so fast and then by laughing so hard when her baby and my pillow encountered each other. Words cannot begin to express my joy at our reunion. Even Henry was laughing as he gently touched Pearl's belly and pretended to recoil in alarm at being given a swift, foetal kick. Laughing with delight, she flung her arms around him and kissed him so fiercely that I had to look away.

There being scant room in the house to accommodate six people, Henry and Cuthbert left again on their mules as soon as they had eaten a meal and unloaded our baggage and all the provisions. They left us not entirely without male company. We have the elderly caretaker, Cato, whose charge it is to maintain the property and to provide us with wood for the fireplace. It is strange to imagine a fireplace in Jamaica, but we certainly require it in the evenings; at this time of year and at this height, the nights are very cool.

We are a happy band. The house is simple but comfortable. All the rooms are on one floor and consist of a parlour, a dining room, two bedrooms — I share one with Pearl; Celia and her baby share the other with Monimia — a kitchen, and a long gallery. Cato lives in a hut, just a short distance from the house. During the day, we spend much of our time on the gallery gazing at the ever-changing play of light and shade on the mountains. The peace of it all; the purity of the air; the sweetness of the water; the joy of friendship! At night, we gaze at the stars and at the antics of the fireflies who challenge the stars themselves for brightness.

I do not suffer from the absence of friends whose education equals mine. Indeed, Celia, Pearl, Monimia, and Cato have scant education of the sort that I have experienced; however, I find myself in the position of student rather than teacher to this band, learning more each day about Africa, about Jamaica, and particularly about the island's vegetation and wildlife. How greatly I prefer the company of Monimia, Celia, Cato, and Pearl to that of the gossips of Spanish Town.

Monimia and Pearl have tamed the luxuriant vegetation around the house and have created a garden that is filled with flowers and herbs. Ginger grows wild and the air is often pungent with its aroma. Pimento trees exude an odour which I imagine vies with that of the spice groves of Arabia. The seed from these trees is sometimes called allspice because the flavour resembles a combination of cinnamon, cloves, and juniper. Monimia sings the praises of its medicinal qualities. For a stimulating plaster to counteract the effects of rheumatism and neuralgia, she recommends boiling the fresh berries until the mixture is thick enough to spread. She also recommends the oil made from fresh pimento leaves as a cure for flatulence and indigestion. I am beginning to see Monimia as a true medicine woman. She has a magic use for every plant I comment on. Were they all as truly invested with the powers of healing as she claims, there would be no illness whatsoever in Jamaica.

Our days revolve quite naturally around the growing of food, the harvesting of food, the preparation of food, conversation about food, and the enjoyment of food. We have already consumed one of the ducks we brought with us and, as I write, I can see Monimia running around trying to catch a chicken for today's meal.

In an effort to continue educating Pearl, I have given her the responsibility for writing down some of Monimia's receipts. In this way, she improves her handwriting and I learn some of the secrets of Jamaican cooking. I encourage her to read aloud to me and am charmed by the melody of her voice as she declares the tale of Moll Flanders. She easily takes on the voices of all the characters in the book — she says she's practising her craft. She is still determined to be an actress and has memorized all of

Calista's part in "The Fair Penitent." She longs to play a scene or two with a suitably gay Lothario but spurns my offers to read his part for her.

"I must have a man to play the part," she insists.

So she has dragooned poor old Cato into joining her. She brings him up onto the porch and I hear her directing him to move in certain ways as he pronounces his lines. We are not permitted to watch them at work as yet, but she promises that they will deliver a performance soon. What an unlikely couple. How I wish that Mr Nicholas Rowe himself could see this particular enactment of his play!

Monimia, whom I have just witnessed wringing the chicken's neck, reckons that the baby will arrive in about two weeks' time. To my eye, the baby looks ready to arrive tomorrow, even though it is not due until February. It is almost impossible for Pearl to find a comfortable position at night. Poor soul, she has to sleep sitting upright in order to breathe. Meanwhile, I have been safely delivered of my pillow. I have nothing to hide from this band of conspirators.

After her delivery, Pearl wants to take me for long walks up the narrow mountain trail that leads towards Blue Mountain Peak. For now, we limit ourselves to strolls that are within hailing distance of the house and Monimia's capable hands.

Even though Celia has her youngest child with her, she misses the two children she left behind; we encourage her with promises that her stay here will not be long and that she will soon have another little one to care for. She is deeply suspicious of the cool air and is convinced that she will die of a chill, so she has taken to wearing a turban at all times, and often goes around wrapped in a blanket. Her Spanish Town appearance, neat and almost European, has been transformed; she now has the air and bearing of an African queen.

Her favourite time of day is the late afternoon when she calls on Cato to come into the house to light the fire. She hovers around him as he works, and when the flames catch and the fire takes hold, she crouches next to it, rubbing her hands in front of it, feeling the warmth radiate throughout her body. Then she comes alive again and starts telling stories of duppies and zombies and shref-shrefs, stories which terrify the susceptible Monimia. Celia has a favourite god called Macoo, who makes zombies climb backwards up trees and poles — a useful skill, and much to be admired. She claims to have seen him shimmying foot first up the tall bitterwood tree, which stands like a guardian beside the house, from where he proceeded to ogle in the bedroom window. The bitterwood tree is interesting; it is said that no insect will spend time on bitterwood furniture because of the intensity of the acridity.

By the time we go to our beds, we are often giggling and clinging to each other in a delicious state of terror, starting at every creak the house makes, fearful of the whirring of insect wings lest it advertise the arrival of Macoo, and terrified by the nocturnal songs of frogs and birds. This terror, however, is a mere *frisson* of fear on the calm and secure passage of our days and nights.

Yesterday, Monimia, Celia, and I were treated to an excerpt from Act IV, scene I, of *The Fair Penitent*, a scene in which Calista and the evil Lothario condemn each other for treachery. Pearl had arranged the porch to be her stage, while the audience of three sat in the garden. She had dressed her hair, painted her face, and adorned her voluminous nightgown with countless flowers in a futile attempt to distract our attention from her distended belly, ignoring the fact that her present condition made her a most unlikely Calista. As for Cato, she dusted him off, scrubbed his face, and pulled his hair back into a bag. The day before, she had sewn him a pair of slippers, which were probably the first footwear he had ever worn in his life. Every so often he would gaze down at them in amazement and mutter "Eh-eh. Looka dem shoe."

Pearl was full of confidence in her own ability and delivered her lines in the most dramatic manner. She also delivered most of Cato's. He could generally manage the first line of a speech, but then his voice trailed off, and Pearl would step in, lowering her voice and uttering his lines, before raising it and becoming Calista again. When he stumbled, he cast his eyes to heaven for help and scratched his head and was visibly relieved when Pearl took over. A few of the lines struck me as particularly apt in regard to Pearl's own experience. When Calista uttered the lines, "Let that night / that guilty night be blotted from the year" and "For 'twas the night that gave me up to shame, / to sorrow, to the false Lothario," I found myself nodding in agreement.

At the end of the scene, Cato was obviously delighted with himself, having managed to deploy most of the final speech that begins "The driving storm of passion will have its way" with Pearl acting as a sort of verbal net to catch him when he tripped. He came back again and again for applause from his audience, while Pearl sank into the deepest and most elaborate curtsey imaginable and was unable to rise until we all heaved her to her feet.

Once upright, she announced, "I *will* be an actress." It is in vain that I try to discourage this idea, claiming that while it is perfectly seemly for her to perform in front of her relatives and friends, it is far from seemly for a young, unmarried woman of her standing to seek a living on the stage. To this she responded tartly: "I shall marry, then, immediately, for I *will* be an actress."

What a strange band of conspirators we are up here in the mountains. In some sense it is an ideal situation for me: a few captive students, my favourite books, time to read, and the opportunity to enjoy the scenery and the cool, fragrant air.

> *Read Homer once, and you can read no more;*
> *For all Books else appear so mean, so poor,*
> *Verse will seem Prose: but still persist to read,*
> *And Homer will be all the Books you need.*

I must confess I do not entirely agree with Alexander Pope that Homer will be all the books I need, but following the stirring performance of "The Fair Penitent," I have indeed needed something powerful to read aloud in order to entertain my companions. Feeling that *Tristram Shandy* might be too heady a cordial, I decided to read Pope's translation of the *Iliad* to Monimia, Celia, and Pearl, and as I read I ask myself what effect this tale of anger and retribution can have on these three women.

Monimia finds parallels in it with an epic from her ancestors, an epic of war between tribes. She understands the malevolence of the gods and the thirst for vengeance among men. Pearl is transparent. She has no interest in tales of heroes biting the dust; she waits impatiently for the appearances of Helen and Aphrodite, in the meantime tapping her foot and rearranging her belly noisily and conspicuously. She is also fascinated by Paris, instinctively understanding that respect for a lover is not a necessary component in matters of desire. Celia listens raptly. She has an uncanny ear, can mimic anything she hears, and has a complete understanding of the form of the Homeric simile. Yesterday I read aloud:

> *As when two Vultures on the Mountain's Height*
> *Stoop with their sounding Pinions to the Fight:*
> *They cuff, they tear, they raise a screaming Cry;*
> *The Desert echoes, and the Rocks reply:*
> *The Warriors thus opposed in Arms engage,*
> *With equal Valor, and with equal Rage.*

Today I heard Celia intoning:

> *As when Monimia, t'rowing out de dregs,*
> *She spy a rat who come to t'ief de eggs,*
> *She shout, she scream, she run all roun' de place*
> *An' Ratty quickly try to hide him face,*
> *So dese two warriors wage dem bitter war*
> *'Til Monimia she chase Ratty out de door.*

Divine-eared Celia knows no limit to her poetic invention. She sits in the rocker nursing her baby as she listens to me read from Pope's *Iliad*. As soon as I pause to close the book, she puts her head back and out pours an epic of her own invention. I try to write it down as she speaks but my pen is not fast enough, and once she has spoken the lines, she never repeats them. She records her own history, uttering her poem in perfect rhyming couplets. She starts her epic telling tales of her ancestors on the Slave Coast and assembling her pantheon. In this pantheon, there is a supreme being, too supreme, in fact, to be at all interested in the pedestrian affairs of men and women. She concentrates more on the lesser gods, those spirits that are associated with rain and wind, with fire and earth, with clouds and the sun; in fact, with any force of nature that is servant to her tale. She also invests humans with magic capabilities and uses the word "medicine" to mean "power" — power to intervene and control. Just as she includes medicine-men and medicine-women who work for the good, so she includes those who are committed to working to hurt, to terrify, and to kill.

At the center of her tale is her own mother's journey from the Guiney Coast. Celia sings — she chants her tale rather than speaks it — of the horror and the shame, but above all she sings of her mother's longing for Africa and for death. The Africans sincerely believe that they return to Africa after they die and, when their longing overcomes them, they sometimes kill themselves as a means of returning to their homeland.

I wish Papa could see us as we gather in the evening, when Celia calls out, "Catch up de fire, Cato. Is time for de epic."

In comes Cato, staggering under a load of kindling and logs. He lays the fire and soon his cheeks are bellows as he blows on his creation. And then Celia starts to sing, rocking backwards and forwards, her shadow looming and retreating in the firelight. Monimia sits straight, her expression rapt, her legs apart, her feet planted solidly on the floor, listening to Celia's every word, saying "Oh yes" when she is moved, and clapping her hands with enjoyment. Cato crouches in the doorway, one eye and one ear to the outside, the proper watchman, but his mind all engaged in the tale. Pearl is restless because she is not the centre of attention, because she cannot make herself comfortable in one position for any length of time, and because there is something about these stories of Africa that frightens her; even so, she too falls under the spell of Celia's gift.

As for me, I am in a permanent quandary between wanting

to write down everything I hear and wanting to listen without the necessity of writing. I have finally given up any attempt to write because my efforts disturb Celia, my inkwell inevitably dries, and my enjoyment is impaired. Alas. Celia's epic, like so much that springs from the human imagination, is written in the ether, and will leave its trace only in the memories of the teller of the tale and of the three people who listen to her.

I wish these days would never end, but of course they will. One has only to glance at Pearl to know that our lives are about to be drastically changed any day now. It is trite to make the comparison with ripe fruit, bursting with the next generation, but it is more than apt.

In the last two or three days Pearl has begun to tire, to complain, to weep on my shoulder. Her feet hurt, she cannot breathe when she lies down, she suffers from indigestion. This indigestion sends Monimia into flurries of concocting herbal remedies. Heaven knows what she will produce at the time of *accouchement*! Pearl is still carrying the baby high up under her ribs, so I do not believe she will deliver in the next two or three days, but her size dictates that the time cannot be far away, even though she still lacks five weeks to complete her nine months.

January the twenty-third, 1764

It has started, even though it is a month too soon. Pearl felt the first thrust of labour this morning after breakfast but she thought it might be just another form of indigestion. Monimia took one look at her and declared that the labour was newly under way. It appears that the baby is in the wrong position and Monimia has tried to turn it, to move its head down, but it was unwilling to cooperate. Poor Pearl will have to endure a breech birth; this means that we have a long and painful journey ahead of us.

We are all in Monimia's room.

Monimia is in her element, in absolute control. She is the queen of midwives, comforting Pearl, rubbing her back, issuing orders, running outside for this herb or that, brewing concoctions to stimulate the action of the womb and concoctions to ease the pain, and killing another chicken to make soup to strengthen Pearl after her ordeal. In her excitement, she cut herself as she cleaned the bird, and her thumb is now tied up in a greasy bandage.

Pearl is excited at this point. I remember my sister Lizzie's confinements and the same rapture. Unfortunately, I also remember how the rapture declines into agony, and I dread the struggle my dear Pearl will have to endure.

While we wait, Celia plays with her baby, an endearing little girl called Daphne, who has just learned to crawl and to pull herself up to a standing position. She crows with delight when she finds herself upright, and Celia sings, "Stan' up, Daphne, stan' up tall, soon you going to walk."

Cato is uncomfortable. This is woman's work and he has distanced himself. All day he has been digging in the part of the garden furthest from the house.

I write this later in the day. We are entering the hard time now, sooner than expected. Celia has taken Daphne outside for Cato to watch over, and he pushes her around the garden in a wheelbarrow. Pearl, never brave about physical suffering — she cries if she pricks her finger or stubs her toe — is appalled by the agony of childbirth. She screams at me to help her.

"You who think you know so much," she screams "Why don't you do something?"

So I find my silver brush and try to soothe her by brushing her hair, only to have her scream, "You're hurting me. Go away."

Monimia closes the shutters and creates an elaborate smoke machine into which she stuffs all kinds of strong smelling herbs that she insists will keep away evil spirits and ensure a safe delivery. She reassures us that our wait will not be long, but every minute of Pearl's agony is like a year for me. Seeing my distress, Monimia gives Pearl something to drink, which makes her fall asleep between her pains.

Celia sings.

> *This gwine be one happy birtha*
> *Welcome, baby, to dis eartha*
> *Out jump baby, up jump Martha*
> *Sing she song, give baby batha*

Night has fallen. The pains are closer together now and there is no sleep for any of us. The whole mountain reverberates with Pearl's agony.

Will this baby never come?

Later. The answer to the above question is, of course, that the outcome was inevitable. For this condition there is always resolution. Suddenly, just before midnight, Pearl began to push and pant. Celia held on to one side of her and I to the other and then Monimia cried out:

"Look. Look. De buttocks!" and then "Is bwoy. I see him blue balls."

He stayed just on the edge of entry into this world for a long time. Then Monimia instructed Celia and me to lower Pearl's legs while she reached with her two index fingers — those fingers that had so recently killed a chicken with such dispatch — into the crook of the baby's hips and pulled gently, delivering his body. His little legs were straight up, his feet reaching for his ears. Shortly afterwards, his head appeared, and there he was, complete, and screaming. All our attention was fixed upon the sight. But Pearl's ordeal was not yet finished. She shrieked again, and Celia turned to lend her comfort. Pearl pushed one more time and delivered another baby straight into Celia's hands. This one was much smaller than the first, but otherwise similar in all respects save gender and the fact that the cord was wrapped tightly around her neck. She did not scream; she never drew a breath.

While Monimia took care of Pearl, I bathed the lusty little boy, and Celia wrapped the silent little girl in the shroud which would become her christening gown. Then we bathed Pearl with warm water perfumed with orange blossom, and left her sleeping peacefully. I will never know if she was aware of having delivered the second baby.

I named the little girl Catherine, as I had promised Henry, should we have a girl. I instructed Cato to fashion a small box for her remains and to dig a grave on the hillside above the house, a grave whose aspect would be Blue Mountain Peak. At dawn he and I laid Catherine to rest. I read aloud the familiar words from the christening and burial services and prayed for the resurrection of her soul. We placed no marker on her grave, but later in the day I transplanted a species of Jamaican lily to the spot.

Her brother alternatively screamed, slept, and nursed at Celia's breast throughout these proceedings. When I returned from burying Catherine, Celia handed him to me, saying, "Take. Is your baby now."

I took him in my arms and immediately fell in love — he is
so beautiful that mere words cannot begin to describe him. I
walked with him onto the porch. Venus was still shining in the
brightening sky, but the air was chill, so I returned inside and
went to my bed. I lay down and placed my baby on my stomach.
He managed to reassemble his legs into his birth position and
slept in a V shape with his feet comfortingly close to his ears. I
never saw such a strange and enchanting sight.

Cinchona, January 24, 1764

Dear Henry,

*I am writing to let you know that you are the father of a
lusty son, born last night. Mother and child are faring well.*

*I trust that you, too, are faring well, and that you will
soon be able to witness for yourself the good fortune that has
been showered upon you. Your son has a hearty appetite and
a loud cry, and he appears to be by far the most beautiful
baby ever born.*

*In expectation of seeing you before too long, I remain yr.
wife, Martha.*

I am writing at the kitchen table while Monimia prepares a
meal for Cato to take on his journey of annunciation.

"Empty bag can't stan' up," she pronounces.

By this she means that if Cato is hungry, he will not fulfil his
task. She fills a small calabash with rice and peas, lays a chicken
leg on top, and wraps the food in a bandana.

"Cato, Cato man, you come here," she bellows, at which
our aged Hermes uncoils himself from the vegetable patch and
limps to the kitchen door. He places the picnic in his bag and
adds to it a jug of water from the well. I hand him my letter to
Henry, which swiftly disappears into the folds of his garment.

"Is safe, Mistress," he promises me, patting it every now and then.

"Gwan, now," orders Monimia, and Cato shuffles outside; we hear him addressing his mule as he mounts and then he disappears down the hill on his long journey to deliver news of Peter's birth.

January the twenty-seventh, 1764

Life here in the mountains has taken on a rhythm that is dictated entirely by the whims of the new arrival. I spend most of my time in a rocking chair, gazing adoringly at Peter, watching his face as little twinges of expression pass over it; it is with great reluctance that I relinquish him to Celia for his meals. Celia's own baby, Daphne, resents the new baby's intrusion on her territory and screams whenever Celia puts Peter to the breast. This morning, Pearl arose and tried to squeeze herself into her favourite dress but retired to bed frustrated and feverish. Monimia concocts brews to stimulate an increased flow of Celia's milk and brews to staunch the flow of Pearl's. She is in her element, stewing, stirring, and humming. She has marked Peter's feet with blue crosses, which she promises will keep away the evil eye, and then she announces to me:

"Twin, him strong. Him luck. You gwine give me him navel string, you hear, and I plant him navel string tree. He gwine have long, long life."

She insists that I hand over Peter's umbilical cord to her when it dries up and falls off. Have you ever heard of such a thing? I have heard of people charming warts away, but never knew there was a charm for the "navel string."

I do not know what to think of Monimia. Does she perform magic? Is there reason to believe in the power of her potions and spells? Has she inherited knowledge of medicine from Africa whose benefits we have yet to understand? Should I agree with Pliny: *Ex Africa semper aliquid novi?*

We are all awaiting the return of Cato with news of Henry and perhaps the arrival of Henry himself.

Later the same day.

Cato has just arrived with his story simply spewing out of his mouth.

"I reach Papine and I greet me fren' dem. We tek some rum, an' I fall down and mash up me foot. I mus' wait two day at Papine. When I reach Kingston, eh-eh, everyt'ing nyaka-nyaka, chaka-chaka, takro-takro, jing-bang. Too much people. Eh-eh. I look fe de warehouse long time. I find Massa close by one big ship. Good morning, Sah! I say. Ah, Cato! You have brought news. Yes, Sah! One fine, hongry bwoy! Massa him smile one big smile an' give me some coin. He tek me to him desk in de warehouse an' him write dis letter I give you now."

January twenty-sixth, 1764

Dear Martha,

I told you it would be a boy. As soon as the Swallow *sets sail, I shall make my way to the mountains to escort you and my child safely home to Beverly.*

I hope that mother and son are faring well. Yr. husband, Henry.

Cinchona, January twenty-ninth, 1764

Dear Henry,

Cato has just returned from Kingston, and now I must send him back again with further news. Pearl has been stricken with childbed fever. The thread that holds her to this life is slim. You must come at once, and you must pray that you will not be too late. Bring a doctor. Yr. wife, Martha

Our joy at the birth of Peter Mason has turned to sorrow over the disastrous illness of Pearl. She encountered a fever soon after she was delivered of Peter and each day sees her decline. Oh, how my heart aches at the thought that we may lose her! Such a quantity of life to be lost. My only hope is that her generally strong constitution will triumph in the end. Yesterday, Monimia set off in search of a special "god-bush" she claimed would be effective for Pearl's condition. She returned bearing it triumphantly — an ugly, parasitic thing she called twistletoe — and spent all last evening in a frenzy of stewing and chanting. I am, however, beginning to lose faith in some of Monimia's potions, although she announced this morning that her medicine had been successful. There was indeed a slight improvement in Pearl's condition.

We are still awaiting Henry's arrival. Peter is thriving, and Celia must eat heartily to keep him and Daphne satisfied. While I am quite overwhelmed with sorrow at the gravity of Pearl's illness, the presence of these two marvellous babies distracts me as soon as I turn my eyes upon them.

Before Peter was born, Pearl and I shared one of the two bedrooms, and Monimia, Celia, and Daphne shared the other. As soon as Pearl became ill, Monimia insisted on sleeping in the room with her in order to care for her during the night. In her role as medicine woman, she jealously guards Pearl and looks askance — one might even say she sneers — at my suggestions for a rather more conservative approach to caring for the sick. When I recommended that we send for a doctor, she whirled on me, eyes flashing, and hissed, "Monimia, she doctress!"

February the second, 1764

Henry approached the house unaccompanied, astride his great stallion, Ajax. My message must have failed to reach him before he set off on his journey, unless Cato and the doctor I requested were to follow later. I lifted Peter from his cradle and went out onto the porch, followed closely by Celia. Henry dismounted, strode up the steps, and snatched the baby from my arms; the young heir let out an angry yell, and set to bawling.

"What a greeting for your father, young man!" exclaimed Henry as Peter grew ever more angry, squawling, squirming, and shuddering with rage. Henry tried rocking him in his arms, walking him up and down, and then put him over his shoulder and patted his back — all to no avail. I must admit to experiencing a tiny sting of satisfaction; Peter has never behaved thus in my arms.

"He hongry," said Celia, coming forward and removing the baby.

"I hope my second encounter with Peter will be more amicable," said Henry, laughing. "Now, where is Pearl?"

Since Pearl had just fallen asleep after a long period in which she had tossed and raved, I decided against informing Henry of her illness immediately. I did not wish her rest to be disturbed, and I had no idea how he might react, so I determined rather to break the news as slowly and gently as I could, playing for time.

"I trust that you had a comfortable journey, Henry. You must be thirsty. May I fetch you something to drink?"

"First permit me to greet Pearl. Where is she?" he demanded again, starting into the house.

"Take a moment to recover. Here, sit down," I encouraged, grasping him by the arm and trying to draw him back to the porch. "Are you not tired after your long journey?"

"Not so tired that I cannot greet Pearl."

"She has just this moment fallen asleep. We should not disturb her."

"I insist. I must see her right away." He moved forward into the house; I grabbed his arm again, pulling him back.

"Henry, please sit down. You must prepare yourself for a shock."

"A shock? Why? What is the matter? What is the matter with Pearl? Let me pass. Let me go to her at once. Let me pass!" insisted Henry, sensing immediately that something terrible had happened, thrusting me out of his way.

Like a bull charging, he rushed inside, with me close at his heels. He did not find the right room directly but flung open each door as he passed. When he found the right one, he first recoiled at the stench of sickness and the fumes of Monimia's brews emanating out of the dark. Then he flung open the windows and in a stride or two was at Pearl's side, a Pearl he hardly recognized, flushed with fever, glassy-eyed with fever, mazed with fever, with Monimia sitting, rocking, keening over her.

"Leave," said Henry, dragging Monimia to her feet and heaving her out the door. And then he turned back to the bed, crying, "Pearl, Pearl, look at me. Speak to me." He flung himself to his knees beside the bed, laid his head on the pillow beside Pearl's, and turned her face towards him. And then he neither spoke nor loosed his hold of her for some five minutes. Pearl opened her eyes but did not speak; her look was flat and glazed as Henry stroked her hair and kissed her again and again.

"Pearl," he whispered. "Oh, Pearl! Oh, my life! How can I bear it?" he cried. "You will recover, you will. I will not permit you to die."

Pearl closed her eyes and drifted away to sleep again, while Henry laid his head upon her breast and wept. When he had shed enough tears, he rose, and still gazing upon her, walked backwards to the door. I placed my hand under his elbow and guided him to the porch. He sat down on a chair and bent his head into his hands.

"How long has she been ill?" he groaned.

"She has been in this state a week; she had not recovered from the birth before she succumbed to the fever," I responded.

"Why did you not inform me of her illness?" he demanded angrily.

"Cato is even now again in Kingston trying to deliver a message."

Henry slapped his hand to his head and jumped to his feet.

"Pearl must see a doctor immediately," he shouted. "You are foolish to depend on the concoctions of a mad medicine woman like Monimia. How can you, an Englishwoman, allow such a creature to have control over Pearl's health? Why have you not sent for a doctor? Why has Pearl not been transported to Kingston?"

It was in vain that I repeated that I had indeed sent for a doctor and that to move Pearl to Kingston on a mule would guarantee her death.

"Pearl must be bled immediately. I shall remove her at once."

"How will you transport her?" I asked anxiously.

"I shall hold her safe in my arms, and we will travel together on my horse."

"The journey must surely kill her," I cried. "And if she should by some miracle survive the descent from the mountain, she will certainly perish when she encounters the heat and crowd of Kingston. Do not remove her," I begged.

"She will not die; she will recover. I will save her. Ready my horse!" Henry shouted at me, as though I were his groom.

"Henry, have patience!" I pleaded. "Just this morning we saw some small improvement in her condition. Wait here at least tonight. If you set off now, darkness will soon fall; the night air in the mountains is cold, and the dew is heavy. Pearl will succumb to a chill long before daybreak. Let Monimia care for her through the night, and perhaps we will see another improvement in the morning."

"Monimia knows nothing! If she could truly save lives, she would have won my father back to health, instead of mouthing gibberish about his spirit leaping from his body and flying through the window."

"Remain here tonight," I continued to beg. "Do not take Pearl from her bed and into the mountain air, where certain death awaits her. Remove her in the morning if you must but remain here tonight."

Henry strode back indoors to Pearl's room, with myself once again at his heels. The room was quiet, and Pearl was sleeping comfortably. Shafts of afternoon sunlight cut through the shutters, making stripes on her coverlet.

"Do not disturb her," I whispered into his ear. "Look how peacefully she sleeps."

Henry stood beside her bed no less than ten minutes, gazing at her, before he turned on his heel and left the room.

Now I will list what happened during the rest of the afternoon:

Cato returned without a doctor.

Henry paced up and down the porch. Up and down. Up and down.

I embroidered a tiny shirt.

Celia nursed Peter and sang lullabies to jealous Daphne.

Cato harvested mountain calalu. This resembles spinach.

Pearl slept.

Monimia killed another chicken, plucked it, and threw it into a pot along with scallions, thyme, and pumpkin.

Henry strode to the door of Pearl's room and gazed in, again and again.

I sewed a tiny, mother-of-pearl button onto the shirt as I rocked Peter in the wooden cradle at my foot.

Celia stood Daphne in a bucket of water and washed her from head to toe. Daphne screamed throughout.

Cato brought the calalu into the kitchen and placed it in the sink.

Pearl moaned in her sleep. I wet her parched lips with water but was unable to make her swallow.

Monimia hurried into the woods, carrying a large bag and a knife. She scraped away loose bark from the cinchona tree and filled the bag with it. When she returned she gave the bark to Cato to pound.

Celia washed the calalu and added it to the chicken stew.

Monimia bustled outside again, her calloused feet scratching on the porch floor. She disappeared to the far end of the garden where she filled her apron with herbs and flowers. Returning to the kitchen, she plunged her harvest into a cauldron of steaming water.

I embroidered the initials "P.M." onto the shirt and snipped off the final thread.

Monimia made dumplings.

Darkness fell.

We dined on a delicious chicken stew.

Celia and I made up a bed for Henry on the settee in the front room. After reassuring himself that Pearl was still asleep, he stretched out, declared himself to be comfortable enough, even though his long legs hung down to the floor and there was scarcely room for him to turn over. He closed his eyes and was soon so fast asleep that I began to wonder if Monimia had not slipped a dose of one of her narcotics into his serving of chicken stew.

I administered several teaspoonfuls of water to Pearl and was glad to see her swallow them. And then I retired to bed, doubting mightily that I would sleep that night, but no sooner had I shut my eyes than I began to dream of a snug nest occupied by a single chick whose mother was trying to feed it a violently wriggling worm. Suddenly a dark shadow loomed above them, and I looked up to see a hawk fold its wings close to its body and plummet like a stone to the nest, where it plucked up the little one with its talons and swooped away. I gathered a stone and hurled it after the hawk, hissing at it as I did so.

"Ssss. Mistress," whispered a voice. An overpowering odour of onions told me that my visitor was Monimia.

"Come wit' me, Mistress."

I found myself obeying Monimia's instructions and followed her to Pearl's bedside. Pearl was twisting and turning, flushed with fever once more.

"Mistress," whispered Monimia again, "We gwine tek away de fever."

"I thought you had already tried every remedy, Monimia," I replied wearily.

"We gwine give Miss Pearl de fever bath."

"A bath! No, no. She'll catch a chill. She will never recover."

"I no gwine dead she." Monimia fixed me with an angry stare.

Pearl was moaning, her face furious with fever, her eyes wide open but blank and glazed with fever's film. Sweat poured from her forehead, her upper lip, her chest. She strained at her nightdress, trying to tear it off. Her breath was fast and shallow.

"She's dying," I said to Monimia, and I could feel the blood drain from my face and the beginning of a loss of consciousness.

"I gwine mek she live," Monimia spat out, grabbing me, shaking me roughly, shocking me, clearing my head. "You mus' help me."

She dragged me out of the bedroom and into the kitchen, where Celia was sitting in a rocking chair nursing Peter, and Cato was lurking in the shadows. I was nearly overwhelmed by the mingled scents of the wood stove, of cinchona bark, of chicken soup, and of a massive infusion of herbs and flowers. Monimia stuck her finger into the huge cauldron.

"De weed water lukey warm now; is ready. You," she said pointing imperiously to me, "pick up dem towel an' follow me." She heaved the cauldron from the stove and set off for Pearl's room. I followed her like a sleepwalker.

Together we raised Pearl up, drew off her nightdress, removed her sweat-soaked pillow-case and sheet, and laid a towel beneath her. Then we washed her down from head to toe with the herb-infused water, from front to back, from back to front, and Pearl grew calmer and less flushed as we worked. When we had finished, we removed the towel, replaced it with a clean, dry sheet and pillow-case, and gently lowered Pearl back down.

"Stay here," Monimia ordered me, and disappeared.

She returned with the pounded bark from the fever tree and sprinkled it thickly over Pearl's torso before covering her body lightly with a top sheet.

"De bark jacket gwine draw de fever out."

"But it looks so uncomfortable!" I cried.

"Look she now! She comfortful."

Indeed, there was a change. The deadly red was fading from Pearl's cheeks. Her eyes began to lose their film and to regain focus, her breathing became regular, her muscles relaxed, she closed her eyes, and fell asleep.

I tiptoed from the room and retired to bed once more.

The following morning, just as the sun was rising out of the mist to the east of our little settlement, I awoke with a start to the sound of wild activity. Henry was shouting at Cato to ready Ajax for the journey; Ajax was snorting and slurping from a bucket of water; Monimia was drawing more water from the well; and Celia was in the room beside me, nursing Peter, who snuffled loudly as he sucked. Daphne was still sleeping soundly.

I hurried to Pearl's room, where she lay limp and exhausted upon her pillow, but when I touched her forehead, I found it cool, and she readily drank a concoction that Monimia had prepared for her. I have no idea what it contained, but Pearl did not seem to object to its mucilaginous nature. The mere sight of it made me feel queasy.

After Henry had taken his breakfast — there was nothing amiss with his appetite — he made ready to leave, first telling me that he would make arrangements to send a carriage to Papine for the rest of us as soon as he reached Kingston and had placed Pearl in the hands of a doctor. He advised me not to spend a night in Kingston on the way, but to journey straight to Beverly in order to ready the house for his return with Pearl.

He admitted that since the departure of Celia, Monimia, and myself, the condition of the house left much to be desired.

Monimia and I dressed Pearl in a day dress, over which we wrapped her cloak and pulled its hood up over her head to keep her warm during the early part of the journey through the mountains where the air would still be cool. She was not strong enough to walk across the floor, so Henry lifted her and carried her outdoors where he placed her in Cato's sagging arms while he mounted Ajax. I had begged Henry to take one of the sure-footed mules in place of the high-strung, prancing Ajax, but he dismissed my suggestion out of hand. Poor Cato sank beneath Pearl's weight, but Monimia and I provided a prop on either side of him. Then Henry reached down, catching Pearl under her arms. As he pulled her up, we three pushed from below until she was seated in front of him. We bound her to him with a broad sash which I had made by stripping one of the curtains. In this manner, Henry had both hands free to control the horse.

Alas, my dear Pearl was lifted from me so suddenly that I had no opportunity to embrace her, to wish her farewell. So I clasped her foot, and kissed her ankle.

Blazing-eyed Henry, full of zeal and determination, sat astride the great, pawing stallion, with Pearl's limp form lashed to his body. As they turned to leave, Pearl slowly raised her hand in the gesture of a celebrated actress bidding farewell to her audience at the end of a magnificent performance; then she slumped against Henry's chest.

We watchers saw that it took all Henry's strength to restrain Ajax to a walk.

"Look at Mister Henry him neck-string!" cried Celia, and indeed, the tendons in Henry's neck stood out in sharp relief, bone white. Prancing sideways, Ajax found the path. His ears went back; he had turned towards home. He sprang forward, and in an instant they disappeared.

That evening, as I was changing Peter into his little nightshirt, I inadvertently knocked his navel string off. It had not completely dried and thus left behind a spot of blood. As instructed, I presented Monimia with it. She tucked it into the pocket of her apron and disappeared. A full moon shone that night, and later I witnessed her in the clearing in front of the house, digging a hole. Next, she reached into her pocket, withdrew the crispy little curl, and dropped it into the hole. Then she vanished into the woods bearing a spade, only to reappear within the hour with a healthy sapling, considerably taller than herself. She settled it into the hole, shovelled the earth back in, and patted it down. She made her way to the well and returned to the tree with a large calabash full of water which she poured over the roots; then she raised her hands above her head and began to chant and dance.

Cato appeared from his hut and accompanied her on his merry-wang, which is his favourite instrument; it resembles a rustic guitar, of four strings, made from a calabash, a slice of which being taken off, a dried bladder, or skin, is spread across the largest section, and this is fastened to a handle, which he has taken great pains in ornamenting with a sort of rude carved work and ribbands.

I watched them until the task was completed, before falling to my knees beside my bed, and praying to my Creator to restore his servant Pearl to health. And then I gave thanks for the precious gift He had bestowed upon me.

Spanish Town, February 8th, 1764

Yesterday saw us safely returned to Beverly. We were quite a procession as we set off on our mules. Cato went ahead on foot, making sure that the path was clear. Celia and I followed him on two of the three mules. Celia had wrapped a cloth around Daphne and herself, so that she carried the baby securely on her back, and she insisted that I do the same with Peter. With another suitable length of cloth she bound him to my back, in the manner of African women. Monimia climbed onto the third mule, which sagged to the ground under her weight and refused to budge. She used every method she could imagine to cajole it: sweet words like "Muley, darlin', you go walk now, you hear"; a carrot freshly drawn from the vegetable patch; several lashes with a switch; and finally a special incantation composed for recalcitrant mules. All to no avail. So she climbed down and then piled various pots and pans, a plentiful supply of herbs, "weeds," spices, and bark, and her own belongings onto the mule's back. This load met with the mule's approval. She then wound a cloth into a tight circle, making a thick mat, which she placed on her head. On that she balanced a basket containing a supply of food and water for our journey.

"Now I go walk," she announced. And off we went.

We left Angela, the goat, behind to keep Cato company on his return to Cinchona and to provide him with a regular supply of milk. We had consumed all the fowl at our final meal, dining on the last chicken, the one whom we had named Prodigious because she laid an egg every day during our stay in the mountains. As Monimia was cleaning and drawing her, she called me to come and look. Inside the body of Prodigious were eggs of ever-decreasing sizes, each ready for the ensuing day, and the next, and the next. I was so moved by the manner in which this one small hen had so efficiently nourished us and was so well prepared to continue doing so, that I did not believe I could eat her. However, when the time came, I was so hungry and Monimia had prepared her in such a delicious manner — with scallions and allspice — that I managed to overcome my reluctance.

The journey was arduous but we survived, largely due to the good humour of Celia, who was overjoyed at the thought of seeing Cuthbert and her other children again. She sang a song with many verses as we descended, a song which she called a jamma, describing the scene we had just left and our adventures on the way down, all in rhyming couplets, mixing African-sounding words with English words, African words like nyaka-nyaka, crang-crang, and jeng-jeng. She sang of the labour of Pearl and the birth of Peter, invoking the spirits of light and darkness who gave one baby and took away another. Oh, little Catherine! I will not forget you. She sang of Cato in the garden and Monimia in the kitchen and me on the porch with my books. She sang of Daphne. In her song, our Blue Mountain home became the abode of the gods and we were the puppets of their pleasure. Celia's was a torrent of poetry extempore such as I have never heard before.

We spent the night in Papine, where we left Cato the following morning. His eyes streamed with tears as he bade us farewell.

"Come back soon, Mistress," he begged. "Me gwine wait for you."

I must admit to shedding some tears, too, on leaving that dear old man. He promised to have the house ready for us at any time and said he would always maintain a bountiful supply of vegetables growing in the garden. I hope that, in our absence, those vegetables will provide him with some income to increase the pittance Henry gives him for caretaking. Monimia has shown him the way to turn a profit. She has a remarkable head for business and a strong propensity for saving, shown not only in the vending of eggs and vegetables, but in the driving of hard bargains.

We accomplished the journey from Papine to Kingston and then on to Spanish Town in two narrow carriages; this part of the journey was easier and less arduous but nearly not as entertaining as the first part. Celia, inhibited by the closeness of the carriage and unaccustomed to its swaying motion, huddled in a corner, wordlessly, as she fed Peter and I bounced the irrepressible Daphne on my knee. Monimia seemed unharmed by the motion of the carriage in which she rode and produced manna from her great basket for us to consume when we stopped briefly for some refreshment. She had made gingerbread, which I persuaded Celia to eat to calm her stomach, remembering how much it had calmed mine on the Bay of Biscay.

It was late afternoon by the time we completed our journey. As we passed through Spanish Town on our way to Beverly, a few of the matrons, ever vigilant on their galleries, flagged us down and begged to examine the child. Peter tolerated their scrutiny, and I accepted their congratulations and good wishes with much aplomb, even though their voices began to riccochet in my head:

> *Have you seen the baby? Isn't he sweet?*
> *Did you mark his skin colour and the size of his feet?*
> *Did you see how his hair curls close to his head?*
> *Not straight like Martha's. What's that you said?*
> *Oh no! Oh no! How could that be?*

I'll never believe what you're saying to me,
and I won't tell a soul.

If I had any reluctance about returning to Beverly, it was overcome by the rapturous welcome we received from the household staff. They came to the front steps to greet us: big and little, young and old, all bearing gifts of fruit and vegetables. Celia's two children leaped up and down, Cuthbert grinned from ear to ear, the laundresses danced a jig, the stable boys strummed on their banjees and toombahs. Work came to a halt in the fields, and the field hands ran towards the house, shouting and laughing, the race horses neighed, the donkeys brayed, and even Hercules, the bull, bellowed from a distant field. How this welcome lifted my spirits, spirits which were a little dashed, I must admit, when I saw the condition of the house. However, it is a condition that can easily be fixed with the return of an efficient housekeeper, careful attention, soap, water, and polish. My first aim will be to make sure the house is cleaned, room by room, from lookout tower to kitchen. I will supervise the rubbing of furniture with beeswax, and the laundering of linens with scented soap. Beverly will shine again!

Peter had been restless and irritable during the latter part of the journey. As soon as I bathed him and Celia fed him, we put him to bed in his cradle, and he fell instantly asleep, looking comfortable and sleek, to my eyes for all the world like the young lord returned safely home to the manor.

Even Henry, *in absentia,* had a welcoming gift for me. In a curious attempt to replace my canary, he had purchased a parrot from the captain of a slave ship who had brought it with him from the Guiney Coast. The bird is grey with a red tail, stands about a foot tall, and fixes me with a beady, intelligent eye.

His wings are clipped, so he cannot fly away, and when first introduced to me, he stepped fearlessly onto my outstretched finger. The captain had insisted to Henry that the bird had a large vocabulary, some of it English, some of it African, but so far all I have been able to coax from him are some piercing whistles, a variety of clicks and moans, and one horrifying curse. The captain called him Zooks, but I have changed his name to Scipio Africanus in acknowledgement of his bravery and his birthplace. While I am loath to own anything that has belonged to the captain of a slave ship, I am glad that Scipio has escaped his life at sea.

We have received no word as yet from Henry about Pearl's condition. I am fearful of this silence but remind myself of Henry's taciturnity and his unwillingness to put pen to paper. I am surprised, however, that no news has reached me via the grapevine, and that Jessica Fraser and her gossips have nothing to say on the matter because, not surprisingly, scandal and gossip are still the rage in Spanish Town.

I wonder when Henry will return from Kingston; I wonder how Pearl fared during their journey; I wonder if Henry's doctor found any treatment more effective than Monimia's. Pearl is constantly in my thoughts and in my prayers.

Before Pearl fell ill, she had started to embroider a petticoat for my sister; she wanted to describe Jamaica to her in something other than words. The garment is like a natural history of the island, filled with colour and life, and I believe that my sister will wear it with great pride, knowing that no one in the world, not even a princess or a queen, owns such a garment. She may even consider wearing it outside her dress! Pearl has already embroidered a doctor bird, a lizard, a coney, and a sea turtle, and intends to trim the hem with images of plumbago, a lovely blue flower, because I have told her that blue is my sister's favourite colour. However, I do not want to raise Lizzie's hopes too much. Pearl's favourite colour is red, and I will be surprised if she can resist embroidering at least a few gaudy red flowers in with the blue.

February the tenth, 1764

My hand shudders as I write. I have an unbearable tale to tell, which I will recount in detail, moment by moment, in order that I myself may begin to comprehend all that has come to pass.

I was at my desk when I heard the sound of a horse's hooves. I ran to the window to see if it were Henry approaching. It was not Henry; it was one of the workers from the business office. He leaped down from his horse as I fled to greet him and we encountered each other on the front steps. Breathlessly, he handed up an envelope, his eyes unwilling to meet mine. I tore it open, and this is the terrible message I read:

Pearl died early this morning. I am bringing her body to Spanish Town today. Please arrange for services tomorrow at St Iago. H.

The jagged words looked as though they had been hacked into the paper by the pen of the writer. I felt nothing but the desire to reject them, to hurl them back at the sender. I crumpled the note in one hand, raised the other as if to strike the messenger, and took a step towards him. Instead of striking him, I tripped, and tumbled down the steps, which knocked me unconscious for a moment. I was choked to my senses at the foot of the steps by Monimia waving a pungent, smoking bunch of herbs under my nose. Then she pried open my clenched fist and removed the note, demanding:

"What dis say?"

I could not answer her; I could not speak.

"What it say, man?" she demanded of the messenger. He knew what it said; he glanced at me, and then whispered into Monimia's ear. She staggered and for a moment I thought she too might fall to the ground. Instead, she let out a roar, a howl such as could crack Heaven asunder, a continuous, deafening wail. And out of the house and from the gardens and fields came running all those who had welcomed us so joyously just five days before. I struggled to my feet, and grabbed Monimia's arm with all my strength, digging my nails into her flesh, and hissing into her ear:

"Stop that noise at once."

To my surprise, her jaws clamped shut. Her bosom heaved up and down; she glared at me; she shifted her weight from one foot to another and thrust out a hip — and her lower lip.

I mounted the steps and stood at the top, gesturing to the crowd to gather around me. I took a deep breath and then broke the news of Pearl's death as gently as I could, asking the people to remain silent and respectful as they dispersed. This was an impossible request; I might just as well have asked the thunder not to roll. They did not disperse; they could not remain silent. Soon the sounds of muffled sobbing and keening broke through. A drummer — someone always has a drum — pounded out a slow beat, and shortly the crowd began to sway in time and then to dance and wail. I turned my back, called on Cuthbert to follow me, and entered the house. As yet, the import of Henry's note had failed to penetrate my heart, and I felt impelled to fulfil immediately those tasks he had set out for me.

I asked Cuthbert to ready the carriage and bring it to the kitchen door so that I could avoid the crowd at the front of the house. Moving in a daze, I climbed the stairs to my bedroom, put on my bonnet and a light shawl, picked up my prayer book, my reticule, and my parasol, and left the house.

Cuthbert had been unable to locate the coachman, so he drove the carriage himself the mile from Beverly to the church of St Iago. It was a relief to step from the heat of the noonday sun into the cool shade of the sanctuary. There I discovered Mr Kenet, alone in the empty church, practising the reading for Sunday's service. As I entered, he was sounding forth the words: "Comfort ye, comfort ye, my people," but he stopped short on perceiving that he had an audience.

I walked down the aisle towards him as he descended from the lectern, and we coincided at the exact point where I had married Henry. Again, I could not speak; I could not pronounce the words "Pearl is dead." I still cannot comprehend them. I will never comprehend them. I refuse to comprehend them. I stood shaking from head to toe.

"Mrs Mason, whatever is the matter?" he asked. "Come. Sit down. May I bring you a glass of water?"

He took my arm and guided me into a pew. After I had sat for a few moments, my shaking subsided, and I withdrew Henry's note from my reticule. As Mr Kenet read its contents, the colour drained from his face. He paused for a long moment, and then took me in his arms. My tears started to flow, a river of tears, endless tears, but oh, the comfort of his arms. We remained in each other's arms until my sobs subsided, and then he took a deep breath, cleared his throat, and said:

"We must arrange the funeral service for Pearl," and we set about it immediately. I regained my ability to think and my voice returned as together we chose the psalms, the hymns, and the readings. Mr Kenet promised to find the organist;

I would invite Mrs Fraser and her friends to arrange the flowers. I knew they could not fail to outdo each other with their floral donations. Pearl, who loved flowers so much, would leave this world embowered.

I had assumed that the tiresome Reverend Mr Rutter would conduct the service, but Mr Kenet informed me that he had departed for England a mere week before my return from Cinchona, in search of a more salubrious climate. Evidently, his health had suffered during my absence, and he blamed Jamaica entirely for this decline. However, when I recalled his eating like a cormorant and drinking like a porpoise on many an occasion, I am more inclined to believe that the wound was self-inflicted. May he enjoy his return to the land of steak and kidney pudding! It was difficult to restrain an expression of extreme satisfaction at the news that none other than Mr Kenet himself would conduct Pearl's obsequies.

Cuthbert drove me back to Beverly, where I immediately sought out the carpenter, whom I instructed to create as beautiful a coffin as he could in the short period of time at his disposal. Then I located two of the gardeners and persuaded them to become gravediggers. I had decided that Pearl's grave should rest directly beneath the tamarind tree, but the gravediggers, one of whom is extremely deaf, sucked their teeth, and muttered about the size of the roots they would have to disturb. I examined the ground closely, chose a spot at some distance from the main trunk that appeared to have few obstacles, and bade them dig.

Monimia, ever believing that the best cure for all that ails a person is food and plenty of it, had prepared a giant meal for me. I pecked at it all alone, each small mouthful choking me as I tried to swallow. I soon retired to my room, where I instantly fell into a heavy afternoon slumber. When I awoke, I heard

Peter crying, and then, and then, and then I remembered . . . I shut my eyes and groaned. When I opened them again, I found Celia standing over me, with Peter squirming in her arms.

"He want you should hold him," she declared, and so I rose and put on my afternoon dress, and embraced the precious living link to Pearl. I carried him out into the garden and made my way towards the tamarind tree. As I drew near, I overheard the following conversation between the gravediggers.

"Where you t'ink she spirit go?" one asked the other.

"What you say, man? Haul out your mout'."

The first man repeated his question more loudly.

"Africa is where de spirits dem go," the second responded authoritatively. Then they considered Pearl's ancestry — Chloe from Africa, Silas Mason from England.

"You t'ink Mr Silas spirit him go to Africa?" asked the first.

"No, man," responded the other, tutting, "bukra spirit don' have home in Africa." There was a pause, and then the first gravedigger announced:

"I t'ink Pearl spirit she gwine rest in Jamaica."

There was silence for a while as they worked, and then the conversation took another turn.

"What colour is spirit?"

"Is blue," came the emphatic response.

"Eh-eh. Blue. How you know dis?"

"You never see duppy?"

"No sah. You see duppy?"

"One time I see me fader duppy."

"What him say?"

"Him don' talk, man. Him fly aroun' all aroun' and him try to cyatch me and tek me away."

"An' him blue?"

"Is what I tellin' you, man. Is why you never see duppy in daytime. Is same-same colour like sky."

"Ahhh."

I left them to their work and conversation and returned to the gallery. I remained there, in a rocking chair, with Peter in my arms, until I heard the noise of horses' hooves once more and saw the swirl of dust as Pearl made her final journey home to Beverly. Henry, astride Ajax, rode beside the carriage transporting her body. He was a Henry I barely recognised, hollow-eyed and dishevelled; under his wide-brimmed travelling hat, I perceived that he wore a plaster on his head, and his face was bruised and scratched. He was followed by the usual crowd of spectators.

We called on four servants to help Henry carry Pearl's body to the dining room, where we laid her out on the table. Her clothes were slashed and her face and arms were covered in cuts and bruises; I noticed a large gash over one ear. The servants gawped and stared. Henry left the room.

Monimia entered carrying a bowl of fresh water and soft white cloths.

"Shoo," she said to the servants. "Shoo!"

When they did not move but stayed transfixed, she put down the bowl, picked up a towel and flapped it in their direction.

"Shoo," she spat at them again. "You want I should medicine you?" she threatened, swelling up, rising up, and raising her arms. At this they turned as one and crowded through the doorway, pushing, shoving, cursing each other in their hurry to leave.

Monimia removed what remained of Pearl's clothes and started to chant as she washed the body. I picked up a cloth and helped her, remembering when we had washed the living Pearl, so few days ago, immediately following the birth of the twins. In addition to the wounds to her face and arms, she was bruised from head to toe, and the area around her ribs was particularly livid and swollen. It was in vain that I assured myself I could not hurt her.

When we had finished, I went to the sea chest on the landing, and removed from it the yellow satin dress with sequins that Pearl had worn at my wedding. Together Monimia and I dressed her in it. I brushed her hair, and around her head Monimia tied a chin-strap, which she made from a bow that had adorned the back of the dress. Then we folded her cold arms across her breast. I accompanied Monimia as she carried what she called the death-water outside and poured it on the ground. She told me that death-water must never be poured down the drain, and that it is bad luck to step over it, so we kept our distance.

Celia joined us as we picked flowers and herbs that we carried indoors to strew around Pearl's body and across the floor. Celia wove a garland which she placed at rather a rakish angle around Pearl's brow, successfully obscuring the gash above her ear.

Henry had disappeared to his room without speaking to me or asking to see Peter; once again he refused all offers of food and drink.

I continued to make arrangements. Monimia and I discussed what should be served to those who returned to the house after the funeral. We readied the platters, the goblets, and the silverware. I retrieved my best black dress from the back of my wardrobe and dusted off my black bonnet. Then I sat with Pearl and read aloud some passages from "Romeo and Juliet," which seemed more fitting for her than Job or the Book of Revelation. When my eyelids drooped and I could read no more, I retired for the night, still moving involuntarily. I had ceased to feel; I was dry-eyed.

Sleep was a stranger. In the darkest hour, I heard the stairs creak, and then, first softly, but slowly louder and louder, rose the muffled sound of a soul in agony. I lit a candle and followed the noise downstairs. As I descended, the sound diminished, as though silenced by my approach. I saw no one. I walked through the house and opened the door to the gallery, but it was evident that the noise came from within and not from out of doors. As I turned my back on the gallery, I saw something stir under the dining room table. I bent down to see what it was and saw a person. I bent further and to my amazement found Henry, prostrated face down, trying to muffle his sobs in the turkish carpet.

"Henry!" I cried.

He did not stir.

I tried to pull him by the hand.

He would not budge.

I stood nonplussed.

The racking sobs continued.

And then, at last, at the sight of Henry's sorrow, my own tearless sobbing started, not gently and quietly, but wrenched, roaring, from the depth of my guts.

I fell to the ground.

I began to wail.

I tore my hair.

Henry grabbed my ankle and dragged me under the table. He wound his arms around me as I heaved and shook, and finally my tears began to flow. All the grief that I had restrained so long surged past the floodgates. In a harmony of howling, Henry and I mourned the death of Pearl.

Although it did not seem possible that we could ever cease

lamenting, we eventually recovered a semblance of calm. Henry rose and fetched us each a drink of rum and water, which we carried out onto the gallery. I never expected to drink rum, nor to enjoy it, but that night it acted like a balm. We sat in the dark, in rocking chairs, gazing out at the stars and at the fireflies dancing in the garden, while a gentle breeze dried our tears. And then I entreated Henry to recount for me the story of the death of Pearl. It took him two more drinks of rum before he was prepared to begin. And then he spoke in a quiet voice, and it was as though Pearl's death loosened his tongue and my usually taciturn husband spared me no detail. I shall endeavour to recount his tale as closely as I can.

About two hours' ride down the steep path from Cinchona, a huge rock dislodged itself from the mountainside above and suddenly tumbled across the path, narrowly missing Henry and Pearl, and causing Ajax to shy in alarm. Rearing up, the horse pitched the riders from his back over the steep slope. They rolled down the cliff, still bound together, until they struck a jagged outcrop.

At this point in his narrative, Henry's voice faltered, and he turned to fortify himself with another swig of rum. As I waited for him to resume, I observed that fireflies had gathered around the tamarind tree.

Henry started again, explaining that he had tried to take the blow with his hands in order to protect Pearl, and with this he opened his palms to me so that I could see the injuries thereon. But as it happened, Pearl's right side hit the rock first, and she took the force of the blow. Henry continued, his voice breaking: "She was beneath me as we struck." He began to sob anew. I left my chair, slipped onto his lap, and held on to him. With one foot I set the chair gently rocking.

"She took the blow," he repeated. "I felt the breath, forced from her lungs. I felt the crunch of her broken ribs, the thump as her head hit the rock, in every fibre of my being."

Henry paused, took a giant breath, and then continued.

"But I also felt the beating of that strong heart. She was yet alive, although unconscious."

At first, he dared not move for fear of hurting her still further, but as time passed he recognized that the only way to save her life was to find help. As carefully as he could, he unwound the cloth that held them together, and tore off a piece to staunch the wound over her ear. He made a pillow for her head with the remainder of the fabric and wrapped her cloak around her. The spot where she lay formed a natural declivity, and he assured himself that she could fall no further if she remained in place.

He scrambled back up to the road, ignoring any injury to himself in his haste to find help, and then hallooed up and down the road, only to receive an echo of halloos in response. Then he began to run down the path in search of a village, stumbling and cursing as he went. He soon overtook an old man on a donkey and asked if a large horse had passed his way.

"Yes, sah. One big t'ing go dat way," the old man responded, pointing down. Henry begged the use of his donkey, pressing a coin into his palm. With encouragement from a switch, the donkey moved forward a few paces, but then, perceiving his favourite dinner by the roadside, stopped abruptly to eat, and thereafter refused to budge. In frustration, Henry dismounted and continued on foot as fast as he could. About two miles down the road, he came across a group of children, and commanded the oldest boy to run as swiftly as he could for help, and not to return without some rope. By this time, Henry could run no further, and sat down on a rock to catch his breath. Some minutes later he heard shouts, and around the hairpin bend hurried a group of four young men, each bearing a length of rope.

Henry pointed up the hill, explaining what had occurred, and describing the spot; then he made further enquiries about Ajax. One of the men said that he had seen him streaking down the hill towards Content Gap.

He set off with the young men but they soon outstripped him on the path. It was in vain that he tried to discourage a group of children from following along. They, too, soon outstripped him, and were leaning over the edge pointing down when he reached the spot where the accident had occurred. He looked over the precipice, and discerned the men below, fashioning a hammock out of Pearl's cloak. Soon they had placed her in it and secured her with the rope. Then they positioned themselves to draw her up to the path. With the utmost care, they lifted her inch by inch up the rocky face.

The four young men carried her in the hammock down to Content Gap, preceded by the group of children who had been advised to run ahead and seek word of Ajax. On arrival, the young men halted by a spring, and Henry splashed cold water on Pearl's face to try to bring her back to consciousness; to no avail. They were soon surrounded by higglers, each vying for a look at Pearl, while at the same time impressing on Henry the importance of buying their fresh fruit and vegetables. He tried to send them away, but they continued to stand around, shaking their heads; then one of them stepped forward with a basin of warm water and washed the wound above Pearl's ear.

Henry engaged the men to continue carrying Pearl down to Papine, where he hoped he might be able at last to hire a carriage. They placed her on a pallet and each took one corner. Just as they were leaving Content Gap, Henry heard a triumphant shout. Two boys had captured Ajax; the horse had paused to drink from a stream just outside the village.

Henry thanked them and mounted the runaway. He bade the men lift Pearl up again and continue on their way. It was a long and arduous journey to Papine. They walked for many hours, and darkness was falling by the time they arrived. Pearl had still not regained consciousness.

At Papine, there being no carriages for hire, Henry procured the services of the bread man's mule-drawn cart. He made Pearl as comfortable as he could — several women crowded around and offered pillows. Relieved of their burden, the young men who had carried Pearl as far as Papine appointed themselves torch-bearers, two running ahead of the procession and two running behind.

They reached Kingston at midnight and found their way to Dr Edgar's house at Half Way Tree. He came to the door in his nightshirt and, immediately recognizing the gravity of the situation, bade them enter. The young men lifted Pearl from the cart, and Dr Edgar invited them to carry her into his dining room and to lay her down on the table. Henry thanked them, paid them, and wished them goodnight.

At this point in his narrative, Henry sighed deeply. I rose from the chair and advised him to stand and stretch. We stepped outside and took a walk along the path in the formal garden. Henry took a few deep breaths and continued.

He told me he had explained the accident to Dr Edgar and expressed his concern about the severity of the blow that Pearl had sustained to her side. He promised eternal gratitude and a healthy remuneration if Edgar could save her life.

The doctor inspected the wound over her ear, felt her pulse, and listened to her uneven breath. Then he untied the ropes that still bound her, unwrapped her cloak, and bade Henry help him undress her, a task which proved to be more difficult than they had expected because she lay on her back with her buttons beneath her. Not wishing to turn her over and risk compounding her injuries, Dr Edgar took up his scissors and sliced open her dress from neck to thigh. The whole of the right side of her ribs was bruised and swollen; her breasts were exuding milk.

At this point, Henry began to sob again. I led him to the garden bench and bade him sit. I sat beside him and patted him gently until his sobs subsided. Then he began again, telling me in detail how the doctor carefully felt each rib in turn, shook his head, expressed concern that one of them might have injured a lung, and then tucked his fingers under her breastbone and tried to push the offending rib back into place. After that, the doctor said that there was nothing further he could do except await her return to consciousness. When Henry asked him if this were likely, he shrugged his shoulders. Henry pleaded with him to let him stay at his house so that he might remain in constant attendance, offering him in return a share of the profits from his business; then he entreated him to tell no one of his presence, offering him a still greater share of the profits.

It took three days for Pearl to die. Each day her breath became more laboured; each day saw her drawing further away from this life. She never moved; she never regained consciousness. On the third night, the fever returned, and her shallow breathing became harsh and rapid. And suddenly it stopped.

I expected silence, a profound hush at the end of Henry's tale, but out of the night poured the sudden, cheerful song of the nightingale.

February the twelfth, 1764

Pearl's funeral went according to plan. Mr Kenet conducted the service with a mixture of authority and kindness. The congregation, which numbered in the hundreds, sang the hymns and psalms with amazing vigour. I thought those who attended might be cowed by sorrow at the death of one so young and full of life, but while the people of Spanish Town are not inured to death — death always provides its store of surprises — they have learned how commonplace and indiscriminate it is, and simply take it as a matter of course. They pay their respects, and then return to the business of getting and spending, eating and drinking.

And they certainly did justice to the funeral meats, as Monimia reported to me. Having so recently been delivered of a child, at least in the minds of the guests, I was able to — in fact, expected to — retire to my room soon after we had welcomed them to Beverly. I left Henry glowering at the crowd, which lacking a hostess and faced with a mute host, dispersed as soon as it had consumed its fill, leaving only Henry's brother to console him. Jonas had arrived from Kingston that morning, breathing hot breath, just in time for the funeral. It is hard to imagine that act of consolation, and indeed Monimia told me that Henry soon retired to his room, while Jonas stayed up all night drinking rum.

He spent two days at Beverly before returning to Kingston, two drunken days, days in which Henry remained in his room, leaving me to spend time in Jonas's company. Limp with sorrow over the death of Pearl, I avoided him as much as possible. He sickens me. I do not trust him, and again I was confronted by the differences between the brothers. He is so much smaller and hairier than Henry, and has a beadier, more rapacious eye. I saw that rapacious eye light on Celia, in spite of the fact that he went to great pains to assure me of his intention to marry Antoinetta Kershaw, the daughter of a neighbouring planter in St Thomas-in-the-East. I made every effort to ensure he had no opportunity to be alone with Celia. I hope I was successful.

He has gone now, taking his stinking breath with him, and the house is quiet and ill-lit without Pearl. I am worn out with grief. In the daytime, effort and occupation distract me somewhat. Reminding myself that music hath charms that soothe the savage breast, I have found some consolation in playing my clavichord. But with the setting of the sun — that precipitous plunge from tropical day to tropical night — the sense of loss pierces me like a dagger. I stand on the edge of a void; darkness consumes me.

A week after Pearl's death, I received a delicately worded letter of sympathy and concern from dear Mr Kenet. He included with it a short epigram from Plato that he had translated and paraphrased, expressing the hope that it would console me for my loss:

> *In Memory of Pearl*
> *She was the morning star while living*
> *before her light had fled.*
> *In death, she's the evening star, giving*
> *new brilliance to the dead.*

Mr Kenet has beautiful handwriting. Mr Kenet has beautiful hands.

February the nineteenth, 1764

I thought Henry might never leave his room once he had retired there following the funeral, but two ships have arrived in Kingston laden with goods from Liverpool, and he has now been dragged back to life by the lure of commerce and the advent of another new horse. He has been away for several days now, supervising the unloading and distribution of goods, but I am expecting his return tonight. Before he left, we discussed the matter of the inscription on Pearl's tombstone but came to no agreement.

In spite of the disapproval of the Spanish Town ladies, I plan to open my school again next month. Again I can hear those whispers of disapproval hissing around inside my head:

> *She's at it again. She's planning to teach*
> *the little black fools. All those in her reach*
> *will be welcome, it seems, to study at Beverly*
> *first thing every morning out there on the gallery.*
> *She'll even takes idiots into her care,*
> *and educate them, but says they'll teach her!*
> *Can you imagine it? What a disgrace!*
> *How can Henry allow it? It seems such a waste*
> *when she could spend more time conversing with us,*
> *or playing at cards, getting out of the house.*

Celia will be my assistant at the school. I continue to teach her to read and write, and she has achieved an extraordinary signature, excelling with her "l," which she loops joyously upwards, far, far beyond her other letters.

Peter offers me endless consolation. I could spend the entire day watching him. He has begun to smile — wide, toothless grins, which stretch from ear to ear. He is chubby and curly, and usually cheerful. However, he shows a passionate nature and his cheerfulness can swiftly turn to rage. In an instant his mood may change from one of sublime happiness and winning chortles to raging fury. In his fury, he becomes crimson from head to toe, clenches his little fists, curls his toes, and howls like a demon.

March the thirty-first, 1764

It is sometimes necessary to be a little devious in order to achieve a higher good. Or am I being Machiavellian? Does the end ever justify the means?

A week ago, I recommended teaching on the gallery at Beverly. All went well until yesterday when Henry suddenly accosted me on the matter while we were having breakfast. I believe that Jessica Fraser and her cronies had alerted him. He questioned me with stern features and a lowering brow.

"I hear that you are, once more, running a school at Beverly," he said.

"I am, indeed," I replied.

"I hear that many children are being taken away from their work in my fields and brought to sit on my gallery, where they sing and make noise all day long. This cannot continue."

I was appalled by Henry's statement, and decided that, in order to persuade him to allow me to continue teaching, I needed to convince him that my motive for doing so was purely for his benefit.

"Henry, dear husband, you must remember that my intention is to create a band of loyal workers for you. The boys and girls I teach are far too young to make much of a contribution to work on the pen. I am preparing them for the future, preparing them to be well-equipped to work in your business, where you are ever at a loss to find trustworthy employees."

"Ah, Martha, you do not yet understand the predicament, or perhaps you refuse to acknowledge it. How often do I have to repeat to you that an educated slave is a dangerous slave? Why, he can use his education to procure his freedom!"

"Would you not be proud to employ free men and women? Would they not have your business more at heart if they were working within it freely, rather than under the lash of the overseer's whip? Only yesterday you told me about the incompetence of your staff here in Spanish Town and also at Reward. I am teaching my pupils the values of honesty and efficiency, along with their lettering and arithmetic. A staff that has been educated by me would believe in your best interests. Come and witness how they learn! They do not merely sing and make noise all day. For sure, we do take a break from reading and arithmetic from time to time and refresh ourselves lightheartedly, but even in their play, the children are learning. Please spend a day with us before you decide to take measures. Can you come tomorrow? My pupils would be overjoyed to have Mr Henry visit the classroom."

"No, no. Tomorrow I must be in Kingston for the arrival of the *Betsy*. Tell me again: is it your strong belief that educating these children is a wise investment and that I would stand to profit from it?"

"It is, indeed. You would be the envy of the other merchants."

"How many pupils attend your classes?"

"There are twelve at the moment."

"Are they all the children of my slaves?"

"All except for two, the children of the curate's housekeeper."

"And you have brought all these children into the house without first securing my permission?"

"I did it only on your account, in the spirit of investing in your business, of contributing valuable booty to the profit of your enterprises."

Henry gave me a sidelong glance and spoke again: "Mrs Fraser tells me that you are looked on with suspicion by the ladies of Spanish Town."

"I don't give a fig for the opinion of the ladies of Spanish Town. Let me teach, Henry. This is my purpose in life, and you stand to gain from it. Your establishment will be a model of efficiency; you will be the envy of the other merchants and planters."

With his eye forever on profit, Henry was grudgingly won over by my argument. And I do believe that Henry can be persuaded by efficient argument — look how his mother persuaded him to marry me! But, oh, how I yearn to shout aloud my true motives! I want to scream that education is the strongest tool of liberation, that learning slices through the miasma of ignorance and is a beacon for the oppressed, that these coarsely-clad little peasants are of flesh and blood as good as the scions of gentlest genealogy; and that the germs of native excellence, refinement, intelligence, kind feeling are as likely to exist in their hearts as those of the best-born. It is my duty to develop them.

"So long as I stand to gain," he said, leaving the room, shaking his finger at me.

"You certainly stand to gain," I responded as I watched him go. And then I smirked.

Later the same day, I once again brought up the question of the inscription on Pearl's tombstone. I learned that Henry was considering the resolute "Resurgam." I was surprised that he had fixed on a Latin inscription, knowing his dislike of the language, but I think he was attracted to the straightforward simplicity of the word.

The wind sharply rattled the pods on the tree that they call "women's tongues" when he uttered the word. I immediately decided to argue against "Resurgam," advising him that it struck me as a thoroughly unromantic word and unsuitable in its plainness for one as colourful as Pearl. He countered that he was determined to include the notion of Pearl's awaking and arising into a better world. I then suggested to him that he consider "Arise, my love, my fair one" from the Song of Solomon, resisting the temptation to offer him "Thou hast ravished my heart, my sister, my spouse" as an alternative. The wind dropped and the air was still as he disappeared, bearing with him my Bible, opened to the Song, which he had never before encountered; this is, of course, not surprising because it is rarely referred to within church walls. He returned the Bible to me yesterday, along with a note which contained the following inscription to be delivered to the stonecutter: "Beloved Pearl. Arise, my love, my fair one."

Because we have so few schoolbooks, my pupils and I are in the process of writing and illustrating our own book. Cupid and Psyche have imagined two heroes, Cocky and Polly Lizard, their names for a pair of real lizards who visit the gallery regularly. Henderson sings loudly of his favourite animal hero, Rat-Bat, and he likes to jump onto my desk and swoop down on Cocky Lizard. In vain do I try to restrain him. If I remonstrate, he cries and runs to me, throwing his arms around my legs, and shaking all over. Rose's character is a bird that she calls Bessy

Kickup, and she imitates the way it flips its tail. Bessy Kickup is the most talkative of our characters so far. Augustus insists that he is Jab Jab Crow, and he surveys us all with a predatory eye. Freddie is a roaring, leaping tiger called Stripe. The new pupils, acquired last week, watch with amazement as Cocky, Polly, Rat-Bat, Bessy, Jab Jab, and Stripe entertain us with their adventures.

Each day I write down the progress of our plot and the following day I read the story aloud to an audience that is rapt by its own creation. As soon as they begin to read and write well enough, they will take turns in being the amanuensis. I predict that it will not be long before Rose and Augustus are capable of handling the task.

Now that they all know how to write their figures from one to ten, I have started to teach them arithmetic, using the characters in their drama as examples: Cocky and Polly are two lizards, but Scipio is one parrot. Bessy Kickup has one tail but two feet. Rat-Bat has one nose but two wings. Jab Jab Crow has two parts to one beak. Stripe has four legs. Today I approached addition:

"If I put Bessy Kickup and Jab Jab Crow together," I asked, "what do I have?"

There was a pause, and then the answers came hard and fast: "Two chil'ren." "Two bird." "A hegg."

The other participant in our endeavours is the parrot, Scipio Africanus, whom the children call Sah Kippy. He lives on the gallery and considers it his domain. He has begun to imitate the voices of the children and can say "Miss Tress" in the exact tone of Augustus. I have told the children that the foul curses the bird utters are gibberish and they should pay no attention to them, but they are entranced by a bird who talks and have now started to imitate him. I cannot but be amused by these children imitating a parrot who imitates them. Just yesterday Scipio perfected an imitation of Henderson's Rat-Bat cries and together they entered into a dialogue of shrieks. Henry is right; my classroom is a noisy place and I am fortunate to be at some distance from our nearest neighbours.

But I must not forget to mention the youngest member of this household. Peter is a man of many talents now. He smiles, he gurgles, he plays with his toes, he lifts his head. He is the admiration of us all. I have noticed that Henry comes home earlier in the evenings these days. I find it difficult to attribute this to my charms.

I have tried to interest Henry in my collection of books in order to widen his world somewhat, but to no avail. We have, however, Henry and I, finally found a common area of interest — piquet. In the evenings when he is at home, and after he has been entertained by Peter and we have eaten our evening meal, we sit at the card table and pass the time playing. He is like so many of the Jamaican gentlemen, who seem to have a far greater affection for the modish vice of gaming than the *belles lettres* and love a pack of cards better than the Bible. In his opinion, to talk of a Homer, or a Virgil, of a Tully, or a Demosthenes, is quite impolite.

Some nights it is very late before we retire to our rooms.

Last night as I blew out my candle, I imagined I heard Pearl's laugh. I covered my head with my pillow and cried myself to sleep.

March the thirty-first, 1768

I notice that it is four years to the day since I last wrote in my journal and more than four long years since Pearl died. Without her sparkling presence at Beverly, my spirits gradually sank lower and lower, and I found it nearly impossible to write anything at all. Letters to my father and to Lizzie became a chore and they ended up being short and dull. Even though Peter continually entertained me with his antics as he underwent the metamorphosis from baby to mischievous little boy, and even though my teaching distracted me from sorrow while I worked, and even though Jamaica remained gloriously beautiful, I would often find myself bursting into tears for no apparent reason. I became more and more convinced that, had Henry not so impetuously snatched Pearl away from Cinchona, she would not have died. The bark bath and Monimia's potions had broken her fever, and Pearl was on the way to recovery. O, stupid, stupid, impetuous man.

As the weeks went by, Henry too became more and more subdued but he, of course, immersed himself totally in his work. He spent little time at Beverly, where even Peter's charms failed to attract his attention and change his mood. I could occasionally catch him scrutinising the child's face in an attempt, I assume, to find traces of Pearl in his countenance. Unsatisfied or displeased, he would turn away from his son with a sigh of irritation.

To compound matters, I fell ill with malaria, shaking with cold one moment only to pour with sweat the next, feeling better one day before falling ill again the next, suffering every symptom of that vile disease: fevers, chills, headaches, vomiting, and even convulsions. This went on for weeks and weeks.

I believe Monimia saved my life. Once again, she found herself in her element, brewing disgusting potions and subjecting me to fever baths and bark jackets. The discomfort I endured from her treatments was mitigated by the gentle ministrations of Celia, who sang to me as I struggled, who sat by me as I slept. The two of them never gave up, and it was their strength and encouragement that brought me back to life. Even so, it was months before I regained my full strength, and longer than that before I regained my spirits.

During the passage of years since my last entry, Celia has borne two more children; Monimia has cured one slave with her potions and killed another; Mason, Mason & Fraser's emporium in Spanish Town has prospered, and on the strength of last year's profits, Henry has imported two more racehorses from England and has given me a horse of my own, a gentle grey mare whom I have named Sally; and, in spite of Jonas's incompetence as overseer, Reward has achieved two record harvests of sugarcane, thanks no doubt to Henry's frequent supervisory visits.

Something began stirring in me just now. I do believe it was the itch of the pen! I dipped my pen into the inkwell again, feeling propelled to record a scene on the gallery in which I have just participated. To my surprise, it began with all the hallmarks of a business meeting between four people. Henry had invited Mr and Mrs Fraser to join us in discussing a weighty matter. Mrs Fraser arrived early and by the time Henry and Mr Fraser joined us, she was already seated plumply in a chair, sipping a glass of lemonade, and regaling me with the latest Spanish Town news.

Henry announced, without any preamble, "It is time for

Jonas to marry. He is in sore need of the steadying influence of a family."

Mrs Fraser sat up straight and sniffed the air, a very bloodhound on the scent of a delicious piece of gossip.

"He needs a strong woman to control him and to manage his household," Henry continued. "Do you have any recommendations?"

"Why, certainly!" responded Mrs Fraser, eyes glinting and mouth almost salivating at such an opportunity. "There's . . ."

I interrupted, feeling the need to amuse myself and to bring order into the conversation before she became too carried away. "Let us approach this matter carefully. Phocylides recommends that we look to animals to guide us in the choice of wife. He places women in four groups: bee, bitch, sow, or mare. Of the four, he recommends . . . "

Mr Fraser chuckled.

"How about Jessie Sinclair?" suggested Mrs Fraser, clapping her hands.

"Too sow-like, I fear," responded Henry.

"Joan Abercrombie?"

"She snaps like a bitch at her leash."

"Phocylides recommends the bee," I continued.

"Annie Crawford is infinitely bee-like," chirped Mrs Fraser.

"Oh, my," I said, suddenly remembering. "Jonas has already informed me who it is he intends to marry."

"My goodness! Who is she? What is she? A bee?" asked Mrs Fraser.

"No."

"A sow?" asked Henry.

"No."

"A bitch?" asked Mrs Fraser.

"No. A mare."

"What does Phocylides say about the mare?" asked Mrs Fraser.

"The mare is healthy, fast, well built — and on the loose."

"Who is this mare?" asked Henry.

"Antoinetta Kershaw."

"Antoinetta Kershaw!" exclaimed Henry, and Mrs Fraser clapped her hand to her mouth.

"Do you mean the daughter of old Kershaw, the coffee planter?" asked Mr Fraser. "Oh, this will never do." He began pacing around the gallery, while Mrs Fraser tut-tutted and shook her head. Then Henry displayed exactly the same kind of intolerance his mother displayed when he was in the market for a wife.

"I have seen Antoinetta at her home, dangling her arms, lolling almost the whole day upon beds or settees, her head muffled up with two or three handkerchiefs, her dress loose."

Mrs Fraser joined the lament, "When we travelled to St Thomas-in-the-East last year, we paid a visit to the Kershaws, and there I found Antoinetta employed in gobbling pepper-pot, seated on the floor, with her sable hand-maids around her. And I know as well that in the afternoon, she takes her siesta, while two of her maidservants refresh her face with the gentle breathings of the fan; and a third provokes drowsiness by delicious scratchings on the sole of either foot."

I tentatively suggested that perhaps her laziness was the result of boredom, and maybe marriage would stir her blood.

"I doubt it very much," Henry responded. "When she rouses herself from slumber and opens her mouth to talk, her speech is whining, languid and childish."

"Indeed, she speaks a broken English, with an indolent

drawling out of her words that is very tiresome," agreed Mrs Fraser.

"My mother would never approve of such a person," said Henry.

"Certainly not!" agreed Mrs Fraser. "Your mother often remarked that those Creole women who have been bred up entirely in the sequestered country parts, and have had no opportunity of forming themselves either by example or tuition, are truly to be pitied."

"Antoinetta Kershaw is out of the question," concluded Henry, and Mr Fraser nodded.

April the seventh, 1768

Henry came back from Reward last week with the news that Jonas has definite plans to marry Antoinetta Kershaw. I was caught completely by surprise by his acquiescence to Jonas's intention. One the one hand, I can understand his being delighted by the notion of adding a coffee plantation to Mason, Mason & Fraser's empire, but I had thought that he was dead set against the woman.

"What made you change your mind?" I asked.

"I was too swift in my judgement," Henry snapped.

"What about the indolence? The drawling? The lolling?"

"She was wide awake when I saw her and made every effort to please. She had dressed carefully, and she promised to encourage in Jonas a more mature standard of behaviour."

"And you believed her?"

"I saw no reason not to. She was as charming as she was beautiful. She has already wrought a change on my brother. Jonas was entirely sober during my stay."

"It is easy to be charming, it is easy to be sober when one

is trying to make a good impression. Should you not have made another visit to see how matters stood if you arrived unexpectedly?"

"No! I am not a spy."

"But . . . " I began.

"See to your own affairs," Henry muttered rudely between clenched teeth.

The marriage comes precipitously, which makes me suspect that we may acquire a little nephew or niece in something less than the standard nine months. Henry has made the decision to hold the wedding here rather than at Reward or in Kingston. It turns out that Antoinetta's mother is "absent," and there are no other female relatives to help. It is unclear whether the mother is suffering from some kind of severe illness and has been put away somewhere, or whether she is permanently absent.

Mr Quigley, the new rector, will officiate. How glad I am that the odious Mr Rutter never returned to Jamaica; Quigley is altogether a much better fellow. We shall have a small celebration at Beverly following the service.

The principal players — Jonas, Antoinetta, and her father, William Kershaw —will arrive in Spanish Town next Tuesday. Father and daughter will stay with the Frasers until the wedding on Thursday. Jonas will stay at Beverly. This gives me precious little time to prepare for the wedding, and Celia, Monimia, and I are scurrying around to have everything in order.

How I wish my dear Pearl were here to help me; she would so enjoy the theatrical element of the wedding — the costumes, the lines recited, the entire *mise-en-scène*. Sometimes I find myself talking aloud to her because even absent she is present, and the memory of her wit and liveliness endure to brighten my days. By my side, but not replacing her, Mrs Fraser is constantly and irritatingly a-twitter with excitement and a-chatter about floral arrangements and receipts for wedding cakes.

April the eighteenth, 1768

I have just returned from the Frasers' house where I made Antoinetta's acquaintance after her arrival in Spanish Town. I dressed neatly, as is my wont, and carried with me as a gift a small likeness of Jonas that I once sketched.

Antoinetta is tall, dark, and majestic in build, and was lavishly — but unsuitably, considering the hour and the occasion — dressed in red satin. She was glitter and gloss from the top of her head, with its gleaming black mane, down to her bejewelled dancing shoes. I could not take my eyes off her, and the more she shone, the duller I became.

She has a loud voice, jangling bracelets, a heaving bosom, and a fat pug, who sat snuffling on a cushion beside her on the settee. Her hands are big, and she has dirt under her fingernails. One button at the waistline of her dress was missing, giving some small proof to my suspicion that she is already expecting.

We discussed the arrangements for the wedding. Antoinetta spoke up with enthusiasm on the topic of her wedding gown, her shoes, her bonnet. She was less engaged, however, when conversation turned to the details of the service, the wedding buffet, and who would travel in which carriage with whom, &c. But when the topic of dancing was raised, she brightened again. At her request, we are holding the ceremony in the late afternoon so that the wedding festivities can include dancing into the night, and she informed me that Henry has engaged the services of the best musicians in Spanish Town.

Just as I was leaving the Frasers' house, Antoinetta's father appeared; a stout, morose man, who barely gave me the time of day.

Beverly was a hive of activity as we prepared the house for the festivities, although Monimia was sullen and irritable, and I heard her mutter the word "trash" several times. To my knowledge she had never met Antoinetta before, but word of people's reputations travels fast on this island. The guest list was relatively short: only the two Kershaws (they have no other relatives in Jamaica, apart from the "absent" mother, and apparently no friends); five of Jonas's cronies from Kingston; six large families of our acquaintance in Spanish Town; and, of course, Mr Kenet, Henry, Mr and Mrs Fraser, and myself. Mrs Fraser offered two rather plump nieces to act as bridal attendants, an offer which Antoinetta accepted with alacrity; it appears that the more people who wait upon her, the better she likes it, so I then proceeded to offer the services of Peter as ring-bearer, an offer she also accepted.

April the thirtieth, 1768

The hours just before the wedding were a nightmare. Monimia behaved like a general on a particularly challenging campaign, her voice booming orders at one and all. The servants scurried from room to room. One stood on the centre of the dining room table to clean the chandelier; the whole thing descended around his ears and clattered in a shower onto the table and thence to the floor.

It was at this point that Henry threw up his hands and went in search of Jonas to make sure he appeared at the church on time; he could find him nowhere.

"Jonas!" he yelled throughout the house. We ran from one room to another, trying to find him. Then we called for the servants to look in the stables, the garden, the pasture. He had disappeared without a trace. Henry's face darkened with rage.

"Cuthbert," he called. "Go into every tavern in Spanish Town. Do not return until you have found my brother."

The calm following Cuthbert's departure was the calm at the eye of a hurricane. An hour later, at the very moment that the wedding service was due to commence, Cuthbert returned with a Jonas who, although perfectly attired in his wedding clothes, reeked of rum and remained upright with the utmost difficulty.

"Jonas, how could you?" roared Henry and cast a glass of cold water in Jonas's face and slapped him about the head, before bundling him into the carriage. We set off in a flurry and arrived at the church ten minutes late.

We need not have worried about our tardiness; the bride herself did not arrive for another half-hour, thus stretching the patience of the congregation to breaking point and exhausting the repertoire of the musicians. But what an entrance Antoinetta finally made — she was a gigantic apparition, all tulle and frills and bows, carrying her pug tucked under one arm. There was scant room for her father beside her, and when he tried to take her by her other arm — the one not pug-encumbered — she pushed him away, leaving him to weave an unsteady course behind her down the aisle. I fear that he, too, had fortified himself for the ceremony with a liberal dose of Kill Devil.

The delay in Antoinetta's arrival had the effect of sobering Jonas, who apart from the occasional hiccough, conducted himself properly during the service. The pug, on the other hand, did not acquit himself as civilly, and snapped at Jonas when he tried to place the ring on Antoinetta's finger. This caused the congregation to burst into guffaws of laughter. I cannot imagine how Mr Quigley was able to control himself and continue with the service. And I heard the voices of the Spanish Town matrons in my head as they passed judgment on the ceremony:

"Who giveth this Woman to be married to this Man?"

We never saw such a sight as that man rolling drunk,
delivering his daughter to Jonas, who's sunk

"I, Jonas . . . "

now, we fear. Did you notice those girls,
Mrs Fraser's two nieces, all satin, all curls,

"I, Antoinetta . . . "

giggling and whispering? It's no wonder that
Antoinetta was angry and gave them a slap.
Did you witness the instant when that miserable pug
bared its fangs at poor Jonas? I think it drew blood!
We have to admit that we could not control
a guffaw when the curate — now don't tell a soul —

"With this Ring . . . "

was completely eclipsed by Little Boy Pete
when he dropped the ring, which rolled under our seat,
and up we all jumped, then down on all fours
while Jonas was waiting to finish the clause;

" . . . I thee wed."

and the bell ringer thought that the service had ended
and out rang the bells, and some guests descended,

"Send thy blessing . . . "

while the minister shouted, "It's not over yet."

We repaired to Beverly after the ceremony, where there
was much feasting and revelry, and I am sorry to say that

Jonas's cronies behaved extremely badly. They applied themselves assiduously to the punch bowl, shouted, and danced intemperately, destroying the processions and breaking down the order of the steps. Henry finally removed them out of doors where they began a wolfish howling at the moon. Soon they disappeared in the direction of Spanish Town, swirling Jonas along in their wake. Antoinetta appeared undisturbed by this development and took Henry instead as her dancing partner. The band continued to play and the remaining guests danced up and down. I remained unpartnered, left to endure Mrs Fraser's incessant chatter as she commented on the idiosyncracies of each dancing pair. I found myself wondering all the while how long it would be before I could to retire to my bed and to the pleasures of Volume VII of *Tristram Shandy*.

Finally, the guests departed and the musicians put away their instruments. Never have I been so glad to return to my quiet room. I flew up the staircase but froze in my tracks at the turn upon catching sight of a glint of yellow silk. I caught my breath and took the rest of the stairs two at a time. I heard a swish from the steps that ascended to the lookout tower. I ran along the landing in pursuit and started up the steps. Just as I reached the top, there was a puff of air, of breath, of life breath, and my candle went out. I thought I heard a giggle, and then — utter silence. Not a creak, not a moan. I drew the matches from my pocket and relit the candle. Its light illuminated the lookout, revealing its wooden beams and rough floor. No glint of silk, no flash of sequin. No Pearl. The little room was empty, except for a table and chair, several dead wasps, and a single golden sequin on the floor. I extinguished my candle and looked out at the night. Under the starry bowl of heaven, I could see the lights of Spanish Town to the south; to the west I made out the shapes of stables and servants' quarters; to the north-east, in the far distance, loomed the Blue Mountains; to the west, I discerned the tamarind tree. From nowhere a breeze sprang up, lifting and then relaxing its feathery leaves. The great tree was dancing.

There was nothing frightening about this experience. Instead, I found myself elated as I retraced my steps and retired to my room. I undressed swiftly, raised my mosquito net, and climbed into bed. I was much too excited for sleep, so I propped myself up with three large pillows and began to read, following Tristram's father as he set about choosing a teacher, one who would neither "lisp, or squint, or wink, or talk loud, or look fierce, or foolish; — or bite his lips or grind his teeth, or speak through his nose, or pick it, or blow it with his fingers." Apart from occasionally looking fierce, I reckon that I can meet Mr Shandy's criteria for a proper teacher. I continued reading: "He shall neither walk fast, — or slow or fold his arms, — for that is laziness; — or hang them down, — for that is foolish; or hide them in his pocket, for that is nonsense." I must admit to walking fast. "He shall neither strike, or pinch, or tickle, — or bite . . . " I certainly do not bite my students. " . . . or cut his nails, or hawk, or spit, or sniff, or drum with his feet or fingers in company; — nor, according to Erasmus, shall he speak to any one in making water . . . " I certainly never do that, although I sometimes speak to myself. " . . . nor shall he point to carrion or excrement." Certainly not!

Retiring to bed with my friend *Tristram Shandy* is as amusing an experience as I can imagine.

St Jago de la Vega Gazette

SEPTEMBER 2, 1768
BIRTHS

To Mr and Mrs Jonas Mason, a son, Richard Silas Anthony. Born early last Saturday morning, at Reward, in St Thomas-in-the-East.

April the second, 1770

Two years after he was married, Jonas died as he lived — intemperately. We were more stunned by shock than consumed by sorrow. In my opinion, his death was just one more we must add to the total of those whose sudden departures from this world are precipitated one way or another by overindulgence. We are regularly informed that so-and-so died of the fever or the flux; all too often the truth is that the person was one of those who lived intemperately.

Henry has been muttering about foul play, but I am convinced that rum was entirely responsible. After all, "Wine is a mockery, and strong drink is raging: and whosoever is deceived thereby is not wise." Jonas was not suffering from any actual malady at the time of his death, but the hand of intemperance reveals itself by the manner in which he died. We have been told that he took a nighttime gallop after consuming a gargantuan meal and, for reasons best known to himself, set off in the direction of Judgement Cliff. His body was found the following morning in a rough pasture not far away. His horse had caught its foot in a coney hole, had fallen, and broken its back. Jonas was pitched forward and landed headfirst on a rock, which split his head open. The doctor who examined him said he probably died on the spot, but if not he was probably immune to suffering because of the amount of rum in his blood.

Sudden death is often attended by rumor, and after Jonas died, a rumor circulated that the horse's accident was arranged, and that Jonas was murdered. To conclude that he was murdered was a quick and easy assumption because he was loathed at Reward because of his cruelty. I do not ascribe to that assumption. As far as I am concerned, his death was the result of debauchery.

Henry left for Reward immediately upon hearing the news of Jonas's death. He buried his brother the following day, a funeral that I was not sorry to miss. It is impossible for me to mourn the loss of Jonas. He was destructive, vindictive, and wicked to the core. Celia's newest baby bears the taint of his evil.

On Henry's return from Reward, he lost no time in having the sign over the store repainted. Now it bears just two names, Mason & Fraser.

Now I turn to happier topics. Positions of responsibility within Henry's empire have now been awarded to three of my students. I have put Rose and Psyche in charge of inventory at Beverly. Augustus works at the store, where he knows the price of every article, and waits nimbly on each customer in proper turn. However, I fear that my favourite, the half-wit Henderson, will never be able to read and write with any facility. He is quite able, however, to perform small tasks, and retains Scipio as his special charge. Henderson feeds him the tropical fruits he so enjoys, provides him with clean water, and cleans his cage most diligently. When I listen to the bird and the boy conversing with each other, they sound remarkably like a couple of old sailors, one of whose vocabulary of curses far outstrips the other. I blush sometimes at the range of foul language at Scipio's disposal, and believe that the captain of the slaver knew precisely what he was doing when he presented Henry with the parrot. I can almost hear him laughing to himself: "This will shock Mistress Mason right out of her shoes," or seamier words to that effect.

Next week, I shall acquire two new pupils, who will, with

the earlier addition of Peter, bring our complement back to fourteen. Peter is proving to be an able and energetic pupil, with his father's particular gift for arithmetic. I am starting to wonder about his future education and whether Henry will decide to send him to England.

April the fifteenth, 1770

Life at Beverly is completely out of control. It feels as though we have been hit by a hurricane.

Henry suddenly decreed that his widowed, orphaned, pregnant-with-her-second-child sister-in-law should come and live with us at Beverly. Because she was prostrated with grief at her losses — and I place the loss of her pug above the loss of Jonas in her mind — and suffering the ill-effects of pregnancy, Henry sent me to Reward and put me in charge of the arrangements for her removal. I was loath to go, being reluctant to leave my pupils, but Mr Kenet offered his assistance and I asked Rose to lend hers; together they taught the classes at my school for the week I was away.

I rode in the new phaeton Henry had recently imported from England, and I was accompanied by Celia and a coachman. The journey was long but not arduous, thanks to the excellent suspension of the coach and a good road. Fine weather had come after weeks of torrential rain — had we travelled the week before, we might not have been able to ford a couple of the rivers. En route we made a stop at Bath to take the waters just before we reached Reward.

The road to Bath is the most beautiful one I ever saw, narrow, and winding for two or three miles up a mountain. A dreadful precipice is on one side, at the bottom of which runs a river; but bamboos and other plants growing thickly up the sides of the mountain lessened my fears about the narrowness and height of the road.

The bathing-house is a low West India building containing four small rooms, in each of which there is a marble bath. Then there is another house for infirm negroes. In fact, it is a kind of public hospital with baths, and they tell you of wonderful cures performed by the water. I drank a glass of it first, which was really so warm that it almost scalded my throat. I then went in for twenty minutes, and had the heat increased till I was familiarised to the bath, which I really found most delightful and relaxing.

Strengthened by my bath, I continued my journey to Reward, reaching there at four o'clock. The house itself is perched on the summit of a steep hill, at the foot of which I had to disembark from the carriage and proceed on horseback. The road followed the swollen, rushing waters of the Plantain-Garden River, and we climbed up through a profusion of bamboos and cocoanut trees, through which the sunlight could barely penetrate. Suddenly we emerged from the trees and presently reached the summit, where all was sunlight and colour as far as the eye could see. The view to the west extends over wooded hills and valleys, reaching back as far as the Blue Mountains. The view to the east is all sugarcane and Guinea grass, some fields green with new growth, some brown where they have been harvested; sugar works and settlements are interspersed here and there. The plantations run right down to the rocky shore, where suddenly the green and brown patchwork turns blue. The sea! The sea! This is not the smooth, turquoise sea with its white sand beaches that you find on the north coast of the island. This is a lively, dangerous creature, which foams as it flings itself upon the shoals and rocks offshore and sends pillars of spray high into the air.

While the plantation itself appeared to be in relatively good working order — the assistant overseer, a fairly recent arrival from England, had taken over on the death of Jonas — the house was in utter disarray. Boxes and baskets and trunks and packages were strewn across the floor, from one end of the house to another. In her bedroom, Antoinetta was in a flurry of hurling shoes at one container, stuffing toilet articles into another, bundling clothes into another, and shouting abuses at the servants, who were running around her in circles, ineffectually trying to obey her commands and her counter-commands. In the midst of it all, crawled a small baby, examining the various articles that fell his way, and gumming on this and that. This was Jonas's son and heir, Richard Silas Anthony Mason.

"My dear Antoinetta," I greeted her, "Please allow me to assist you."

She cast a baleful glance in my direction, sank down into a chair, and remained there, like a great, gravid queen, while Celia and I set to work on the task of packing up all her goods. What an assortment! I have never before encountered so much gimcrackery, which included a huge collection of rag dolls; the notion that it was all to be stowed — or, more likely, strewn around — at Beverly made my blood run cold.

James Johnson, the new overseer, came to call, and I invited him to join us for dinner that evening. He is a forthright young man with a kindly air. I pray that he will prove to be both a competent and benevolent ruler. I hurried to the kitchen and advised the cook that we would be three instead of two. She is a sullen person with a fearsome scar which runs from one ear, across her cheek, and down to her chin. Her kitchen looked ill-equipped to provide anything appetising, and I shuddered at the sight of a giant cockroach, which sauntered across the kitchen table. She idly flicked a cloth at it, and it fell unharmed to the floor, where it continued its travels, having suffered not a jot. However, she promised to provide something very delicious for our meal.

I was surprised and horrorstruck, therefore, when the three of us sat down for dinner and were presented with roasted peacock, complete with tail feathers arranged as though it were still alive and putting on its courtship display. I was totally incapable of consuming a single morsel and contented myself with a few vegetables. Antoinetta, however, fell upon the bird with the enthusiasm of a lion devouring an antelope.

The dinner conversation soon turned to the subject of books, and Mr Johnson promised to lend me several volumes that he had transported from England. I, in turn, promised to lend him some of mine. It has been a long, long time since I have had the pleasure of such a conversation. In Spanish Town, only Mr Kenet can provide any articulate discourse, but his conversation, naturally, often has a religious bent and we regularly find ourselves arguing about St Paul or Moses and sometimes, if matters become really spirited, about Mary Magdalene.

Antoinetta did not try to conceal her boredom at our conversation. She yawned, she drummed her fingers on the table, she rolled her eyes to the ceiling. The ladies of Spanish Town will have much to comment on when they see her mealtime performance. She completed her meal, collected the peacock feathers to bring with her to Beverly, and left the table to retire to her bed long before we had finished eating. In so doing, she granted us a favour.

Our conversation then turned to the subject of sugar production, a subject about which I admitted I was woefully ignorant. I asked Mr Johnson if I might tour the sugar works with him the following morning. He was horrified at the idea, insisting that the works were no place for a woman.

"Why not?" I asked.

"The works are a place of danger, violence, and scorching heat, the very manifestation of hell itself. I should not care to take you there."

"But how can I ever learn about the production of Jamaica's most important commodity?"

"I will describe the works for you. This will serve your purpose."

And with that, Mr Johnson launched himself into a lengthy and careful description of what it takes to produce the sugar that pleasures our taste for the sweet and the intoxicating.

"The mill is turned by water, and the cane, being put in on one side, comes out in a moment on the other, quite like a dry pith, so rapidly is all the sweet juice expressed, passing between two cylinders, turning around contrary ways. You then see the juice running through a great gutter, which conveys it to the boiling-house. Four negroes stuff in the canes, while others are employed continually in bringing great bundles of them. After the juice is expressed, the pithy stuff, which is called trash, is conveyed to a place below the boiling-house, to keep the fire going constantly. In the boiling-house there are nine coppers; three of them merely simmer the sugar. This throws up all scum and useless particles to the top of the copper. The pure liquor then runs into the first boiling copper, and so it is conveyed to another, till it granulates. After that, it is carried by a large gutter into a large trough, called a cooler, from whence the negroes take it in pails-full, and put it into the hogheads. Those casks have holes bored at the bottom, and being on stands, the coarsest part, called molasses, runs through, and is used in the distilling of the rum.

"At each copper in the boiling-house stands a man, with a large skimmer upon a long pole, constantly stirring the sugar, and ladling it from one copper to another. The man at the last copper calls continually to those below, attending the fire, to throw on more trash, for if the heat relaxes in the least, all the sugar in the copper is spoiled."

"How often are these people relieved from their duties?" I asked Mr Johnson.

"Every twelve hours," he responded.

"How dreadful to think of their standing twelve hours over a boiling copper and doing the same thing over and over again!" I exclaimed.

"They do sometimes fall asleep," he owned, "and get their poor fingers into the mill." Then he mentioned a hatchet that was always at the ready to sever the whole limb and was the only means of saving the poor sufferer's life. I shrank in horror and covered my eyes as I imagined such a scene.

"Now perhaps you can understand why I am unwilling to have you visit the works," concluded Mr Johnson. "Let us turn to other topics."

It turns out that he was as interested in the natural history of Jamaica as I was, and that his particular area of interest was the endemic birds of the island. He had recently sighted the Jamaican woodpecker, a bird I have never yet seen. He told me that it sported a scarlet head, black and white barred wings, and a black tail. A lucky sighting would allow a glimpse of the patch of orange on its lower abdomen. But he admitted that the

Jamaican oriole was his favourite, with its jaunty yellow body and black markings, a bird that I too have seen. After the last storm he found an oriole's nest lying on the ground, resembling a little purse woven from the dry fibres of palm leaves. He had even managed to encourage an oriole to come to a feeder where he could watch it ripping into a ripe banana.

Then Mr Johnson stood up and burst into the call of the oriole, uttering ""tie-tiewu, tie-tiewu," his throat trembling just like a bird's. I asked him if he could imitate other birds and he admitted that, as a recent arrival on the island, he had not yet had time to identify and learn the calls of other birds, but that was his intention.

On this happy note, we bade each other goodnight.

Because we had stayed up so late, I overslept the following morning and when I arose I found that Antoinetta had had preceded me to the breakfast table. I joined her, and we ate — she much, I almost nothing.

"Mart'a," she drawled, "You eat small, small. Here, tek dis," she said pronging a piece of fried bread and shoving it at my face. I felt so silly as I opened my mouth like a little bird to its large, assertive mother.

I tried to eat a little more on my own account, and then I helped her to make plans for the day. With the assistance of the household servants, we would complete the packing in the morning; in the afternoon, we would arrange for two mule carts to be loaded with her possessions. I suggested that we invite James Johnson to join us again for our evening meal. We would then retire early, rise at four o'clock, and be under way long before the heat of the day.

Everything went according to plan, except that I did not retire early; Mr Johnson and I once again remained at the table until nearly midnight. I had not appreciated quite how starved I had become for true conversation, and how much I enjoyed conversing with an educated Englishman of my age and background. What a contrast it made with those long, silent dinners I have spent in the company of Henry.

The journey back to Beverly was accomplished in spite of the various small disasters that attended us. The first problem occurred before our departure. Sylvia, Antoinetta's maidservant, who also acted as baby Richard's nurse, was nowhere to be found; she was eventually discovered bidding a tearful farewell to her large family. I suggested to Antoinetta that she should bring along her youngest offspring with her to ease the pain; Antoinetta would not hear of it.

Our second problem came when one of the sumpter mules lay down on the ground in protest rather than agreeing to pull a heavily laden wagon. His will was adamantine, and he won the point; we had to send for another mule.

The third problem arose after we had proceeded a mile down the hill; Antoinetta suddenly insisted that we return to Reward — she had forgotten something. On arrival back at the house, she removed Richard from his nursemaid's arms, thrust him at me as she descended from the carriage, and bade the wretched Sylvia follow her. Richard promptly puked on my dress — he is a very mewly, pukey baby, unlike my Peter. Antoinetta hurried to the foot of a tree where she stood imperiously and commanded Sylvia to dig amongst its roots. They soon unearthed a small box and returned with it to the carriage. As we continued our journey, Antoinetta opened the box and revealed its contents: a very fine ruby necklace that had belonged to her mother. She immediately strung it around her neck and called on me to fasten it securely.

Our arrival at Beverly brought with it an invasion of Spanish Town matrons the following day, come to gaze upon the new arrival. They gathered in a swarm on the gallery where Antoinetta had spread herself out, still wearing her rubies, yawning, and complaining. I could tell immediately that in Antoinetta they saw a perfect opportunity to play Pygmalion.

Have you seen the arrival in Spanish Town?
She's beautiful, yes, but that ugly frown
quite ruins the impression she needs to give
if she wants to succeed here, if she wants to live.
Never have I seen such a flashing at noon.
Were those genuine rubies? We'll find out soon.
But there's always a chance that she'll turn out well;
she has the potential to be quite the belle.
But what of the way she yawns in our faces?
She has yet to acquire some social graces.
She's been stuck in the east with nothing to do
and no one to teach her everything you
and I take for granted. I make you a dare:
Let's make a silk purse from this pregnant sow's ear.

My joy at returning to my orderly, gleaming home was somewhat tempered by the onslaught being inflicted upon it. However, Henry has promised to build a separate establishment for Antoinetta and her children. In the meantime, she will reside in the house with us. We are fortunate in having two extra rooms she can use, one in which to sleep and one in which to store some of her myriad possessions. Peter will share the nursery with Richard. I wonder how he will take to this invasion of his territory.

PETER

Peter Mason lies on his back on the floor of Martha's bedroom, resting after running round and round the house in his excitement at her return. His young eye muscles are still so flexible and strong that the detail he gazes at is more startling than the grand sweeps within his range. While he notices that the roof soars upwards and the large windows yawn open, he is far more interested in the dust and the infinitessimally small dancing creatures he sees in the solid bolt of light cutting through the room. In the corner of a window, a spider makes a web, and Peter watches intently as it twirls out ropes of silk from its spinnarets and anchors them. He sees a mad ant running and halting, running and turning, running thiswaythatway, across a floorboard, thiswaythatway, until it reaches a crack, where it flails its front legs over the chasm and reaches across. Peter stretches out his hand to touch the ant and away it hurries, thiswaythatway, thiswaythatway.

He hears with childhood sharpness the sound of a termite munching, flies buzzing, and the terrible drone of a lone diurnal mosquito. He slips his thumb into his mouth and drifts off to sleep.

Peter dreams that Cocky and Polly Lizard are chasing Anansi and when they have him cornered, Rat-Bat bares his fangs, and Jab Jab Crow and Bessy Kickup start to peck him. Peter struggles up out of his nightmare and screams. Martha comes running, and he throws himself into her arms. She is home again.

May the ninth, 1770

The disruption to our household is tremendous. I would never have believed that one person could so totally transform a smoothly running, pleasant domicile into such a garish madhouse. Antoinetta is everywhere in evidence. She is loud, she is imperious, she is slovenly, she is strewn from one end of the house to the other. She has received no training in neatness, and expects everyone in the household, including me, to wait on her hand and foot, using the condition of pregnancy as a convenient excuse for laziness. She constantly requires refreshment, she changes her clothes five times a day, leaving those she steps out of lying on the floor. The work of the laundress has tripled. If Antoinetta were achieving any end, if there were any purpose to her day, if she read or thought, or sketched or stitched, or sang or wrote, if she at least mourned — for heaven's sake, Jonas has been dead a mere six weeks! — I might feel differently about her, but her only preoccupation is her self, her self, and nothing but her self.

She has begun to complain to Henry that the noise from my school on the gallery disturbs her in the morning and that my playing the clavichord disturbs her in the afternoon. She insists that she needs absolute quiet for her rest now that she is in the seventh month of her pregnancy Henry has intimated to me that he and I need to discuss the issue, and I fear this bodes ill. I remind him of the bargain we made, but Antoinetta has complete hold of his ear, always going first to him when she desires some change in the household. He is as soft clay in her large hands. She has declared to him that she desires to take over my room because it is larger than hers.

"After all," she concludes, "Martha, poor soul, has so few possessions; she does not need the space."

Informing me that the move is, of course, merely for the short term, Henry has insisted that I have pity on Antoinetta and that I change rooms tomorrow.

"Why should I have pity on Antoinetta?"

"Because she is with child."

"You had precious little pity on me when I was 'with child'," I muttered. Henry grabbed my right wrist and twisted my arm behind my back.

"Tomorrow," he insisted.

I kicked him on the shin until he let go. Henry has reduced me to behaving like an ass.

In the end, I decided I could not win, and changed rooms the following day.

I think that Pearl is sulking; I have seen no glints of silk, heard no tinkling laughter. The leaves of the tamarind tree lie flat and still.

In order to remove myself from the confusion — I cannot oppose it, and I must instead wait patiently until Antoinetta's house is completed before I can reclaim my authority over Beverly — I take Peter for walks in the afternoons. He brings along his Coromantee flute, given to him by Monimia, and plays it vigorously as we walk along. Could this be Chloe, his Coromantee grandmother, asserting her influence? The instrument is a long black reed that has a plaintive and melancholy sound and is played with the nose. It is made from the porous branches of the trumpet-tree, is about a yard in length, and of nearly the thickness of the upper part of a bassoon: it generally has three holes at the bottom, and is held, in point of direction, like the haut-boy.

In truth, the Coramantee flute is much too big an instrument for such a little fellow, but Peter strives determinedly to sound the notes, sometimes blowing with his mouth and sometimes with his nose. Thus piping and squawking, we make our way down to the Rio Cobre, where we are joined by several children from my school.

It has been imagined that the Spaniards gave the river the name of Rio Cobre from its passing through a vein of copper. But it is more probable that they christened it after some river in Old Spain, although its water does appear to have a fine bluish tinge, which has confirmed many in their opinion of its being tinctured with copper. But others have conjectured that the original name was Rio Cobra, from the Portuguese cobra, which signifies a snake, and might with great propriety allude to the serpentine course of the river.

My pupils have taught Peter to swim in one of the almost still pools formed by its turns. The children that are born upon estates abundant in water very soon become almost amphibious and it is astonishing to see to what depths they will dive, from what cataracts descend, and for how long a time they will continue submerged without the necessity of aspiration. Peter has become a little fish. When it is time to return home from our expeditions, he leaves the river with the utmost reluctance. I have to drag him back home. Last night, when I entered the nursery to assure myself that he and Richard were tucked in soundly, Peter was talking in his sleep. I drew near to his bed to listen. He was whispering "Fish, fish, fish."

I wish I could swim. I wish I could strip off my clothes and join those children splashing in the water.

May the thirteenth, 1770

The axe has fallen. Henry announced last night that I may no longer conduct my lessons on the gallery at Beverly. I see the hand of Antoinetta in this decision. I reminded him of his bargain and marshalled every argument to convince him that he was short-sighted. He had only to look at the excellent way that Augustus performs at the store as a result of his having received some education; at Rose and Psyche's smooth management of the household supplies; and at two more students coming along, also preparing to become valuable members of his staff.

"No," he insisted, his face hardening, his mouth turning down. "You may not continue to run a school at Beverly."

"Traitor," I shouted.

Henry flinched but stood his ground.

I decided to try another tack and threw myself at his knees and began to weep.

He cursed and turned on his heel, which had the effect of dragging me across the floor. I let go and lay there for a while, staring at the ceiling, drumming my feet on the floor. I would not, I would never give up my school as long as I remained in Jamaica.

I rose. I washed my face and hands, straightened my dress, put on my bonnet, picked up my parasol, and in order to burn out my anger, walked the mile to the church of St Iago in search of Mr Kenet. When I arrived, he was conducting a funeral, which is his regular sport these days, there being a terrific number of fatal cases of yellow fever. I entered the church and sat in the last pew, where I remained until the service was over and the body was buried. On his way from the church to the churchyard, Mr Kenet noticed me and received the unspoken message that I was seeking help. As soon as the burial was completed, he hurried back to the church and sat beside me in the pew. My tears welled up again, choking me as I tried to recount Henry's sudden interdiction.

Mr Kenet listened carefully before speaking.

"Is it your opinion that Henry made this decision in order to please Antoinetta or did the command come from his own heart?"

"I sincerely believe that Antoinetta is at the root of the matter," I responded.

"Come with me," said Mr Kenet, rising from the pew. "We shall find Mr Quigley and ask him if you may conduct your lessons in the church hall."

"But Rutter said that I might never teach slaves within the precincts of the church," I responded.

"Mr Quigley is cut from a different kind of cloth."

We found him at the rectory, stretched out in a hammock on the gallery, reading his Bible, humming to himself. He is a man of medium height, with a shock of ill-behaved, sandy-coloured hair, bushy eyebrows that appear to have a life of their own, and a stirring wit which is belied by his usually earnest expression. He looked up and swung to his feet, greeting us with:

"The earth is the Lord's, and the fulness thereof; the world, and they that dwell within."

I wished him a good morning, in a voice that was still shaking with emotion.

"Why art thou cast down, O my soul?" he asked.

With Mr Kenet's help, I explained to him about my school, about Antoinetta, and about Henry's decision. It all poured out in a torrent of anguish.

"Fret not thyself because of evildoers, neither be thou envious against the workers of iniquity," he responded.

I decided to reply in kind: "Deliver me out of the mire and let me not sink."

"Serve the Lord with gladness; come before his presence with singing," he responded, gesturing to me to follow him to the church hall, and humming loudly as he proceeded. He opened the door and bade me enter.

"The children of thy servants shall continue," he said, throwing wide his hands and beaming beneficently.

And so it is that my pupils now assemble for two hours each morning in the church hall. Scipio, however, has remained on the gallery at Beverly. Henderson visits him twice a day, before school in the morning when Antoinetta has not yet arisen and after school when she is taking her siesta. He feeds him and cleans his cage, and then allows Scipio to climb onto his finger and they go for a stroll together in the garden.

As I left the rectory, Mr Kenet pressed a paper into my hand, telling me it was his latest translation from Theocritus, and asking my opinion of it. I find it altogether charming and include it here because it reminds me so much of Peter.

The Honey Stealer

When Cupid once the little thief would play,
And search'd a Hive to steal the Combs away;
A watchful Bee that in her waxen Cell,
To guard her Nectar then stood Centinel,
Wounded his Fingers as they still drew near,
And to the head bury'd her poyson'd Spear;
He cry'd, and stamp'd, and frisk'd, and blow'd his hand,
And to his Mother of the Bee complain'd;
He sobb'd, and wonder'd how there could be found
A Fly so small to make so great a wound;

But Venus laugh'd to see how Cupid cry'd,
And thus at length she smilingly reply'd:
Thou'rt like this Bee, my Child, a little Brat,
But great the wound you make, I'm sure of that.

June the third, 1770

Peter has recognised that Antoinetta is a rival for his father's affection. He recognises, too, that he can disconcert her. When in her presence, his eyes never leave her face, and he particularly delights in crawling into Henry's lap and silently examines her from the safety of his father's embrace. Antoinetta complains of this to Henry. "Tell de child him not to stare," she commanded yesterday, her voice ringing out in the vernacular. We were seated on the gallery in the early evening, Peter on Henry's knee, Richard on hers. Peter turned his gaze on his father, smiled at him, and snuggled down in his arms.

"He means no harm," Henry replied.

"He discomfort me with dat staring. I t'ink he hate me."

Henry laughed and insisted that Peter would learn to love her as soon as he came to know her.

Antoinetta glanced at Peter, at me, and then at Peter again. She is obviously fascinated by his appearance and has commented on two occasions that he resembles many of the children of mixed parentage on the island. Again she glanced at me and then back at him, at his curls, at his long, strong legs, at his light brown skin. And then she glanced down at Richard with his straight hair and paler skin covered in the red weals of mosquito bites.

She changed the conversation and began to provoke Henry into suggesting names for her shortly-to-be-delivered baby, whom she insisted would be a girl.

"How about Catherine?" Henry suggested. I flinched.

"No."

"How about Harriet?"

"No."

"How about Ellen?"

"No."

Antoinetta finally concluded that the child should be named Bertha, in memory of her grandmother whose only other memorial was a gravestone which bore the simple inscription "Wife." And so Bertha it will be.

As Antoinetta approaches her ninth month, she is distended with fluid, and regards herself in the mirror with disgust. She has no patience with a self that moves slowly, that is unable to bend, that suffers constant heartburn. She calls on Celia and on her maid, the eternally lachrymose Sylvia, to fetch and carry:

"Bring me water."

"Bring me crackers."

"Fan me."

"Buckle me shoe."

"Button me dress."

"Brush me hair."

"Trim me toenails."

"Wash me face."

More and more housebound and more and more irritable, she is never content. She intones a daily litany of complaint to Henry:

"Your servants dem don' do what I say. Dem say: 'Dis how Mistress Mart'a she do it.' Tell dem to do what I say. Especially dat meanface Celia. Replace dem."

Henry will replace Celia over my dead body.

Antoinetta's feet are so swollen that she is unable to make

use of them. She stays in bed all day and needs constant bedside entertainment. Sometimes she calls for Richard, and for a few moments she is amused by the little fellow's attempts to walk, but as soon as he falls and starts to cry, she commands that he be removed.

From her window, she watches Henry exercising his race-horses, but she soon becomes irritated with watching and not participating. She has informed me that she is an excellent horsewoman and will resume riding as soon as she has recovered from the birth of her baby.

June the thirtieth, 1770

Finally, more than two weeks late, Antoinetta has given birth to a little girl. She refused Monimia's services as midwife, and we had to call on a woman from the town. Antoinetta screamed her way through the delivery, starting in the early evening, and rising to the most enormous crescendo of groans and moaning at dawn when suddenly all was quiet except for the shocked wail of a baby drawing its first breath.

Bertha is big and healthy, and Antoinetta's mood has shown an improvement since the birth.

Mrs Fraser and her cohorts come daily to call on the new mother, who receives them regally from the settee on the gallery. They have intimated to me that they are planning a campaign to "improve" her as soon as she is out of mourning and recovered from the birth. Ah yes! I wish them the best of luck. I, too, have plans to improve her by helping her with her reading — she is almost illiterate and signs her name with the greatest difficulty — but I am not convinced that she will submit to any lessons from me.

Contributing to the brightening of her spirits has been the

removal of my school from Beverly. She ooohs and aaaahs to Henry about the difference it has made to her composure. It seems, however, that she is always in need of something to whine about.

"Dat damn parrot, Henry. T'row it away," she insisted last night.

"But . . . " I interposed.

"What is the problem?" Henry asked.

"When I trying to rest, him squawk all the time. When I tell he to stop, he cuss me. Eh-eh! How come a bird can learn such bad language?"

I stifled a laugh.

"Yesterday, he bite me finger," said Antoinetta, her voice rising with irritation. She held out her index finger that did, indeed, have a nasty, curved cut on it.

"My dear Antoinetta," I cried, professing sympathy, "what on earth caused him to bite you so hard?"

She avoided my question.

"Soon you will be sleeping less in the daytime and going out more," I continued consolingly. "A few whistles from Scipio will no longer bother you." And I reckon that now that he has drawn blood, Antoinetta is unlikely to approach him again.

Antoinetta gave me a look that could stop a charging bull in its tracks and turned to Henry.

"Get rid of the bird!"

I stared at Henry, who shuffled his feet. Scipio had been his present to me.

Just then, we were interrupted by Cuthbert, announcing dinner. Antoinetta is so powerfully attracted to food that she was quickly diverted from live parrot to roast chicken.

August the twelfth, 1770

Hooray and hurrah, the carpenters are nearing completion of Antoinetta's new dwelling, a little house set at some distance from the main house. I visit them each day as they work, and compliment them on their efforts, encouraging them to finish as soon as they can.

I am much amused by the efforts of Mrs Fraser and her cohorts to transform Antoinetta into a beautiful lady, although I am unconvinced that they will succeed in fashioning anything truly virtuous out of such unpromising clay. However, they are indomitable when they are on such a mission, and they may well be able to create at least a veneer of good manners and charm. Their technique is to invite Antoinetta to their houses to take lemonade each morning, and there they set about bribing her. They have an arsenal of ammunition at the ready: sweetmeats from England, outings in their carriages, and the services of an excellent dressmaker.

Mrs Fraser has created a schedule for the bribes. In the morning, if the time spent on elocution is successful, Antoinetta is offered refreshments. If her table manners improve, they call on friends. If she restrains her naturally volatile temper, they visit the dressmaker. Gradually, Antoinetta's use of language is improving as she begins to leave the vernacular behind. However, she has now adopted an unusual manner of speaking, lifting her naturally deep voice into a higher, piercing register even as she cocks her little finger to raise a glass of lemonade to her lips.

"How vairy, vairy kind of you to visit us," she pipes, "I am deeelighted to make your acquaaaaintance."

Mrs Fraser at first avowed delight with Antoinetta's progress, but yesterday she called on me, looking worried.

"Martha, my dear, may I have a word with you?" she enquired.

"Of course," I responded as gracefully as I could. She had interrupted me as I was working on a translation of Ovid's creation — *Ante mare et terras et, quod tegit omnia, caelum / unus erat toto naturae vultus in orbe, / quem dixere Chaos* — which I planned to use as a topic for comparison and debate with Mr Kenet. More and more I wish to spend time in his company; more and more I make up excuses to do so.

"I have recently become a little concerned . . ." she said and then paused as though it were painful to carry on. My heart sank; I was convinced that Peter was somehow the cause of this concern.

"Pray continue, Jessica," I entreated.

"Have you noticed . . . ?" Again she paused.

"Have I noticed what?" I asked. I found myself holding my breath.

"Has Antoinetta . . . ?"

"Antoinetta?"

"Yes. Has Antoinetta shown any signs of temper with you?" I tried to stifle my sigh of relief.

"Temper?"

"Yes. Irritability. Even rage."

"I have noticed, once or twice, the ship of her emotions lacking an even keel," I responded, as cagily as possible.

"Now, Martha, I do not mind — and nor do my friends — expressions of the liveliness of her character, for they only add to her charm. But on occasion she becomes so irritated, so enraged, that she stamps her foot, she lashes out at the servants, and I have even seen her strike the dressmaker when the unfortunate woman accidentally pricked her with a pin.

"But in spite of these little moments, my dear," she

concluded, "we are making excellent progress. I ask about her temper merely to ascertain whether you, too, are aware of it, and if you have any advice for controlling it."

One might just as well ask the thunder not to roll.

"Dear Jessica, I am delighted that you are making such excellent progress, and indeed I have noticed how much Antoinetta's manners and speech have improved. As for how to deal with her temperament, I am just as at sea as you."

"How are you coming along with her reading and writing lessons?"

"She has no patience for reading and wishes merely to learn how to write a gracious note of thanks, something which you and your friends have insisted she must do."

"Good!" cried Mrs Fraser.

"She has an extraordinary hand; the letters of her alphabet lean backwards, are circular in form, and driven powerfully into the page. Her handwriting carries a stronger message than her words."

"But what can we do about her temper?" Mrs Fraser asked again.

"You already bribe her and reward her. I can only suggest regular appeals to her vanity — tell her that bad temper makes her look ugly. Withhold rewards when she behaves badly. Let us reinforce each other's efforts," I recommended, wondering whether one of Monimia's strong concoctions might not be more effective in controlling that wild temper than Mrs Fraser's tepid, genteel efforts.

I, too, am deeply concerned about Antoinetta's temper. Here is a scorching example of her behaviour. When I returned home from teaching this morning, I went onto the gallery to greet Scipio only to discover the most horrible sight. Someone had wrung that excellent bird's neck and hung him by a string from the back of a chair. I could think of only one person cruel enough to perform this act, only one person who hated him enough, and a rage flared up in me, not unlike the rage that overcame me when I struck Henry with the letter opener. I flew upstairs and flung open the door of her room — my room — and found her stretched out in a deep post-prandial stupor.

"How dare you?" I yelled, approaching the bed.

"Wha . . . , " she mumbled.

"How dare you?" I repeated and reached out and grabbed a handful of her hair and pulled it as hard as I could. That woke her up.

She wrenched away my hand and shouted "How dare I what?" back at me.

"Kill the bird."

"What you talkin' about, woman?"

"You killed Scipio."

"I did not. I have been away from the house all morning."

Lies, lies, lies.

I turned on my heel and slammed the door behind me. I retreated to my room in a fury. I threw myself down on my bed and punched my pillow. I tried to steady my breathing, but each time I recalled the sight of that dear bird hanging by its neck, I felt a choking anger rise again. I will have my revenge.

Henderson wept copiously on learning of the loss of his avian friend. He cradled the limp, feathered body in his arms, murmuring, "Sah Kippy, Sah Kippy." I decided to conduct a small burial ceremony and instructed Peter and Henderson to dig a hole beside the hen house — they had agreed that Scipio would enjoy the company of hens. As we laid that proud, foul-mouthed bird to rest, a single red feather fell from his tail. Henderson grasped it, and stuck it into his mat of hair, where it has remained ever since. In an effort to console him, I have persuaded Monimia to appoint him Chief Egg Collector. He has acquired a large basket and bears the air of an important official as he makes his rounds to all the likely places where he may discover eggs. While he works, he clucks to the hens, and they march in file behind him, seeming to enjoy his company.

I shall never recover from the death of Scipio nor from my anger at his murderer.

September the twenty-eighth, 1770

Antoinetta (I can barely write that word) removes to her cottage tomorrow, along with her children and Sylvia. It is not a moment too soon. The floorboards creak each night, and I fear that Henry has heeded the Biblical injunction "her husband's brother shall go in unto her, and take her to him." Am I, her husband's brother's wife, distressed by this turn of events? I am not. I am merely disgusted. Let them wallow in carnal filth for all I care.

As far as Peter is concerned, I witnessed him early yesterday morning from my bedroom window as he crept stealthily across the garden to the new house where Antoinetta lives. On arriving, he stood on a flower pot, and pulled himself up until his chin rested on the windowsill. He peered through the half-closed curtain; even from that distance I could witness his jaw drop, and I can only imagine what he saw: Antoinetta, naked, stretched out on her bed, such mountains of breasts, such dark purple nipples, such a carpet of black hair. He kept on staring. And then I heard a roar as Antoinetta awoke and saw him peering in. Peter fell off his flower pot, scrambled up, and streaked back to the main house, followed by a hurled shoe.

October the second, 1770

While I am still boiling with rage about the death of Scipio, I am truly delighted to have my school in the church hall. Because it is not as cool as the gallery at Beverly, we hold our classes early in the morning. When we have finished our lessons, dear Mr Kenet escorts the children into the church, where he shows them a different feature of the building each day, and then teaches them to sing a hymn or a psalm. In this manner, they are not only learning to read and write, they are also beginning their journey as Christian soldiers. Occasionally, he strays from Christian teaching to another, more pagan, age. This morning, he could not resist reading a translation from Oppian that he had made especially for them about the hermit crab, a creature we often meet by the seashore in Jamaica.

The children clapped their hands with glee when he finished reading, and begged him to start all over again, chanting "The Hermit-Fish, The Hermit-Fish, read for us the Hermit-Fish."

> *The Hermit-Fish, unarm'd by Nature left,*
> *Helpless, and weak, grow strong by harmless Theft.*
> *Fearful they strowl, and look with panting Wish*
> *For the cast Crust of some new-cover'd Fish;*
> *Or such as empty lie, and deck the Shore,*
> *Whose first and rightful Owners are no more.*
> *They make glad Seizure of the vacant Room,*
> *And count the borrow'd Shell their native Home:*
> *Screw their soft Limbs to fit the winding Case,*
> *And boldly herd with the Crustaceous Race.*

When the children disperse, Mr Kenet often invites me to join him for some refreshment. While I am always sorely tempted to accept his offer — he is the one person in Spanish Town to whom I can turn for conversation and encouragement — I do not usually take advantage of his invitation. Tongues wag like dogs' tails in this city, and all eyes are on the curate. The matrons have been trying for years to find him a suitable mate. The irony of the matter is that I can say quite unabashedly that I, of all the women in Spanish Town, am the most suitable mate for Mr Kenet and he for me. Had we met in another place at another time, I believe that there would have been no obstacle to our union. As the ultimate test of his worth, I have introduced him to *Tristram Shandy,* to see what his response might be. It is as I had suspected: while he as a churchman feels the obligation to appear shocked by the frankness of Sterne's matter, he allows that he is most profoundly amused and provoked. We have much to discuss these days. Spending time in his company gives me more pleasure than I dare to admit.

Peter, at seven and a half years of age, is irrepressible and handsome; he demands far more attention than his other classmates; he knows precisely how to make me laugh; he stretches my imagination; he is everywhere at once. He has an ardour about him, which I have no desire to dampen, but he is relentless in his search for entertainment, and does not wish to stay seated in order to learn to read and write. He is the showman of the church hall. I must rein him in.

I find it touching that whenever Henry is away in Kingston or at Reward, Peter wears his father's straw hat, the one that Henry sports when he visits the horses and cattle here at Beverly. Peter refuses to take it off all throughout the day, wearing it for classes and at meal times, even wearing it when he climbs trees. Only at night does he remove it; then he places it on the pillow beside him. I have heard him singing it to sleep. As soon as Henry returns from his trips, the hat is cast aside, and we are once more treated to the sight of Peter's shiny curls.

October the fourth, 1770

Antoinetta's move to the little house has been far less successful than I had hoped. While she spends each night there, she complains that she finds her dwelling cramped and confining and prefers to spend her days, when she is not parading around in the company of the Spanish Town ladies, on the gallery at Beverly. She is also showing a great interest in Henry's horses, and has selected one, Flame, as her special favourite.

"Henry, I wishhhhhh to accompany you on Flaaaaame when you tour the grounds, visiting your cattle," she announced the other day, stretching out her syllables in her newly-affected manner of speech.

"But Flame is a racehorse. He is far too big and highly strung for a woman," Henry responded. "Let me choose another horse."

"At home in St Thomas-in-the-East, I used to ride my father's horse and it bigger and livelier than Flame," retorted Antoinetta, sulking, pouting.

"But it was not a racehorse. Let us proceed step by step. First you shall ride a gentle horse — she would like Sally, wouldn't she, Martha?"

"Sally is my horse," I snapped.

"But I am sure you would be kind enough to let Antoinetta ride her," countered Henry. I glared at him. "And when I have been convinced that Antoinetta is competent . . . "

Antoinetta stamped her foot and flounced from the room, shouting over her shoulder, "Sally too slow for me."

"Bring her back, Martha. I have something of interest to tell her — and you, too."

I had no time to leave the room before Antoinetta had returned. She had overheard what Henry said.

"The only t'ing of interest to me is Flame," she announced.

"This has to do with Flame. I thought you and Martha might be interested in going to the races at Montego Bay. Flame and another of my horses will be competing."

Antoinetta paused. She looked at the floor, and then at Henry. Her eyes were dancing.

"The races at Montego Bay! How absoluuuuutely deeeeelightful," she cried. "How soon?"

At first I was surprised that Henry had invited me to go along too, but then I realised that he needed me to function as a cover. Apart from having to spend time in Antoinetta's company, I do not care that Henry uses me in this way for I shall at last have the opportunity visit Montego Bay, a town which many call the most beautiful in Jamaica. Mrs Fraser will accompany us, seeing the occasion as a dress rehearsal for Antoinetta's social debut, which will occur at the Governor's Christmas ball. She is in a flurry of activity and instruction before our departure, and Antoinetta's temper improves steadily as more and more attention is lavished upon her.

I hope that Peter will not get up to mischief while we are away. He is a very mischievous little boy, and I am constantly having to reprimand him. His particular delight is in taunting Antoinetta, with which I can easily sympathise, and I have to steel myself to scold him. I have also found him teasing animals — pulling the cats' tails, firing his slingshot into the henhouse, and mooing at Hercules. I fear that one day he will regret this behaviour.

He is physically fearless. He dives from a cliff into the Rio Cobre, he climbs the tallest trees at Beverly, he wrestles with boys far bigger than himself and usually wins the battle, and he makes his pony gallop as fast as its little legs will carry it. Yesterday, in a fit of pique, he stamped on his father's foot, and Henry — usually mild and tender toward Peter — struck him in retaliation. Peter was appalled; he opened his mouth and howled and then sobbed bitterly for an hour.

For all his naughtiness, he maintains a look of utter innocence. He is absolutely charming, and far too clever for his own good. He is the apple of my eye, my heart's darling.

October the fifteenth, 1770

We have just returned from Montego Bay. I am both enlivened and exhausted by the experience; it was all sensation of one kind or another. First there was the intolerable aggravation of spending many hours in the carriage with Mrs Fraser and Antoinetta. Henry wisely donned his large travelling hat and spent most of his time above with the coachman. What a rattle of gossip and wrong-headed nonsense those women spewed! Never once did they pause to draw breath, never once did they glance outside to admire the landscape.

To escape their chatter, I hung my head out the window and gazed with amazement at all I saw — the plantations, the villages, the mountains, the gullies with huge ferns overarching, and then finally the coast, with its white-sand beaches, tall palm trees, and turquoise water in the shallow part, reaching out to the dark blue seas of the deep. How I wished that I had been able to bring Peter along with me. How my little fish would have loved to swim in that turquoise water.

Having crossed the island by the main road to the north,

we turned west and proceeded along the coast to Montego Bay. The town is situated in an amphitheatre of very high hills. In front lies a most beautiful bay, full of vessels, and open to the sea. On the hills are all the gentlemen's houses, and these are interspersed with gardens, palms of all sorts, &c., so that, from the town, quite up to the tops of the hills, you see nothing but villas peeping out from among the foliage.

Upon arrival we took up residence with Mr Cunningham, another racing aficionado. Henry's two racehorses had travelled in advance of us, and having survived the journey without mishap, were stabled beside Mr Cunningham's horses. From the moment of our arrival, the gentlemen's talk was of nothing but the races. Mrs Fraser and Antoinetta retired, demanding the attention of an ironing woman to care for the various garments they planned to wear to the races and to the ball. I had brought with me just one day dress and one evening gown, apart from my travelling clothes. It matters not a whit to me if the crowd should gather to gawp at Mistress Martha Mason who has the audacity to sport the same garment three days in a row.

The race-course is exceedingly picturesque, bounded on one side by gentle sloping woodlands, intermixed with cane-pieces and pasture-grounds, and on the opposite side by the deep blue sea, from which comes a refreshing breeze. The excitement amongst the mulatto and negro population who were present was infectious; they were dressed in the extreme caricature of English fashion, the females in muslins and ribbons of the gayest colours, with caps and turbans of the smartest silks and stuffs, silk stockings, and always red shoes, to which the shortness of their dresses gave ample display, and, above all, the gay parasols of green or pink, which they displayed with infinite pride. The gentlemen shone forth in superfine blue coats, with large brass buttons of the fiercest mode and fashion; waistcoats of silk or satin, set off by trousers of the whitest; their feet were seldom troubled with the encumbrance of shoes or stockings, though their heads were adorned with hats, usually white.

After great delay, owing to want of arrangement on the part of the stewards, the horses were saddled and mounted, and ready to start. Many of the horses were in the highest condition, showing the care that had been taken in their breeding. The jockeys, as regards costume, were the same as in England, but without shoes, and, in this case, it enabled them to follow their invariable custom, when on horse-back, of taking one side of the stirrup-iron between their toes. On the word being given, off they went, and, as the course was circular, the horses passed in front of the stand twice during each race, which afforded the most favourable opportunity of observing the struggle.

The grandstand was the site of much conviviality. I found myself delighted by the colour and excitement of the races, and Mrs Fraser rejoiced in reunions with several old friends. Imagine my delight when a gentle hand tapped me on the shoulder, and a soft voice asked:

"Mrs Martha Mason?"

I turned at once and encountered the lady with whom I had spent so much time on board ship during my journey to Jamaica. She told me she was no longer Julia Jamison, she was now Julia Henriques because she had remarried shortly after the death of her first husband. We passed the long intervals between races comparing notes on our experiences in Jamaica during the seven years since our first meeting. After the loss of her first husband, she suffered dreadfully from grief, and was on the brink of returning to England, even though she, like me, had fallen under the charms of Jamaica. She had in fact booked her passage and had removed to Kingston to await the sailing of her ship. She was detained there by an ardent admirer in the form of her banker, the wealthy widower Jacob Henriques. He refused to let her return to England, courting her with every enticement his generous and genial character could imagine. She succumbed, and with her marriage to him and the birth of their two sons her spirits rose again. In fact, she was blooming with happiness. She now lives in a large house surrounded by a beautiful garden up at Stony Hill, just above Kingston. She invited me to visit her there whenever I should happen to be in Kingston. "Any day, any week! You are always welcome. You do not need to inform me ahead of time."

We turned our attention back to the races, and she and I placed small bets together. I advised her to wager as much as she could spare on Flame, and we were immoderately overjoyed when he far outran his competition.

I spent no time at all playing chaperone. Antoinetta accompanied Henry wherever he went — to the stables, to the ring, to the betting shops —a giant, vulgar bauble hanging on his arm.

At the balls, I danced a few turns with Henry, but most of his time was spent partnering Antoinetta. Did I mind? Certainly not! There being a surfeit of men because of the presence in Montego Bay of the 55th regiment, even Mrs Fraser and I did not lack opportunity to dance. Each night saw me retire to bed pleasurably exhausted. Henry came back many hours later to the room we were obliged to share — we were keeping up the pretence of living a normal married life — and fell on the bed fully dressed, soon sawing his way through the night with snores. I would silence him with a sharp kick.

After three days of non-stop revelry, we set off on our journey home. In the carriage, Antoinetta slept like the dead, her mouth hanging open, leaving me alone to endure Mrs Fraser's ceaseless prattle. Night had fallen by the time we reached Beverly. I ran to Peter's room to see if he were still awake. He slept peacefully, spread out on his stomach, his black hair curling on his white pillow, his eyelashes soft crescents on his cheeks. I kissed his warm face, called him my little angel, and crept from his room.

"Mistress, Mistress," cried Celia, knocking at my bedroom door as I unpacked my clothes.

"Come in, Celia," I called.

Celia stood hesitating in the doorway.

"Peter is one wicked lickle boy," she said.

"Oh, dear, what has he done now?" I asked.

Celia stood straight, placing one foot in front of the other, and raised her arm. Then she opened her mouth and declaimed:

> *As when de monkey him climb up de tree,*
> *An' t'row down sticks on every man him see,*
> *An' jump from branch to branch and play all day,*
> *An' won't come down, no matter what you say;*
> *So Peter climb the stairs up to the top*
> *An' out de window. 'Stop,' I cry, 'Stop, Stop!'*
> *He walk along de ridge and look right down*
> *An' see de garden man him dig de groun',*
> *Den Peter laugh and den him start to pee*
> *An' water fall on Michael's head an' he*
> *T'ink it raining . . . "*

And here Celia stopped and we looked at each other. We both tried to look horrified but try as we might we were unable to contain the waves of laughter that overcame us. We laughed till we cried.

"What happened then?" I asked when I could speak again.

"I beg Peter to come in, but him say, 'No, no. I won't come in till Mama come home.' So I go find Cuthbert, and Cuthbert him walk out on de roof wi' one custard apple, and him sit down and start to eat. Den him offer one piece to Peter, holdin' out he hand, and Peter tek it. Den Cuthbert offer him another, and dis time him grab hold of Peter hand, and him catch him and bring him back inside."

I congratulated Celia on her quick wittedness and Cuthbert on his courage.

"Were you a good boy in my absence?" I asked Peter the following morning.

He looked at me with a mischievous smile.

"Yes, Mama," he said, hugging me and pulling my face down to his to deliver a big kiss. "I love you, Mama!"

What could I do?

My school had not suffered in my absence, thanks to the efforts of Mr Kenet and Rose. I recounted for Mr Kenet my experience at the races, and he listened with the utmost concentration and enjoyment. How delightful it is to have a friend with whom one can converse with ease. He then expressed to me how he had welcomed the opportunity to work in the school and to be in service of the living rather than the dead; he is becoming more and more saddened by the relentless parade of funerals passing through the church of St Iago. He held my hands in his as he told me this, and when I turned my back to leave I held my hands to my lips and kissed them. If I had not felt such a stirring of emotion, I might say it was an involuntary act.

After I recovered from my conversation with Mr Kenet,

I went to the rectory to express my thanks to Mr Quigley and found him once more strung up in his hammock, snoring gently, with his Bible resting on his chest. He stirred as I approached. One of his magnificent eyebrows twitched, and then he opened one eye.

"Thou hast searched me, and known me. Thou knowest my downsitting," he said, beginning to swing himself upright.

I apologized for disturbing him, bade him remain in his hammock, and offered my gratitude for his assistance. He spoke of his belief in the power of education — "Whoso loveth instruction loveth knowledge" — and we drank a glass of tamarind water together before I departed.

Since Mr Quigley's arrival, the congregation has swelled and the pews are crowded, the organist is proficient, and the congregation sings lustily. We sit in a pew near the front of the church for the Sunday morning service, placing Peter at the end of the pew, so that Celia can remove him before the sermon. Henry sits between me and Antoinetta.

"As pants the hart for cooling streams, when heated in the chase" sings Antoinetta, *à haute voix,* tossing her head so that several dark curls cascade from her bonnet, dabbing her handkerchief to her gleaming throat, swishing her fan. The eyes of the men of the congregation, when not cast down in prayer, invariably land on her. The women cough, and nudge the men back to their prayer books.

December the second, 1770

As Christmas draws near, Mrs Fraser announces that the Spanish Town ladies' lengthy project is now reaching fulfilment. Antoinetta has been thoroughly groomed in the social graces. Her wardrobe is complete. They have found ways to restrain her hair. Her social demeanour has improved to the extent that she has become capable of delivering a steady stream of mindless, charming chatter, neatly punctuated by girlish giggles. These giggles, however, have an unfortunate whinny to them which her social instructors have failed to suppress. Nonetheless, Mrs Fraser proclaims Antoinetta fit to make her appearance at the Governor's Ball on the day after Christmas.

In spite of myself, I find I am caught up in the enterprise, and have ordered for myself a new ball gown of dark blue silk. Henry, too, has visited his tailor.

In the Christmas season here, even the slaves are given new clothes and time off in which to celebrate the birth of that distant, desert baby, whose existence means little to them. And celebrate they do; already the musicians are roaming the streets, fantastically costumed, led by a John Canoe, dancing to strange, throbbing African laments, music which both thrills and frightens the wives of Spanish Town. I have finally learned that John Canoe is the anglicised name for a famous African warrior.

This year they have several tall robust fellows dressed up in grotesque habits, with ox-horns on their heads, sprouting from the top of a horrid sort of vizor, which about the mouth is rendered very terrifying with large boar-tusks. The lead masquerader, complete with wooden sword, is followed by a numerous crowd of drunken women, who refresh him frequently with a sup of aniseed-water, whilst he dances at every door, bellowing out "John Canoe." His retainers all dance, leap and play a thousand antics. Their leader sings a sort of recitative and seems to regulate all their proceedings, the rest joining at intervals in the air and the chorus. The instrument to accompany the song is a rude sort of drum, made of bark leaves, on this they beat time with two sticks, while the singers do the same with their feet.

Yesterday I saw a party of actors with a little child, supposed to be a king, who stabbed all the rest. I was told that some of the children who appeared represented the kings and queens of Europe and Africa. One actor played Sundiata, the great king of Mali, another played Henry the Fourth of France, while yet another appeared as Richard III, grotesquely humped, fighting for a queen rather than a kingdom. When his victor carried her off, he surprised me by crying: "A whore, a whore, a kingdom for a whore." What a *mélange*! All were dressed very finely, and many of the negroes had real gold and silver fringe on their robes. After the tragedy, they all began dancing with the greatest enthusiasm.

I thought I caught a glimpse of Pearl the other night, twirling in the ballroom at Beverly. I called her name — I received nothing but the sound of swishing silk in return.

December the seventeenth, 1770

Last night was finally the occasion of the Governor's Ball. Antoinetta went early to Mrs Fraser's, where she spent the afternoon wallowing in self-beautification. Mrs Fraser informed me later that her cohorts gathered around their work of art, each offering suggestions for primping this and preening that. Antoinetta suffered this with a fairly good grace, until she turned on them as she was about to step into her ball gown, requesting them in a manner far from civil to remove themselves from her sight. Once dressed in her pink satin gown, with her mother's rubies glinting at her throat and her ears decorated with a pair of fine ruby earrings, she regained her composure, apologised to Mrs Fraser's friends, and declared that she was ready to face the world. I cannot help wondering where she acquired the earrings, for they were not in the package she retrieved from Reward.

Henry and I proceeded to the ball in the phaeton, his latest carriage just acquired from England. Guests streamed up the steps to the columned portico of the King's House, which is the governor's brand new, spacious brick residence, considered by some to be the noblest edifice of the kind in all the colonies. In the grand ballroom, three huge chandeliers blazed with candles, and the regimental band sawed and blew its way through cotillions and highland reels while British ladies and gentlemen minced up and down to the latest dances imported from Europe. We joined in the dancing, but Henry was somewhat distracted and missed quite a few steps. Everyone was in a flurry about Antoinetta's arrival; all Spanish Town was a-twitter with anticipation.

Suddenly the grand door of the ballroom flew open, the musicians faltered, everyone stopped dancing, and all eyes fell on the apparition within the doorframe: Antoinetta, a vision of delight in pink satin and gleaming rubies, surrounded by her attendants. There was a pause for the intake of breath, and then loud applause. Just as suddenly, an inimical roar came from the other end of the ballroom, followed by a gasp of surprise from the dancers as a giant figure entered, shaking his feathers and beads, tossing his horns and twitching his tail, shouting "John Canoe, John Canoe!" This apparition made music by running a stick along the teeth in the jawbone of an ass, and he was followed by a crowd of rowdy retainers playing on drums and flutes and horns. He led the procession in and out, in and out, snaking along paths through the astonished guests, graciously accepting some coins from the governor, and made to leave via the grand door, where he finally came face to face with Antoinetta. Her face was like thunder; he had stolen her moment.

"Eh-eh!" he cried, and grabbing her by the waist, swirled her around and around into the middle of the room. She started to scream, a piercing sound which caused the crystals in the chandelier to rattle and roused the members of the 20th Light Dragoons to action. They started for Mr John Canoe, who quickly released his hold of Antoinetta, evaded their grasp, and disappeared into the night as suddenly as he had appeared.

All eyes were on Antoinetta as she collapsed onto the dance floor. Henry ran to her aid and she recovered almost immediately, rose to her feet, regained her poise, thanked him politely for his help, made a gesture to the orchestra to resume playing, and then began to dance. All night she was never without a dancing partner; the officers of the 20th Light Dragoons jostled each other for the privilege, and Mrs Fraser and her friends beamed with pride. In my head I heard their cries of self-congratulation:

> *What a success! What a glorious success!*
> *Antoinetta's succeeded in passing the test;*
> *Did you see how she conquered the 20th Light?*
> *How she danced and she danced far into the night*
> *with each man in turn? And how each lost his heart?*
> *Antoinetta's a marvel. She's our own work of art!*

January the fourteenth, 1771
I had wishfully presumed that Antoinetta's success at the

Governor's Ball would improve the manner in which she behaved at Beverly. I was wrong. Her success has gone to her head. She has become even more demanding. Quaco, the head stable hand, is terror-stricken because she insists on riding a different horse each day; she has frightened Rose and Psyche into handing over the keys to the pantry and has raided its contents; Cuthbert shakes from head to toe at her commands; and Celia and Monimia are on the verge of mutiny. They have every right to be. They know how I wish Beverly to be run; Antoinetta countermands my instructions; they refuse to perform her wishes; she complains about their refusals to Henry; Henry reprimands them.

I have never had any difficulty in talking to Henry about business matters, and I decided to tackle the issue of Antoinetta's behaviour as though dealing with a business transaction. I approached him at early breakfast — the only moment during the day when the house is free of her; she is a late riser, and it is not until late morning that she makes her way from her cottage to take up residence on the gallery.

"Henry, may I speak to you for a moment about a matter that concerns the household?" I asked.

"Certainly," he responded.

"While I am in sympathy with Antoinetta's desire to spend time in the big house," I started, well aware of the false ring to my voice, "and it is, after all, a more suitable venue for her to receive the various members of the 20th Light Dragoons who come to call," and here I thought Henry flinched, "I hope that she will respect certain rules."

"I thought you wished to talk to me about the household; instead you berate me with complaints about Antoinetta," accused Henry.

"I come directly to the household. I am having difficulty keeping the staff happy, and I beg you to help me enforce some rules where Antoinetta is concerned."

"You know yourself that Antoinetta does not respond well to enforcement."

"You are correct. She is, however, more likely to respond well to a request from you than from me."

"What sort of request?"

"Could you first designate a single horse to Antoinetta, so that Quaco is not intimidated into allowing her to ride horses that are unsuitable or dangerous?"

"I have determined that Antoinetta is capable of riding any horse she cares to, except Flame," he responded.

"Could you, then, reclaim the pantry key from her and return it to Rose and Psyche? They maintain the inventory of our stock, but Antoinetta removes whatever she wants without informing them."

"And why should she not?" asked Henry.

I ignored the question. I continued to appeal to Henry as one person trying to run a business would appeal to another.

"As you are well aware, no man can serve two masters, Henry. Please make it clear to Antoinetta that my word is law at Beverly, and that Celia and Monimia are my lieutenants."

"As my brother's widow, Antoinetta has every right to make a few requests of the servants. As far as I am concerned, she may have complete freedom to exercise her wishes, and if I have to hire servants to replace Celia and Monimia, I am prepared to do so."

"Should you do so, the same problem will recur with new servants," I responded.

"Perhaps you should be the one to change your *modus*

operandi. Can you not learn to be more tolerant?" he asked. "Have you no compassion for the recent widow?

I have been completely eclipsed by that woman; I am diminished day by day.

Last night, I heard the stairs creaking again. I heard the door to the gallery swing open. I went to my window and by the light of the gibbous moon, I watched a man's figure make its way across the garden to Antoinetta's cottage. A shudder rippled from the top to the foot of the tamarind tree. At breakfast this morning, Henry appeared listless. He did not speak to me. Nor did I speak to him, violator of his own sister and now of his already-much-violated brother's wife, that wallower in carnal filth, that vulgar bauble.

January the fifteenth, 1771

This afternoon I took a walk with Peter to the carriage house. He loves the carriages, and in particular the kittereen. We climbed into it together, and he took me for a pretend ride, imagining himself the driver with reins in his hands and the horse between the shafts, and whooping at the speed the animal galloped along the road. "Giddyup. Giddyup," he cried, as we whirled along. Eventually, he pulled on the reins and told his imaginary horse to slow down and we came to a stop.

"Thank you. That was a lovely outing," I said.

"Now for the stables," he said and jumped down from the kittereen. Like a gentleman, wanting to impress me, he held out his hand and helped me down, in the manner of his father. Then he ran full tilt over to the stables. I followed him and caught sight of him as he swarmed up the ladder to the hayloft. I walked around below, stroking the soft muzzles of the racehorses, breathing in the acrid odour of horse piss and hay. Suddenly I heard a yell nearby. It was Antoinetta calling for Quaco.

"Flame," shouted Antoinetta. "Quaco, saddle up Flame."

Quaco, who had been snoozing in the shade of a nearby tree, jumped up and said, "But Mistress, Master him say . . . "

"Flame," insisted Antoinetta, preceding him into the stables. She was blinded for an instant as she stepped from the sunshine into the dark. I shrank into the shadows.

"Booo! Duppy gwine get you!" shrieked Peter, leaping from the top of the ladder onto her back and knocking her to the ground. Then, like a streak of lightning, he ran from the stables. Flame pawed the ground and snorted, and the other horses whinnied anxiously. Antoinetta, shaking with fury, shrilled to Quaco, "Catch that boy at once!"

"I don' see no bwoy, Mistress," Quaco replied.

"Catch him. He's running away in that direction."

"I don' see no bwoy. Perhaps him ram puss."

"Stupid man! I know the difference between puss and boy! Catch him!"

Antoinetta switched her whip at him, and Quaco loped off. He was too late, of course. His delaying tactic had been successful, and Peter had disappeared.

Flame was still snorting when Antoinetta approached him. He shied and tried to kick her, and then would not allow Quaco to saddle him. She had to content herself with Silver instead, a gentle grey mare, and together they set off at an irritable trot.

I emerged from the shadows, trying to control my laughter. Quaco saw me, and we both let out the most tremendous guffaws. Oh, that naughty little boy!

January the seventeenth, 1771

While others drowse, Peter spends his afternoons outdoors, climbing higher and higher trees. He doodles with his stick in the sand; he chases and traps lizards and watches their tails wriggle after they shed them; he drops bread crumbs on the ground for ants and observes them as they marshall forces to drag the crumbs back to their nests. That is not all. Peter has a slingshot. He collects stones and practises zealously. He can knock tamarind pods down from the huge spreading tree, can pick off lizards on the ground from the heights of the tree, and can fire stones straight into ant nests. He once struck a scorpion dead with a single shot.

Today Antoinetta decided yet again to ride Flame. Once more she ventured out to the stables in her riding habit, swishing her whip; once more she called to Quaco, "Saddle up Flame."

From the gallery I could see Flame dancing around as Antoinetta mounted and adjusted the stirrups. I could tell she was feeling strong and eager; Flame is the horse of her dreams. As they left the stables, Antoinetta kept him on a tight rein. Suddenly, I caught sight of movement on the stable roof. Oh no! I watched as Peter aimed his sling, and his shot was deadly accurate. The stone hit Flame on the rump; the horse reared and whinnied and snorted and kicked and flung Antoinetta from his back to the ground, and then he was off galloping galloping galloping through the astounded streets of Spanish Town galloping galloping galloping out into the plains beyond. Antoinetta lay in the dust, winded, with her right arm broken. I watched as she gasped for breath, and then:

"AIEEEEE! AIEEEEE!" she screamed, and the quiet afternoon was torn asunder.

Quaco came running, Monimia came running, Sylvia picked up Bertha and came running, and all the other slaves gathered around the furious figure writhing on the ground. Peter told me later that as he gazed down on the scene, he thought it looked like a giant ant colony, and Antoinetta for all the world resembled the great queen ant surrounded by her soldiers. I reprimanded him rather lamely for what he had done.

February the sixth, 1771

The house stews as Antoinetta convalesces. She sits on the gallery, stretched out on the swing seat, with her arm in a sling, issuing orders to the servants, or pacing up and down, up and down. In the late morning, the ladies of Spanish Town come to call, bearing sympathy and sweetmeats. In the late afternoon, the officers of the 20th Light Dragoons march in, and their voices resonate throughout the house. Antoinetta's mood is transformed by their visits, but as soon as they leave she reverts to bile and gloom.

With astonishing drive for one so young, Peter has started a John Canoe band with four of the children from my school. His ability to lead others, at a mere seven years of age, is impressive. In addition to his Coromantee flute, the instruments are drums, whistles, calabashes, jawbones. Unfortunately, upon the insistence of Antoinetta, Henry has forbidden the children to play their instruments near the house, so they have made their headquarters in the shade of a spreading lignum vitae tree out in the cattle pasture.

They have collected calabashes big enough to fit over their heads and have made holes in them for their eyes. They have fashioned bracelets and necklaces from seeds and pods. They have collected chicken feathers and palm fronds. Celia has helped them sew the palm fronds into skirts and has made a headpiece of gaudy feathers for Peter, who cannot sport a calabash like the others because he needs freedom to play his flute. The headpiece hangs down over his face, completely hiding it, except for a small gap where his nose protrudes for flute-playing. When they are fully costumed, the children are completely disguised, and they make such a shusshing and rustling as they dance that their costumes themselves become another musical instrument; they call this the swish-swish. They practise constantly. How delightful it is to witness a group of children engaged in such activity! They tell me that they are preparing to celebrate "pickney Christmas," which is what some of the slaves call Easter.

Easter Sunday, March the thirty-first, 1771

On Good Friday, that most quiet of all Christian holy days, in the late afternoon, just as the sun was setting, the children made their move. Dressed in full regalia, they left the haven of their lignum vitae tree and wound their way through the fields towards the house, past the chicken coops and pig pens, past the slave quarters, past the stables, through the formal garden and then, drumming and swishing and fluting, burst onto the gallery where Antoinetta was stretched out on the chaise longue in a disagreeable, late afternoon slumber, her newly-mended arm arranged languidly behind her head.

"King oooo, King oooo, Kimbebe King," sang the children, swishing, rattling, and drumming.

Antoinetta's eyes flew open and fell on the little group of grotesques dancing wildly in front of her. She screamed, a shriek so loud and so piercing that I sprang up from my chair, Henry rushed out onto the gallery, and Monimia came running from the kitchen.

"Duppy gwine get you!" cried Peter, as he and his followers scurried down the steps and swished out into the quickly falling night, giggling with pleasure and fear. They ran as fast as they could back past the stables, the slave quarters, the coops, the pens, the fields, and made for the safety of the lignum vitae tree. They swung themselves up into its branches and were swiftly hidden from sight.

"It's that child again. I know it is. Catch him, Henry. Catch them all. Run after them! Punish them!" screamed Antoinetta.

Her face was purple and bloated with rage; she looked as though she might suffer an apoplectic fit. Henry attempted to calm her, and Monimia brought water, while I stood on the sidelines scarcely able to control the bubbles of laughter trying to escape from my mouth. And still Antoinetta screamed at Henry to hunt the children down. He set off into the fading light, but he did not know about the haven in the lignum vitae tree.

May the seventh, 1771

"Papa is not very well these days," my sister writes in a letter that arrived on the latest packet. Does "not very well" imply that he is deathly ill or merely that his rheumatics are more than usually troublesome? Oh, my dearest Papa, should I return to England immediately? What should I do?

I am torn asunder. My love for Papa and my sense of duty stir me to go, but my practical head tells me there are two reasons to wait until I hear more. The first reason I should not leave immediately for England is that he might die before I get there — and perhaps, even now, I am already too late to see him again. The second: he might recover and wonder why I had gone to all the trouble of crossing the Atlantic. How can I possibly decide when is the proper moment?

I do not want to go. I do not want to leave Jamaica. I do not want to part from Peter for even an instant. Heaven knows what cruelties Antoinetta might inflict on him were I not here to act as his defender. I do not want to leave Mr Kenet. There I have said it. I adore him. He came to my classroom today, bearing with him a silver snake to show the children. He had it in a box, and when he lifted it out and gently stroked it, I fell in love with his hands. I confess, I wanted those hands to stroke me instead of the snake.

The silver snake is interesting. Some people call it "Amphisbaena," after the mythological two-headed snake, because of its uniform thickness and its ability to move both backwards and forwards. The country people simply refer to it as the worm snake. Whatever its name, it proved a great success with the children as it proceeded first this way and then that way.

"Snakey darlin'," they cried, and added its name to their growing list of Jamaican animals and birds. Mr Kenet, however, decided not to leave it in the classroom, but told the children he intended to set it free in the ditch where he had found it. He returned it to its box and closed the lid. His hands, his hands.

While I desire to spend more time with him each day, I notice that we have recently become tongue-tied in each other's presence. Whereas before, I often found myself chattering like a girl, and he would engage me at length upon some weighty topic like the difference in metre between sapphics and alcaics or the size of Solomon's temple, we now sit together in almost total silence. At the mere sight of him, longing pierces my breast, my voice shakes, my tongue is frozen. A current runs through my body; there is roaring in my ears. I think I am dying.

How will we ever converse once more with ease? If I left for England now, we might never speak again.

I decided to stay in place.

May the twenty-third, 1771

I heard screaming.

"Mistress, Mistress!"

I jumped up from my desk and looked out the window to see Sylvia running towards the house. I hurried outside.

"Mistress, Mistress! Help! She ga'an, she ga'an!" she cried as we came together.

"Sylvia, calm yourself. What are you talking about?"

"Mistress gwine kill me!" Sylvia was shaking from head to toe; her eyes starting from their sockets in fright.

I grabbed her arms and held them to her sides to control her shaking. Tears streamed down her face.

"Tell me what's the matter."

"The baby ga'an!"

"Bertha?"

"Yes, ma'am. She ga'an. I can't find she. She ga'an, ga'an, ga'an. Duppy take she away," she blurted out hysterically.

"Now, Sylvia, calm yourself," I said in a voice like a slap. "Tell me what happened."

The harshness in my voice stopped her short. She looked at her feet and then spoke up.

"I go to she room because is long time she sleep, an' she ga'an, she ga'an," and here Sylvia started to weep again.

"Stop that," I snapped again to hold back the floods. "We

shall find her. Come with me," I commanded and we set off at a run for Antoinetta's cottage. I knew that Bertha was of an age when she could easily climb out of her crib and crawl off on her own little adventure, and I was confident we would discover her somewhere nearby.

There was no sign of her indoors, and we had just begun to search outside when Antoinetta returned from her afternoon outing on Flame. She saw us in the garden, recognized that something was amiss, and rode over to us.

"What are you doing?" she demanded. "What is the matter, Sylvia?"

Sylvia covered her face with her apron and shook from head to toe, while I explained as calmly as I could that Bertha had vanished from her crib and that we had just started to look for her.

"Fool!" shouted Antoinetta, swinging at Sylvia with her horsewhip.

"Leave her alone, woman," I shrieked, lunging for the whip but failing to grasp it. "Help us search!"

Antoinetta paused and looked around her, and then, struck by the lightning of inspiration shouted, "The stables!"

She wheeled Flame around and cantered off. Sylvia and I hurried after her on foot. When we arrived, she had dismounted and had sent Quaco up into the loft in search of Peter.

"There's no sign of the little fiend," she spat. "Where else does he hide?"

"Why are you looking for him? Do you really believe he had something to do with this?" I asked.

"I know he's the culprit," she responded between clenched teeth. "Where is he?"

"He could be in his room, or he might have climbed the tamarind tree," I suggested.

"You search his room; I'll go to the tree," she directed, setting off at a run, trailing the miserable Sylvia behind her.

I hastened to the house and took the stairs two at a time, but found Peter's room empty. I checked under his pillow where he usually kept his slingshot; it was missing. And then I heard the screams coming from the tamarind tree.

I fled outside, crossed the garden to the tree, and entered the penumbra. There I came upon the most terrifying sight. Antoinetta was flogging Peter with her horsewhip, again and again and again. Her teeth were bared in a snarl and her face was purple and bloated with rage. Peter was screaming, Bertha was screaming, Sylvia was screaming. The tamarind tree was shuddering, and pods were dropping to the ground.

I grabbed at Antoinetta's arm, trying to stop the whip, but she was too strong for me and flung me off. My attempt at intervention only deepened her rage and, growling like some strange wild animal, she doubled her effort. I jumped up, grabbed her by the other arm and bit it as hard as I could. Ugh! I too had turned into a wild animal; she had reduced me to her level. At that she swung away from Peter and brought the whip around so that it caught me in the face, drew blood, and I fell to the ground. Antoinetta laughed, picked up Bertha, gave Peter a parting kick, and shouted to Sylvia to accompany her back to the cottage.

I crawled over to Peter, who lay on Pearl's tombstone, howling and bleeding. He screamed and pulled himself up into a kneeling position.

"Mama! Mama!" he cried and flung his arms around me. I hesitated to embrace him for fear that I might injure him further, but he held on to me so fiercely that when Cuthbert arrived on the scene, my dress was soaked in Peter's blood. I sent Cuthbert back to fetch Monimia and Celia and to bring clean water and bandages.

Monimia took charge immediately, ordering Celia to look to my injury while she took care of Peter's. She removed his shirt, and gasped when she saw the lashes on his back. It is frightful to imagine the damage that might have been inflicted had he not been wearing his favourite blue shirt. Having washed Peter's wounds, she spread a salve on them made from the weed she calls "fresh-cut," and bound up those that still bled. She then applied fresh-cut to my cheekbone and bade me hold a cloth to it to staunch the bleeding.

Celia and Monima made a chair with their arms and carried Peter back to the nursery in that fashion. I retired to my room, and when my cheek stopped bleeding, I stepped out of my blood-stained dress, and washed myself from head to foot. I asked myself if I had need of a surgeon to sew up the cut on my face but could come to no conclusion. Then I went along to the nursery.

Peter was in his nightshirt, sitting up, straight and silent, on his bed. He refused to speak. I lifted down a copy of Aesop's fables, and began to read to him. I read for an hour, choosing all his favourites; then I closed the book and put it away. He had no desire to sleep, so I took him by the hand, and we walked downstairs together, and out onto the gallery. Celia brought us tamarind water and two slices of Monimia's magnificent cocoanut cake — Peter's favourite food — and we sat on the gallery, sipping and nibbling. This revived him enough to tell me why he and Bertha happened to be under the tamarind tree.

Here is the story he told, through renewed sobs. (I have been unable to resist adding some coherence and colour to his jerky tale.) He recounted that, in the afternoon, he was lying stretched out on a limb high up in the tamarind tree, sucking on one of its sour pods. He looked down on Sylvia taking Richard for a walk, on Monimia gathering herbs, and on Quaco brushing Flame until the stallion's coat gleamed like polished ebony. Suddenly, Antoinetta burst from her cottage in her riding habit, and ran to the stables. Quaco saddled Flame for her. He helped her mount and adjusted the stirrups, and then with a slash of her whip to Flame's rump, Antoinetta disappeared up the road in a cloud of dust. Quaco shook his head.

Peter let himself down to the lowest branch, dropped to the ground, ran to the house, up the front steps, crossed the cool tiles of the gallery, the hard expanse of polished floor, the soft nap of the turkish carpet; he climbed the wide mahogany stairs, creak by creak, holding onto the fat stair rail; he entered his room, and gathered all he had been saving that might be useful for a journey: an orange, a banana, a small gleaming coin found on the seat of the kittereen, a blue bandana stolen from Monimia, a kitchen knife, his slingshot. He stowed the orange, the banana, the coin, and the slingshot in his pockets, tucked the knife into his belt, and tied the bandana around his head. He fancied himself a pirate.

He held his breath as he slunk along the corridor and descended the stairs. He disembarked from the house and voyaged across the garden seas to Antoinetta's cottage. Its doors and windows were open to catch any available breeze. He sailed straight in, over the forbidden threshold, past Antoinetta's room, to the entrance of her children's room. He gazed at the crib; the gauze was in place. He floated along a single floorboard across the room and drew back the mosquito net. Bertha was sleeping on her back, on a lambskin, and her hair was fluffy around her head. Antoinetta's collection of rag dolls was arranged at the foot of the crib. Peter drew the knife from his belt and cut off their heads one by one. He tucked the knife back into his belt. He breathed softly onto Bertha's face and her eyelids fluttered. He touched her hand with his finger and she grasped it. When she opened her eyes, she smiled at him in recognition.

Peter picked Bertha up and carried her over his shoulder, just the way Sylvia did. He pulled off the bandana and draped it over her head to shade her from the sun; he left the cottage and skulked to the tamarind tree. There he had already prepared a nest for Bertha by digging a bowl in the earth beside Pearl's tombstone and filling it with feathery leaves from the tamarind tree.

He spread the bandana over the leaves, placed Bertha in the nest, and sat down beside her, on Pearl's tomb. He tickled her feet, which made her chuckle and kick them wildly. He clapped his hands, and sang and danced for her, and then he picked her up and swung with her gently on Martha's swing. When she tired of this entertainment and started to cry, he sat her down again and peeled the orange, pulled off a segment, carefully removed the membrane, and put one end of the segment into Bertha's screaming, sparsely-toothed mouth. The crying stopped as Bertha tried to suck the orange. Peter was worried about her lack of teeth. He himself had just lost two and could feel the sharp points of the new ones coming in. He soon realised that Bertha was having trouble chewing the orange and was frustrated in her attempts to suck it, so he carefully squeezed the juice into her open mouth, ate the banana himself, and then he picked her up and they swung again together on Martha's swing.

And then Antoinetta found them.

Darkness was falling by the time Henry returned from Kingston — he was later than usual because he had been supervising the unloading of the *Destiny* — and the lights were on in Antoinetta's cottage. Like a moth drawn to a candle, he went straight there. Ten minutes later he stormed out again like a charging bull, traversed the garden, and mounted the steps to the gallery. I rose to speak to him, but he pushed me aside and addressed Peter directly.

"Why did you steal Bertha?" he roared at Peter.

"I don' t'ief she. I tek she for walk," shouted Peter in return, fortifying himself with the vernacular, and addressing his father squarely. I could not help but admire the child's courage as he faced down his inquisitor.

"You know that you are forbidden to enter Aunt Antoinetta's cottage. Why did you disobey?" thundered Henry.

"Please lower your voice, Henry," I begged.

"She ga'an ridin'," Peter shouted back. "Sylvia she tek Richard for walk. Bert'a she want to go for walk. Why Bert'a she cyan go too, Papa? I tek she for walk." He paused for breath, and then said meekly, "I am a good boy, Papa."

"You are not a good boy, Peter Mason. You disobeyed Aunt Antoinetta's orders."

"Look, Papa, where Auntie done hit me. She tek she whip, and she hit me, one, two, t'ree, fifty, eighty, one million time."

"Silence! You deserve your punishment, young man. You are a vile, wicked, evil thief."

Peter had never heard his father address him thus, and he looked astonished. Then he gasped and spat directly into Henry's face, "Pah!"

Henry turned purple with anger, and then he sprang. I leaped from my chair as he took Peter by the hair. In that instant an image flashed before my eyes: Pyrrhus as he swung Astyanax above his head and flung him over the battlements of Troy to his death below. I screamed and jumped forward to grab Henry's arm just as he flung Peter down the gallery steps. This had the effect of pitching me to the ground also. I screamed again. Henry turned on his heel and entered the house. Before I knew it, Celia was by my side. She helped me to my feet, and together we made our way down the steps, fearful of what we might discover. I was shaking with rage.

Peter lay at the foot, stunned and winded, but had suffered no broken bones. He had tried to save himself with his hands, which severely grazed them. The fall had re-opened a large wound on his upper arm, and it was once again bleeding copiously. Celia produced a cloth, which we pressed down on the wound, and when Peter had regained his breath enough to wail "Mama!," we lifted him, and carried him up the stairs to the nursery, once again in chairlike fashion.

When I tried to put him to bed, he started to scream that there was a duppy hiding beneath it, so I examined the situation, and declared that he was mistaken. He then agreed to go to bed on the condition that I remain in the nursery until he had fallen asleep. This did not seem too big a favour to grant.

Poor little fellow. Henry has broken his heart but has steeled my resolve.

It was a long time before Peter finally succumbed to sleep and I was able to retire to my room. I flung myself on my bed and pounded my pillow. I bit into it to prevent myself from screaming aloud.

There was a tap at the door. It was Celia, bearing a jug of warm water. She helped me remove my second bloodied dress of the day — I was still shaking so much that I could not undo the buttons — and stayed with me while I washed and donned my nightdress. I sat at my dressing table and she unpinned my hair and brushed it gently until I had regained a veneer of icy calm. Then she disappeared, only to return a few minutes later with a bowl of callalu soup and some warm bread. We did not speak, but she remained with me until I had finished my meal, mouthful by angry mouthful, and had retired under my mosquito net.

I could not fall asleep. My mind was racing and the words of hurricane chant kept going round and round in my brain: "June, too soon. July, stand by. August, must. September, remember. October, all over." But even May was not too soon that night. A freak of Nature sent a hurricane wind tearing through Spanish Town. I first heard it soughing in the trees, I heard it rattle the shutters, I heard it fling open doors and bang them shut again. I crawled from my bed and looked out into the garden. The trees blew steadfastly one way, never writhing around, so continuous was the strain bending their branches. I spoke to myself: "I hear the wind blowing. I will go out of doors and feel it."

It was not without wild pleasure that I ran before the wind delivering my trouble of mind to the measureless air-torrent thundering through space. I raised my arms as though I were flying, and my nightdress filled with air. I leaped over flowerbeds and shrubs. I flew towards the tamarind tree, and suddenly the wind stopped. I, too, stopped, and my heart stood still to an inexpressible feeling that thrilled it through, sharp, strange, and startling. It was like a shock that acted on my senses as if their utmost activity hitherto had been but torpor, from which they were now summoned, and forced to wake.

I heard a voice cry, "Martha! Martha!"

I held my breath and listened, and listened, and listened with every fibre of my being.

The voice came again: "Leave Jamaica!"

The voice did not come out of the air, nor from under the earth, but I heard it, and I knew it was Pearl.

Suddenly, the sky was rent by lightning, and the tamarind tree shivered and glittered in the brilliance. The wind rose again and set the branches swirling. Thunder snapped and rolled and bounced. And then it started to rain, and I began to dance, all by myself, in the downpour. I had found my resolve. My road lay straight ahead. It was my time to assume ascendancy. My powers were in play, and in force. I mounted to my chamber; locked myself in; fell on my knees; and prayed in my own fashion. I seemed to penetrate very near a Mighty Spirit, and my soul rushed out in gratitude. I rose from the thanksgiving, and lay down, emboldened — eager for the daylight.

Exhausted, I slept a hard, dark, dreamless sleep. Very early the following morning, I awoke with my cheek throbbing. I felt battered and limp. I staggered to my feet and scrutinized my face in the mirror. Although the gash no longer bled, a dark purple bruise covered my entire left cheek and surrounded my eye. Nausea rose in my throat as I recollected the scenes I had beheld. I started shaking from head to foot. My teeth chattered. And then I recalled Pearl's voice telling me to leave Jamaica, convincing me that there was no longer room for me on my beloved island. I realised that the forces of evil were greater than I could withstand. With a sinking heart, I tried to plan my departure, but my mind flittered and gibbered and I could gain no foothold on my thoughts. I needed help, but to whom could

I turn? Who hated Henry enough to help me fulfill my resolve? Who hated him enough to want to destroy him?

As though moving through molasses, I dressed myself and went downstairs, clinging to the banister. I staggered around the rooms, touching dear familiar objects, and then I left the house for the garden, drawn back to Pearl's grave. Under the tamarind tree, it was still dark, but I found my swing and sat on it, gently swishing to and fro. My shaking abated; my mind cleared and through the wreckage came a vision of the one person whose hatred for Henry was so great that I knew she would stop at nothing to help me.

Mrs Perkins.

After I had reassured myself that Peter was still sleeping comfortably — Celia had stayed in his room all night — I went out to the stables. The stable boy was not yet awake, so I coaxed Sally's bit into her mouth, threw a saddle over her, and grabbed the reins, all the while wishing I had the courage to ride fleethooved Flame. Sally needed much encouragement to break into the gallop I wanted for the journey from Beverly to Government House. On our breathless arrival I rode around to the back of the building, dismounted, and handed over the heaving mare to a groom; then I entered the kitchen and asked for Mrs Perkins. The kitchen staff was astonished to see such a hideously disfigured woman trespassing on their territory. They remained mute until the head cook stepped forward and told me I would find Mrs Perkins in the butler's pantry, counting the silver. She showed me the way.

There I found Priscilla Perkins, stooped over the gleaming forks and spoons, a little greyer, a little gaunter, but still the same crisp-moving, deliberate woman.

"Good morning, Mrs Perkins."

She stood up straight and, without flinching or batting an eyelid in surprise, snapped, "Good morning, Mrs Mason."

"May I talk to you?"

I could see her distaste at my request and her desire to deny it. But I also perceived her taking note of the bruise on my face.

"One moment," she said, making me wait and placing herself in control of the situation. She took her time to finish counting the silver and then locked the wooden coffer in which it was held. "Follow me."

She led me to a little room with a small, high window, a room used for the storage of linens. She brought in two stools, and we sat down among the sweet-smelling sheets and towels and stared at each other.

"Why are you here?" she asked peremptorily.

I began shaking again. I could not speak. We sat in a heavy silence until she broke it with a stark question.

"Henry?"

I nodded.

"Hmph," she sniffed and pursed her lips so hard they turned white.

Again, a long silence. I felt a single tear slide down and sting my cheek. Salt in the wound.

"What has that devil done now?" She spat the words.

I opened my mouth and tried to speak, but not a sound came out.

"Swallow."

I did.

"Now breathe slowly."

I did.

"Now speak."

I tried to but the floodgates opened, tears streamed down my face, my nose ran, I tried to breathe, but the breath choked in and out of my breast.

Mrs Perkins reached in her pocket for a handkerchief, removing one that I recognised immediately as having been embroidered by Pearl. My tears redoubled.

"Pull yourself together," she snapped.

I could not. The sorrow roared out of me, on and on. I thought it would never end. Eventually, Mrs Perkins stood up and slapped me hard on my right cheek, stunning me. I was so shocked that I stopped crying. She left the room and returned shortly, bearing two glasses, one of rum and one of water.

"Drink this," she ordered, handing me the glass of water. I took a spluttering sip.

"Now this," she said, handing me the rum. I sipped and choked on it, but a small amount slid down my throat and I felt its warmth spreading throughout my chest.

"Now speak." She sat back down on her stool, folded her hands on her lap and crossed her ankles.

And speak I did, haltingly at first and then, as the whole horrible story unrolled, in a seamless narrative. As I spoke, she nodded and pursed, nodded and pursed, sniffed and groaned, sniffed and groaned. When I came to the part when Antoinetta whipped Peter, I witnessed her gorge rise. She turned aside and I thought she was about to vomit, but she did not. When Henry cast Peter down the stone steps, her face went bright red with anger, a sight I had never seen in one who was usually so pale. Her jaw clenched, her eyes narrowed, and she balled her fists.

As I finished the tale, I slid off my stool and sank onto the ground in exhaustion. I lay there silent, almost senseless. Mrs

Perkins uncrossed her ankles, stretched out her feet, and gave me a few moments of rest. Then she stamped on the floor and spoke.

"Get up!" She rose and reached out her strong, stringy hand and hauled me to my feet. We glared at each other.

"Solve my problem," I shouted in her face.

Given the task of at last taking revenge on Henry for despoiling her treasured Pearl, her eyes glinted, her back straightened, she paced back and forth in that little room, and she began to mutter and plot. She agreed with Pearl that I must leave Jamaica at once, and she insisted I take Peter with me. This idea of depriving Henry of Peter caused her every possible delight; in so doing she and I would wreak a deep-cutting, never-ending revenge, a sorrow for Henry that even the antics of the slattern Antoinetta would not be able to assuage. The very thought of this pasted a hideous smile on Mrs Perkins's face. It stuck there as she gloated.

Then her brain took over her gloating and she started plotting again. "Can you find transportation to England for Peter and yourself immediately and without Henry's knowledge?"

This seemed like an impossible task. I waited for inspiration, but none came.

"Hurry up, woman. Think hard!"

Her steeliness fortified my brain and I thought as hard as I could. At first nothing came to me, but slowly an image of Mr Fraser emerged.

"Mr Fraser might be able to secure us passage on a ship."

"Indeed. Now, is there someone who can help you travel from Spanish Town to Kingston?"

That was easy. My thoughts immediately fled to Mr Kenet, whom I could trust to do anything in his power to help me.

"Yes."

"Good. Now, is there anyone with whom you can stay in Kingston as you await the departure of your ship?"

I paused. This was harder. I thought and thought, but I could bring forth no one. In desperation, I listened for Pearl's voice. Nothing. But then a gust of wind blew the small window wide open and it creaked as it swung, and I swear I heard the word "Henriques."

"Yes, there is someone," I replied. I could hide Peter and myself at the home of my dear friend Julia Jamison, now Mrs Jacob Henriques.

"Very well. All is in place. You are free to go. I can see nothing standing in your way except your own weakmindedness."

"I am not weakminded," I shrieked indignantly. "How dare you say that?"

"You are weakminded because you didn't leave Henry when I did."

"I am not weakminded. I had important reasons for staying."

"Hmmph."

"I am not weakminded. I am leaving now."

"Very well," said Mrs Perkins again. "I see a glimmer of resolve. Go now."

We glared at each other and then — I still cannot believe this — we held each other in a long, tight, bony embrace.

"Go immediately. Do not waver," she said as we pulled apart. She turned her back to me and I left.

When I arrived back at Beverly, it was still early morning, and I found Monimia preparing Henry's breakfast.

"Good morning, Monimia," I called, surprising her at her work.

"Eh-eh, Mistress! Where you come from den?" she exclaimed.

"Please help me, Doctoress Monimia." She preened herself at the title.

"I need your skill," I continued. Again she preened. "Can you insert a strong narcotic into Henry's breakfast, one that will make him sleep throughout the entire day? Do you have such a thing?"

Monimia's eyes glinted devilishly. She did not answer but reached a heavy arm to the highest shelf in the kitchen and lifted down an unassuming earthenware jar. She grinned and nodded.

"I have de t'ing."

When breakfast was ready, Celia carried a tray to Peter in the nursery. He had, not unreasonably, refused to eat with his father. I, on the other hand, forced myself to eat with my husband, wanting to flaunt my wound at him, wanting him to acknowledge the injury he had inflicted, wanting a final encounter with him to strengthen my resolve. In silence I stared at him as he gobbled his repast, willing him to look at me, but he never once glanced up from his plate. Coward. When he had finished, he wiped his mouth, yawned, rose from the table, turned his back on me, and staggered to the settee in the drawing room. With all the dignity he could muster, he sank down on it, and was soon snoring, flat on his back, his cheeks slack, his mouth wide open. The "t'ing" had gone to work.

Now I could act. Now I could wreak my revenge. I was filled with a maniacal determination. I ran upstairs and packed two travelling bags, one for me and one for Peter. At the last moment I slipped Peter's slingshot in amongst his clothes. His

Coromantee flute was too large for his bag, but I managed to wedge it down the side of mine. Then I relieved Rose of her household duties, and begged her to make haste to the church hall, explaining I needed her to work at the school that day. I asked her to summon Mr Kenet to come at once to Beverly in his kitereen. She left for the church hall immediately. I instructed Monimia to pack food and plenty of water for Peter and me and Mr Kenet. Then I washed and dressed my dear little boy, who was all black and blue and crying. I told him we were going for a real ride in a real kitereen, and with that his eyes lit up and he stopped sobbing. We collected our bags, and then hand in hand we tiptoed down that lovely staircase and made our way to the kitchen.

I was not concerned that Antoinetta might witness my flight. She never rose before noon. Lazy cow.

"Where you goin'?" demanded Monimia.

"You gwine lef' we?" cried Celia.

"Where you goin'?" repeated Monimia.

"You can tell your master you believe I have gone to Cinchona."

"Is true?" Monimia can smell a rat faster than anyone I know.

"You must believe it," I said.

"I gwine come too," said Celia.

"No, no. Not this time, dear Celia."

"Who gwine cook for you?" asked Monimia pushing out her lower lip and sucking her teeth. "You gwine starve up in dem mountain all by you self."

"Don't worry. Just tell your master that you think I have gone to Cinchona."

"You gwine someplace else. You cyan fool me."

Celia started crying. "You gwine le' we," she sobbed.

We had reached a stalemate. To let them into my confidence about my real destination would be to endanger them; having them intimate to Henry that I might have gone to Cinchona was an entirely reasonable thing to suggest and would protect them at the same time as it would buy me time. Henry might not even bother looking for me there for several days.

I took their hands, and we stood in a little ring.

"This is our circle of friendship, and it will never be broken, no matter where I am," I assured them.

"Mama," whined Peter, "Can we go now?"

Monimia showed me the contents of the brimming picnic basket she had prepared for us: rice and peas, boiled eggs, pickles, jars of water, a flask of coffee, and enough fruit to feed an army.

We continued to stand around, with Peter pulling on my hand and whining, but it was not long before we heard the sound of a kittereen approaching. I ran to the door and down the front steps and beheld my dear Mr Kenet climbing down from the carriage. He stepped towards me and then halted in shock at the sight of my face.

"Oh, my dear Mrs Mason! What terrible thing has happened to you?"

I could not speak, but as we stood there looking at each other, he raised his right hand to my face, and with a touch as gentle as that of a butterfly's wing, he traced the perimeter of the wound. He asked me again what had happened.

How I wanted to confess everything to him — to confess that I was a wife in name alone; to tell him about Pearl and Henry, and about the birth of the twins; to recount for him the death of Pearl; to explain to him how life at Beverly had become intolerable since Antoinetta's arrival and how I feared for Peter's life; but there was no time for all that. Instead, I said, "For now, I will tell you that I fell on the front steps," and glanced away as I spoke.

He knew I was lying but did not try to persuade me to tell the truth, recognising that some terrible cruelty lay behind my fabrication. Instead, he asked me if he could help me in any way. "Tell me what you need. I will do all I can to help you"

This time I told a half-lie. "My father is ill and I must leave for England immediately. I beg you, dear friend, to transport Peter and me to Kingston, and thence to Stony Hill."

"Now?" he asked.

"Yes, as soon as I have bidden my farewells."

"I shall await you in the kittereen."

I clasped his hand and kissed it fervently. I did not want to let go.

"Please to stop talking," called Peter to Mr Kenet from the top of the steps. "Mama and I wish to go for a ride in your carriage. Come along, Mama."

I dragged him back into the house to make our farewells while Mr Kenet climbed onto the driver's seat of the kittereen. We found Monimia and Celia standing in the kitchen, looking baleful, and Cuthbert looking anxious.

"Where you go, Mistress?" asked Celia again with a turned-down mouth. "Why you don' tell we?"

"Where you go, Mistress?" echoed Cuthbert.

"I do not want trouble for you. Please do not look for me, but remember, wherever I am, you three are always with me."

Monimia started to bawl. Celia stood as still and silent as a rock while tears poured down her cheeks. And I, too, began to weep. Cuthbert cleared his throat awkwardly.

"Mama!" cried Peter impatiently.

I pulled myself together and asked Cuthbert to place our travelling bags and the picnic basket in the carriage, and to raise the hood. As we left the house, Peter ran down the steps and jumped into the kitereen while Monimia and Celia clung to me so hard that the breath was squeezed from my body. They clung to me even as I tried to descend the steps. When at last we reached the ground, they freed me and lifted me high in the air, calling out that I was their dolly princess for ever and ever, and then they lowered me and placed me gently on the seat. Peter and I blew kisses to our beloved companions as we set off at a busy trot down the avenue of yokewood trees. I took my last look at Beverly, and then sat back on the seat and told Peter that, as we were pirates, no one must see us, and that we must squeeze ourselves into the dark corners under the hood as we left Spanish Town.

Mr Kenet, sitting above us on the driver's seat, turned around.

"Where to, Madam?" he asked, grinning.

"To Kingston."

May the twenty-fourth, 1771

The distance between Spanish Town and Kingston is thirteen miles, and as we journeyed along the road past the many sugar plantations, I was reminded of the first time I had travelled the road eight years before. In my wildest dreams, I never could have imagined the twists and turns that Fate would deal me in those few short years.

We stopped once, beside the Rio Cobre, to water the horse and to eat our picnic. Peter begged to swim in the river before we ate, but I reminded him this was unwise because of the wounds on his back. He sulked but then settled for fishing, using a rod he fashioned from a stick, with a liana for the line, and a pea for bait.

Mr Kenet and I decided to eat in the kittereen rather than on the ground, for fear of predators such as stinging ants. As I set up the meal, he did not press me for information, but slowly I began to tell him the history of my life in Jamaica, feeling I owed him the truth and knowing I would never find a more sympathetic listener. Not wanting pity, I tried to tell my story as though it were a mere list of facts. However, as the facts mounted up, I could see his eyes widen in horror. When I finally told him about Antoinetta beating Peter, his eyes flashed with rage.

"You were quite right to leave," he insisted, pounding one fist into the opposite palm. "When I consider the depth of treachery you have endured, I am surprised that you did not quit long before now."

"I did not quit because I did not want to leave Jamaica. I did not want to leave my school." And then I whispered, "And I did not want to leave you."

He took my hands.

"You know I would never leave," I continued, "were it not for that malicious woman. If I stayed, I would murder her — or Henry — or both." I was stabbed again by the memory of Henry's beating Peter. "I thought Henry was going to kill Peter," I gulped. "Antoinetta has driven him raving mad."

"I hungry," said Peter, returning to us, fishless, and we turned our attention to the contents of the picnic basket.

Having unburdened my sorrows to Mr Kenet, I felt relief. We settled down to Monimia's meal, and even I, whose appetite is usually so small, relished our picnic. Being in the open air, in the company of someone I admired, whose presence had the effect of calming my spirit, allowed me to actually taste the food I was consuming. Food had tasted of nothing at all, and even that taste of nothing was nauseating when I dined with Henry during my last few weeks at Beverly.

"Where now, Madam?" asked Mr Kenet as we climbed back into the kittereen.

"To Mason & Fraser's place of business on Harbour Street."

He cracked the whip, and we set off again, arriving in Kingston in the afternoon, a Kingston that was rousing itself from its post-prandial nap, taking on noise and colour and all the ragged excitement of a port city. I knew exactly in which office I would find Thomas Fraser, having visited Mason & Fraser's quite a few times. Meanwhile, Mr Kenet said he would find water for the horse and then wait outside with Peter while I transacted my business.

Mr Fraser answered my knock with a reassuring "Why, it's my dear Martha! Have you come to borrow more books?" He stood up and came from behind his desk to greet me as I entered.

I rushed across the threshold and threw myself, sobbing, into his arms. He patted my back, and then held me at arms' length, scrutinising my face.

"Martha, my dear, whatever has happened to you?" he asked.

Even my bonnet could not hide the wound on my face. On first seeing it and the massive bruise surrounding it, he was aghast, but then he examined it carefully, with great concern, before remarking on the rainbow of colours.

"There, there. Calm down, my dear. Tell me what happened to you."

I blurted out the whole gruesome tale of Antoinetta's cruelty from the moment of her strangling Scipio to her seduction of Henry to her whipping of my precious boy and to my fear that she would kill him if she ever set eyes on him again.

He sat me down and passed me a large linen handkerchief with erratically embroidered initials. In an instant I remembered that handkerchief; Pearl had embroidered it for his birthday just a few months before she died. Pearl, always Pearl. I wiped my eyes with it.

"Now, tell me what may I do for you?"

He returned to his desk and sat down across from me, the perfect merchant, ready to transact new business.

"I hesitate to ask your help, knowing you must feel some loyalty to your business partner. I suspect that he would take ill to the notion of your assisting me." I twisted the handkerchief in my lap.

Mr Fraser snorted. "How can you imagine I would not help you after what Henry and that . . . " and here he was at a loss for words. The only word he could come up with was " . . . person," which he uttered with such an explosive "p" that the air moved and I saw a little flick of spittle land on his desk.

He began again, "How can you imagine I would not help you after what Henry and that — person — have done to you? Do you think that Mrs Fraser and I are completely blind to what has been going on?"

I was sure, although I did not say it, that Mrs Fraser had a very good idea of what was going on. Was she not alert to scandal? Had she not witnessed Antoinetta's anger at first hand? Had she not accompanied Antoinetta and me to Montego Bay? Had she not witnessed Antoinetta's behaviour at the Governor's Ball? Would she not have confided this gossip to her husband?

Reassured that I was not calling on him to perform a task that he might be unwilling to undertake, I put forth my request.

"I need a passage to England for me and Peter immediately."

He was taken aback for a moment. "People generally book their passages months in advance, and I may not be able to satisfy your wish for an immediate departure." My shoulders slumped.

"But," he continued, "I shall do my very best. The *Destiny* leaves for Liverpool three days hence. We are in the process of loading her right now. I shall try to find you a berth, but do not allow your hopes to rise too much."

Then he asked me if I had a place to stay, a place where I would be invisible. I told him about Mrs Henriques's invitation to stay with her at Stony Hill any time I wished. Henry had never met her, and he would never think to track me down there.

"Stony Hill. Good. Lie low. I will send word to you if I meet with success."

Mr Fraser rose to his feet and came from behind his desk. I rose too and tried to return his handkerchief to him.

"You must keep it. You may need it again," he said with a gentle smile as he escorted me from his office and out into the hustle and bustle of Harbour Street. There I encountered a very hot and irritable Peter and a patient Mr Kenet, who was trying to entertain him with a game of cat's cradle.

"Where to now?" Mr Kenet asked.

"To Stony Hill, to the home of Mr and Mrs Henriques. I have the address." That good horse, which must have been exhausted after the journey from Spanish Town, responded to Mr Kenet's "Giddyup," and off we set through the hustle and bustle of the city of Kingston. We proceeded up the Hope Road and soon found ourselves climbing towards Stony Hill.

Julia Henriques's home was indeed as she had described it, a charming stone building, embowered in flowers. She was able to grow plants on the hill that would fail to flourish in Kingston or Spanish Town. Her garden was ablaze with colour, but the house was cool, shaded by giant trees. It was a very private retreat.

On our arrival, she greeted me with open arms, and when I explained my unfortunate situation, she told me that Peter and I were welcome to stay with her as long as necessary. I introduced her to Mr Kenet, and she offered him a glass of lemonade, a cup of coffee, some fruit. He thanked her but said he must return to his duties in Spanish Town. She forbade him to go, saying he must stay, he must rest, his horse must rest; he must eat; he could leave at dawn. She forbade him to refuse her hospitality, and he relented.

"Let me call the children," she said, turning into the house.

At her call, her two sons came running. They stared at Peter, sizing up whether he was a threat or a gift and, deciding that he was the latter, grabbed him by the arms and dragged him away. We could hear them all laughing as they chased each other around the garden.

And so it was that Mr Kenet spent the evening with us, and ate dinner with Julia and me and her fine Mr Henriques, whose stories of fortunes gained and lost on the island of Jamaica had us all amazed. It was hard for me to realise that, in the mere span of a day, my life and Peter's had been subjected to such intense violence and cruelty that we were forced to flee our home, and now all that had changed, and here I was, talking and laughing among dear friends as though this were the most natural occurrence in the world.

Since Mr Kenet planned to return to Spanish Town at dawn, I decided to bid him farewell before going to bed. When our hosts retired, we stepped onto the gallery to gaze at the full moon and breathe the scented air of Julia's garden. Holding hands, we agreed to write to each other frequently, and I promised to send him such books as I knew he would enjoy. And then he placed his arm around my waist and pulled me to him.

"'And wilt thou leave me thus? Say nay, say nay, for shame,'" he uttered, sounding strangled. I could not speak.

"'And is thy heart so strong, as for to leave me thus?'" he continued, and the tears poured down his face. I wiped them with the handkerchief that was first Pearl's, that became Thomas Fraser's, that became mine, that was still damp with my tears, and he kissed it before he blew his nose and pocketed it.

"If I had not married you, I should have married you," he said with an attempt at humour.

"If you had not married me, I should have married you," I replied, and we could not help but laugh. And then we kissed each other again and again and again. My heart felt so empty and so full at the same time, empty because of the coming absence from such a friend, but at the same time full of joy at the admission of our love for one another.

"Take this now," he said, pulling a folded paper from his pocket, and handing it to me. "I have carried it with me for weeks, always wanting to give it to you but never daring. Do not read it now, but read it often as you travel, never taking it amiss, but always remembering your friend."

I took it from him and placed it inside my dress, close to my heart.

We did not go to bed that night. We remained on the gallery, entwined in each other's arms until the moon set and the sky began to gather colour. Only then did John Kenet leave for Spanish Town.

May the twenty-fifth, 1771

After John left, I wandered around the garden, and noticed the colour shifting from grey to rosy-fingered dawn. The sudden screech of a cock's crowing broke into my reverie. I climbed the steps onto the verandah, and tiptoed my way to my room. I knew that Peter was spending the night with the Henriques boys in the nursery, so I threw myself down on the bed, and sobbed for all that I had lost and gained. And then I was aroused by a sudden stirring of the heart, and found my thoughts going back to the tamarind tree. I was transported to a spot underneath its sweeping branches. The wind picked up and the canopy above me was dancing. I had the feeling of being in the presence of something greater than myself. I paused and listened. I sat down on Pearl's grave and listened again. I could sense that she was nearby, and encouraging me to leave. The tamarind tree faded from green to yellow to white, and I drifted back into the soundest sleep I had had in years.

I awoke with a shock. Where was Peter? It was already noon. I felt panic rising and ran from my bed, shouting for him. Julia was instantly by my side. "Look out the window. He's playing happily with my boys." Indeed he was, and at the sight, I collapsed into her arms with relief.

She took me by the hand and led me to the dining room, where she fed me a meal of breakfast and lunch all rolled into one, and then rolled me back into bed. I slept again until dinner. She and her good Mr Henriques did their best to entertain me, but I was soon back in bed again, safe in the knowledge that Peter was well taken care of.

May the twenty-sixth, 1771

Today Peter was playing so hard with the Henriques boys that he did not have time for me. Julia and I talked and talked and talked, filling those seemingly endless hours with conversation, cramming more confidences into that short interval than most people cram into a lifetime. Suddenly, in the late afternoon, Jacob Henriques came hooting in, waving a piece of paper. "Here it is! The letter from Mr Fraser." I snatched it from his hands, but I was trembling so much that I could not read. "Read it to me," I begged.

May the twenty-sixth, 1771

Dear Martha,

I have secured a passage for you and Peter on board the Destiny, *Captain Richard Manesty. This freeing-up of a cabin came about as a result of the sudden death from yellow fever of the wife of a Kingston merchant. You must share the cabin with Peter, so your quarters will be close, but such was your desperation that I decided to take the opportunity of securing this berth for you.*

The Destiny *sails tomorrow at noon. Please ask Mr Henriques to make plans for your transport to the dock so that you arrive well ahead of time.*

I am delighted to have been able to make this arrangement even though it deprives my wife and myself of your dear company. We wish you a safe and comfortable voyage and pray that you may be able to return to Jamaica one day.

Ever your devoted friend,
Thomas Fraser

All that remained was for me to pack my case and Peter's, to eat a farewell meal, and then to leave under cover of darkness. I was all of a dither. My hands were shaking with excitement as I folded our clothes. At eleven Mr and Mrs Henriques and I ate our last dinner together. It broke my heart to leave my dear Julia. We clung to each other until Mr Henriques said we must leave. He had to tear us apart, and then he bundled Peter and me abruptly into the waiting carriage. We trotted all the way down Stony Hill and through the almost silent streets of the outskirts of Kingston. When we came to the harbour itself, there was such a racket coming from the roaring of the rum houses that no one noticed us as we passed by. Jacob Henriques wrapped us in his cloak, ushered us up the gangplank, and when Captain Richard Manesty received us, came with us to our cabin, where I am now writing this last entry in my diary.

While the two men are enjoying a glass of Madeira, I take this opportunity to write down the translation that was John Kenet's farewell gift to me:

> *Silent he went,*
> *and stood against the Maid,*
> *In sidelong glances*
> *faintly he convey'd*
> *His crafty eyes about her;*
> *with dumb shows*
> *Tempting her mind to Error.*
> *And now grows*
> *She to conceive his subtle flame,*
> *and joy'd*
> *Since he was graceful.*
> *Then she herself imploy'd*

Her womanish cunning,
turning from him quite
Her Lovely Count'nance;
giving yet some Light
even by the dark signs,
of her kindling fire;
With up and down-looks,
whetting his desire.

I shall hand this diary over to Jacob Henriques to take to his wife, to whom I entrust it. I hope she will tell my tale.

Now I commit myself and my dear son Peter into the hands of my merciful Creator. Life and love are yet in my possession, with all their requirements, and pains, and responsibilities. The burden must be carried; the want provided for; the suffering endured; the responsibility fulfilled. And so I set out.

Annals of Liverpool

JULY 30, 1771

Dreadful storm of thunder, lightning, and rain, a perfect hurricane which filled the river with wreck and destruction; many rooms in the lower part of the town laid under water; the mainmast of the ship Destiny *shattered by lightning and the bowsprit driven through the middle window of a house at the bottom of James-street; surge so great as to prevent assistance being sent to those on board, all of whom perished. The tide rose six feet higher than the calculation in the tide-table.*

Peter Mason who loves to climb to the top of trees is riding the storm at the top of the mizzen, clinging to it like a monkey, screeching with terror and exhilaration, growling back at the thunder. Suddenly, lightning strikes the main mast and the *Destiny* splits in half. A huge wave sends her bow forward and flings the bowsprit through the parlour window of a James Street house belonging to one Mistress Clark, milliner. As the stern sinks, the mizzen mast snaps free. It swings out and flies up in the air. Flung loose by the snap, flung high, Peter soars in an arc, shapes his body like a swallow, and dives into the dirty water of the Mersey River, which sucks him under, rolls him under, drags him down, scrapes him along the bottom, gathers strength, rolls forward, and throws him up again, swimming for his life.

There is a sudden stillness as the wind drops and the tide is at the slack. Peter Mason paddles ashore, and drags himself up through slime, through weed, past barnacles, past swimming rats and all the stinking muck of Liverpool harbour, onto George's Dock.

Wuthering Heights
by Emily Brontë
Harmondsworth: Penguin. Ch. 4, p. 78.

"The master tried to explain the matter," said Nelly Dean, "but he was really half dead with fatigue, and all that I could make out, amongst Mrs Earnshaw's scolding, was a tale of his seeing it starving, and houseless, and as good as dumb in the streets of Liverpool, where he picked it up and inquired for its owner. Not a soul knew to whom it belonged, he said, and his money and time being both limited, he thought it better to take it home with him at once, than run into vain expenses there; because he was determined he would not leave it as he found it . . . I later found they christened him 'Heathcliff': it was the name of a son who died in childhood, and it has served him ever since, both for Christian and surname."

The West Indian is typeset in Williams Caslon Text, with *Poppl Exquisit* used for display. These types were chosen for their ability to evoke the feeling of the period. The few portions of the narrative not in Martha's voice are set in Magma.

William Caslon (1692–1766) produced what many scholars feel are the quintessential English types. His foundry exported tens of thousands of pounds of printing types to English colonies all over the world, and printer's cases in Jamaica would have been filled with Caslon. William Berkson (1944–) completed his electronic revival in 2010, basing his designs on Caslon's Pica Roman No. 2 from the 1760s. Williams Caslon Text succeeds in capturing the personality of the original metal types: highly readable, warm and inviting, and authoritative.

Although Friedrich Poppl (1923–1982) designed Exquisit in 1970, it echoes much of the spirit found in the penmanship of an educated person in the eighteenth century.

In Magma, Sumner Stone (1945–) succeeded in merging the minimalist contours of a sans-serif design with the humanistic qualities most often associated with serif types.

Design and typography by Bruce Kennett.

41807884R00175

Made in the USA
Lexington, KY
11 June 2019